autumn DAWN

THE LONDON TRILOGY: BOOK I

autumn
DAWN

DAVID MOODY

Author's note:
Although many of the locations featured in this
novel are real, I have taken fictional liberties with them.
This is a work of fiction, not a travel guide.

First published in 2021 by Infected Books

A CIP catalogue record for this book
is available from the British Library

ISBN 978-0-9576563-8-3

Cover design by Craig Paton
www.craigpaton.com

www.davidmoody.net

www.lastoftheliving.net

www.infectedbooks.co.uk

When I came to London last April, I felt like I was drowning in people. Now I'm the only one left alive.

I never got used to living here. London was completely different from home, different from pretty much everywhere, actually. It had its own rules, masses of unexpected complications that were always catching me out. It did my head in. Travel was a good example. Back in Leeds, getting to and from work was never a problem, but getting anywhere by public transport here needed an encyclopaedic knowledge of every street, train, bus route and tube line, as well as military-grade logistical skills. I didn't stand a chance, really. Some days I just couldn't face trying and I'd walk instead, but even then I felt like I'd done the wrong thing. The walk took me less than an hour, but when I got to work people would look at me like I was from Mars. *Are you mad, Helen?* they'd say. *You walked?!* Then they'd bore me shitless talking about how I should have got there, how *they* would have got there, telling me all the best shortcuts and traffic dodges.

Doesn't matter now. There are no more tubes or buses or trains running. No more patronising co-workers; in fact, there are no more people. There's no more work. No more anything.

Tuesday morning. First week of September. Bright but cool.

I left the house about an hour before my shift. I'd been living in a house-share with two other people. Shanice worked in the same hospital as me, doing opposite shifts, and there was a guy called Yan who had the ground floor bedroom. I'd only ever seen him a couple of times. He did something important in finance somewhere, apparently, but I reckoned he was probably up to something dodgy.

I hadn't wanted to get up, and I certainly didn't want to go to work. Bottom line: I was a fish out of water. I didn't fit in. I'd left Leeds because I thought my life was going nowhere, but here there was nothing but dead ends. I'd given it almost six months, but I'd come to accept that leaving home had been a huge mistake.

You know that feeling when you know what you've got to do, but you've got no idea how you're going to do it? I'd reached that point. My grand experiment was over, and it had failed spectacularly. I walked down the Romford Road with my head down and my hands in my pockets, trying to work out how I was going to get out of London and back to Leeds. I was thinking about how I was going to tell my employers, what I would say to my folks and everybody else who'd been telling me I'd made a mistake moving down here in the first place. I felt completely alone, despite the chaos of the rush hour streets, or maybe because of it. That was something else I couldn't work out – how was it that everybody else could walk along the pavement in a straight line at double speed without ever looking up from their phones? I was always the one left to swerve, to change direction to avoid collisions with zombies who had their headphones in, eyes glued to their screens. It was like being stuck on the first level of a particularly hard and particularly shite video game.

Then everything changed.

I moved to sidestep some random guy – drunk at seven in the morning, for Christ's sake – who was zigzagging across the pavement with his eyes bulging, drooling from the corner of his mouth. Someone else collided with me from behind, and I was about to turn around and give them hell when an out-of-control Ford Focus shot across in front of me, wiped out the drunk, then crashed into the front of a takeaway.

Everything fell apart so fast after that that I didn't know where to look first, who I should try and help... I caught my breath, and when I turned around and saw the full extent of what was happening, I realised it didn't matter. I couldn't help anyone.

Whatever it was, it rolled down the Romford Road like a wave. People were dying all around me. I was too busy trying to work out why they were dropping dead to even consider why I was the only person left standing, but that was the truth of it. Within a few minutes, for as far as I could see in every direction, I was the only one left alive.

I was numb with shock, and when that shock wore off, I went to pieces. It was the absoluteness of everything that got to me at first. There was no one else left. I remember wanting to find just one other person so I could check with them that what had happened had actually happened, that I wasn't going mad. All the live broadcasts on TV had stopped mid-flow, grim faces frozen on the screen. I checked the internet, kept pressing refresh on the news sites, but the headlines stayed the same. The only thing that changed were the timings after each link showing how long it had been since the stories were last updated. I watched the minutes turn to hours turn to longer.

I was just distracting myself, biding time, I realise that now. I locked the door to my little room in the little house and did everything I could to block out the fear that what had happened in London had most likely happened everywhere. When I couldn't avoid it any longer, I picked up my phone and started to call the people who mattered, Mum and Dad, my brother, a couple of friends. Then I tried the people who didn't matter so much: my ex, the hospital, my old boss, my GP surgery, my dentist, the gym, my bank... every number I could find. But no one picked up. Even 999 rang out unanswered.

I knew they were all gone, but I couldn't accept it because it didn't make sense. First night, I took some tablets to help me sleep. Second night, I contemplated taking all of them. That would have been the easy way out, but I couldn't do it. Instead I locked myself in my room and didn't move again until the dead bodies began to walk.

Christ, it sounds so bloody stupid when I put it like that, but there's no other way to describe what happened. It wasn't *all* of them, and it didn't all happen at the same time. It started early on Thursday, the third day. I'd just got out of bed with a bitch of a headache. I opened the bathroom window to get some fresh air and they... god, it's hard to describe, but they were peeling themselves up off the pavements then staggering around like new-born animals, legs buckling under the weight of themselves, tipping sideways, swaying like drunks. It was like they were relearning how to walk. Some stayed on the ground but, by dusk, the majority were up and about. And after that, they never bloody stopped.

I thought it was the bloody sleeping pills screwing with my brain. I mean, zombies, for Christ's sake. It was as hackneyed as it was inconceivable. And the thing was, no matter how many pulpy novels I'd read or shitty films I'd sat through (and I'd sat through plenty, believe me), I couldn't help myself going outside and getting closer to them. They were so slow and unresponsive that I didn't think they were a danger, not like in the films. I guess it's the medic in me, but I wanted to work out what was making them tick. I knelt beside one that hadn't figured out vertical movement quite yet. She had no pulse, and she wasn't breathing, so even though it was impossible, I had no doubt she was dead. Was it some kind of residual nervous reaction to whatever had killed them? They ignored me. They didn't react if I stopped them nor when I let them go; they just lumbered around all slow and useless, walking into things and each other, oblivious to their surroundings, not paying any attention to me, not paying any attention to anything.

I could have just about handled that and left them to their own devices, but after a couple more days I realised they were changing again. This was different to the books and films, because in those stories the zombies are always one note – they're the same at the end as they are at the beginning, just a little more decayed. But I watched those things outside continuing to reanimate, and it was frigging terrifying. They were getting quicker, becoming more alert. At one point I threw out a bag of rubbish. There must have been some glass at the bottom of the sack and when it smashed, half a dozen of them stopped and turned around to see what the noise was. Until then I'd felt invisible or at least inconsequential. I panicked. By the time I got up to my room there must have been more than thirty of them outside the front of the house.

And that was where they stayed.

After I got over the shock, they really started to get under my skin. It was like they were taunting me, waiting for me to come out and play. It was starting to drive me out of my fucking mind. I tried chucking glass bottles and other breakables as far as I could from an upstairs window to distract them with noise, but those few that took the bait wandered right back. Because the rest of the world was so completely, utterly, deathly silent, the damn things just kept on coming back no matter what I did. If I rolled over on the bed, coughed, took a sharp intake of breath, fetched a drink or something to eat, went to the loo... the slightest sound was enough to attract their attention. I hadn't realised it before, but everything I did made noise. They couldn't see me, but it was getting impossible to hide from them. Sometimes I stayed silent for hours thinking they'd leave me alone. Sometimes a few of them would drift off but all it took was one slip to bring them shuffling back again and more. And they were so bloody clumsy and uncoordinated that they made enough noise themselves, so what I did or didn't do didn't matter. It seemed I'd become the star of the show. The rest of the world was a vacuum, and with nothing else to occupy them, they'd become a self-perpetuating mob on my doorstep. One time I had to run to the nearest shop for food, and though I was quiet and outran them easily, by the time I got home there were more than a hundred of them behind me.

My mobile died (not that I'd heard from anyone) then the internet gave up the ghost. More and more sites started to disappear and were replaced with error messages. That almost felt like a relief, because I'd got addicted to checking random people's social media feeds, clicking from profile to profile, looking for signs of life but finding none. Then a couple of days later the electricity went off, and by then there was no gas supply either. Each new loss made me feel a bit more disconnected from my old life and slightly more paranoid. It felt like the dead were taking over. It was like they were rebooting – no, *defrosting* – as I was shutting down. The more cut off and abandoned I felt, the more they seemed to single me out. They didn't want to eat my brains or pass on their infection or anything like that... they just wanted to make what was left of my life as terrifying and lonely and completely fucking miserable as they could. That's how it seemed, anyway, and I took it personally. That was their revenge, I decided. I'd survived and they hadn't.

And eventually I snapped.

I'd had enough. There was only so much I could take and, after seventeen days, I'd had a fucking gutful.

I left the house by the back door and walked the length of the driveway down the side. They didn't even notice. Dumb bastards were still crowding around the front, clustered round each other. There was a loose metal railing in next-door's fence. I grabbed it and held it like a baseball bat, and when the nearest of them stumbled into range, I nearly took its head off.

Oh, it was beautiful.

I shouldn't have enjoyed it, but I really did. The tip of the railing cut through its skin with ease, and its skull cracked like an egg. I know it shouldn't have, but it felt good. Once the first one had gone down with such ease and pleasure, I lashed out again. Then again. And again. And again and again and again and again and again.

In the space of a couple of minutes it was as if my whole life had been inverted, tipped on its head. In the old world, my job had been to keep people alive. Now it felt like my business was to wipe out the dead. It made perfect sense, and also no sense at all, but it gave me something to hold onto and made me feel like I had a purpose again. I kept (re)killing them for as long as I could until I was soaked with sweat and my arms were numb. I felt on fire. I felt *alive*.

Later, back in the house, I looked down from an upstairs window, expecting to see a real difference. But it was as if I hadn't been outside at all. For every one of them I'd hacked down, another ten had turned up to take its place.

I realised I had a lot of work ahead of me.

I slept really well that night, and I woke up early and ready to get going. I finally had a reason for getting out of bed. I got ready quickly and forced some food down, not bothered about the noise anymore, then I went out to the landlord's shed in the back garden. I prised the padlock off with the metal railing I'd used the day before, then mooched around in the gloom for something more effective. I was thinking I might find an axe, a machete, or a spade, but I ended up with something much better. I found a chainsaw. A bloody chainsaw! I'd done some volunteering with the Forestry Commission in my uni days, so I knew how to handle the wicked machine. It had been a few years, but I managed to get the chainsaw going. I got a kick out of making such a damn horrible racket after mincing around, staying quiet for so long. It felt like I was taking back control.

The driveway between my house and next-door was a useful funnel. It let me deal with the monsters with a bit of authority. The gate at the end of the drive made a bottleneck and only three or four of them could get through to me at a time. To be honest, I could have handled more. The chainsaw blade cut through the advancing bodies like something out of a video game, gloriously graphic and completely satisfying, and I never felt like I was in any real danger. I sliced upwards through one of them at an acute angle from its hip to its opposite shoulder, and the head and everything else above the waist slid clean off and landed at my feet. I put the chainsaw blade between the legs of the next one mid-step and brought it straight up; the right side of the body parted from the left like something out of a cartoon. I never stopped to consider whether it was wrong because it felt like so good. It felt like it was them or me.

I don't know how long I was out there, but I barely broke a sweat getting rid of the crowd in front of the house and I just kept going. I must have walked a mile down the Romford Road, hacking down anything that got in my way. When I looked back towards the house, hundreds of them were following. Didn't matter. I just turned around and walked right back into the heart of them, the chainsaw still buzzing.

When I got up next morning, it was like yesterday's bloodbath had never happened. The street outside was packed again, the dead rammed up against the garden fence like they'd been waiting all night to see me. I felt nervous, all those people watching. Then it struck me, *they're not watching*. Then, *they're not even people*.

But there was something different about them.

It took me a while to put my finger on it, then I realised, they were showing more control than before. They weren't wandering around aimlessly like they had been, getting in each other's way. It might have been a gradual thing – I'd been too busy trying to get rid of them to notice – but there'd been a definite change, and it worried me because I was thinking if they're like this today, what are they going to be like tomorrow? I knew I was going to have to pick up my pace.

I sold my car before I came to London. There wasn't any point bringing it here. The roads were too busy, you had to pay a premium for using them, and even if you did manage to get to where you were going, the chances of finding anywhere to park when you got there were non-existent. But I did miss my knackered old motor, and it felt good to get behind the wheel again. The Nissan Navara I plumped for was about as far removed from my ancient Corsa as it was possible to get. It was more pick-up truck than car, and its power and size was exactly what I needed.

I'd got used to thinking about the dead things as exactly that – things, not people – but now and then I was forced to remember who they used to be. I found the Nissan double-parked outside a school with the door open and the keys in the ignition. I assumed the driver had been there for the morning drop-off, and that their child was likely one of the horribly sad little figures now doomed to stagger round and around the enclosed school playground forever. It was heart-breaking. The dead kids were like forgotten zoo animals, putting their hands through the fence and reaching out whenever I got close. Pretty much all the bodies I'd seen up until that point had been adult sized. I cried when I saw the lifeless little ones. I should have done something to help them, to put them out of their misery, but I just couldn't bring myself to chainsaw a child.

Weirdly, thinking about the kids made me angry more than anything, and I drove my new truck straight into the crowds, determined to get rid of as many of them as I could. The first few collisions made me feel sick to my stomach, but I quickly got used to the size of the truck and to the *thump, thump, thump* of bodies bouncing off the bumper.

I accelerated back towards the house and down the Romford Road again, driving at stupid speeds and carving a relatively clear path virtually all the way back. I turned the truck around in the mouth of a side-street, then made another pass. I was starting to hate the dead people now. I blamed them for the solitary shitstorm my life had become, and getting rid of them was the only thing that gave me any pleasure. It gave me a focus, a reason for being. By eliminating the dead, I'd found a justification for staying alive.

On the third charge, things started to get a little hairy. Although there were fewer of them left standing, my windscreen was filthy and the amount of once-human waste covering the tarmac made it increasingly difficult to keep control. I skidded around the corner into High Street North, then aquaplaned straight into the back of a Post Office van. I smacked my head on the steering wheel and wrenched my neck. Whiplash. If I hadn't had my belt on, I'd have ended up just another corpse.

I walked back to the house and it seemed to take forever because of the sludge on the ground and I got lost because everywhere was starting to look the same. The dead people were ignoring me, and

I guessed that was because I was walking as slowly and awkwardly as they were. Also, I was covered in as much muck and decay as every other creature. When I got to the house and saw the ever-present crowd milling outside, I just kept walking.

They were really starting to piss me off. There was no escape from their irritating blankness. No matter where I went, there they were. Every road I walked down, every building I went into, every crashed car I looked at, every bloody London bus I passed... they were *everywhere*. I started to imagine wiping out the entire urban population. It seemed a daunting task, but one thing was clear: if I wanted to get rid of more of them, I was going to have to up my game. From my studies I knew they'd rot down to nothing over time, but we were talking months, and I just couldn't wait that long.

I walked further into the city, passing landmarks I recognised. The Olympic park from 2012 was really grim, the buildings like tombstones. I remembered the games, how busy and vibrant everywhere had been, how crowds of people had filled this place, the whole world coming together for a fortnight. Naturally, all that made me feel worse than ever, because now there was no world, there was only me.

I was hungry and cold, and it was either lose the dead crowd following me or lose my mind. I had no plan. I broke into a Co-op next to a petrol station on Bow Street, kicked six corpses out the door (two dead staff, four dead customers) then blocked the entrance and hunkered down out of sight behind the counter with some food and drink and a pile of magazines to remind me how things used to be.

It was like the sun had forgotten to rise. I'd lost track of what time it was, what day, even, but I knew it had to be late enough for daylight. When I got up and looked outside, I saw it was the dead people again. Hundreds of them, it looked like, packed tight around the outside of the Co-op, their faces pressed up against the glass, blocking out the daylight. I said to myself, *Helen, you know what you've got to do*.

I set fire to the supermarket.

It was a calculated risk, but it worked. I started a blaze by the entrance and then, when I was sure it was going strong and wasn't going to fizzle out, I opened the door and let them in. They were fighting with each other to get inside, focused on the fire that took hold swiftly, ripping through the innards of the dusty, dried-out store. I escaped through a back door while they continued to pile in through the front, and for once they didn't pay me any attention. The fire was so intense it was the only thing they could see, and I stood in front of the shops on the other side of the road and watched as it drew hundreds more of them out from the shadows. Thousands, even.

It was pitiful to watch. I couldn't help grinning.

The fire was really raging, and it jumped the gap between the supermarket and the overhanging canopy of the petrol station next door. I was hypnotised by the way it destroyed everything it touched, eating through the plastic signs and licking against the sides of the pumps. It was beautiful, like a solitary blossom on an otherwise dead tree.

The explosion blew me off my feet and into the front of a charity shop. My face was burned, and my eyelashes were gone, and I just sat there with the dead still advancing all around me. I started laughing and couldn't stop. The roar of the fire drowned out my noise, so I leant back and watched the show for hours until the pissing rain put out most of the blaze. By then I'd counted more than seven hundred rotting bastards reporting for duty and being reduced to ash. The stink of burnt meat hung in the air like a barbecue. I was starving.

I stayed there until I got cold, then I started walking again.

I'm near Shoreditch now, and the rain is still hammering down. I've lost the cover of dark and I'm soaking wet and freezing, but it doesn't matter. I'm not scared anymore; there's no need to be. I'm better than the dead people, more complete. I'm still human. I feel sorry for them, I mean, it must be horrible being dead-ish. Imagine being able to feel your own body rot. Imagine the fear and pain and not being able to scream out. I keep thinking about the way they walked into the fire yesterday, and it makes me think maybe they were consciously trying to bring an end to their misery. And now I'm feeling pretty good about myself, because I'm starting to realise that I'm actually doing this to help them, not hurt them. I swore an oath to help the sick, and I've never come across people as sick as this before. I have to keep helping them; I'll help as many as I can.

I could start another fire out here, but that's too random, too dangerous. It could easily get out of control. No, there has to be a better way. Whatever I do, it has to be contained.

They follow me wherever I go now, and that's convenient. Sometimes I stop and smash a window or make some other noise to let them know where I am. I know I'm taking risks, but all I have to do is walk as slow as they do and stay quiet, and they assume I'm just another poor dead nobody. I'm thinking the more of them I can help in one go, the better. I'll just keep them following me like rats until I've got enough of them together in one place, then maybe start another fire or just lock them all away. I'm thinking I'll start small, use a theatre or a cinema perhaps, then maybe work my way up to an arena or a football stadium even. But I'm getting ahead of myself. I need to build myself up. And this place looks perfect.

This is Commercial Street, and the covered passageway ahead of me, between the fancy restaurants and boutiques, is the entrance to Spitalfields, a massive traders' market. I remember coming here once, before the end of everything. I remember thinking it summed up London in a nutshell: old, functional buildings that had been buffed up and turned into something overpriced and chic. After paying my rent and the essential bills each month, I was having to survive on bland food and charity shop treasures. Because it was a market, I thought I might be able to pick up a few bargains here, but I was so wrong. Shabby chic, I think they used to call it, "vintage." The sandwiches were all gourmet, the coffee priced like fine wine. Oh, there were still charity shops, but the second-hand clothes weren't bargain priced castoffs anymore, they were upcycled designer one-offs that cost a bloody fortune. I remember it really angered me at the time, watching people wasting all that money on overpriced nonsense. It will give me great pleasure to burn the whole damned place down to the ground.

I screwed up at the supermarket yesterday. I should have set the fire deeper inside the building so more of the dead would have been caught. I won't make the same mistake again. I'll be more thorough today.

It's like a maze in here, perfect for trapping them. It's quite light inside, because most of the roof is glass and there's loads of metalwork holding it up, industrial-looking girders and crossbeams. I walk up and down the rows of stalls, blocking some walkways and opening up others so they'll follow me deep inside and won't be able to get back out. And it's working because as I'm walking up one row, I can already see them coming into the building, following the ones who followed me. I pick up things I might need on my way through and shove them in a bag: bottles of acetone from a nail salon, paper and strips of cloth to burn, cigarette lighters, candles...

It's starting to fill up nicely; looks like a busy Saturday shopping day in here now. There are plenty of hiding places and cut throughs, so I won't get caught out. I light a few candles and make a bit of noise now and then, so they don't lose interest. Don't want them drifting off. Don't want all this effort to go to waste. I bang a hammer against one of the huge supporting pillars and it's like I'm ringing a church bell. With everywhere else so quiet, I bet they can hear it for miles.

I work my way back through to the middle of the building. They're too busy focusing on the candles and other distractions I've set up to pay any attention to me. Their eyes are poor, and a little bit of brightness makes everything else disappear. It helps me get on without interruption.

This is where I'm going to do it. Right in the heart of the place. It's a designer clothes stall, bespoke jackets created from military surplus and ancient upholstery fabrics. I look at one price tag and nearly choke. This is going to go up a treat. Such a rush. Seriously. I've been through so much crap recently – before and after the apocalypse – and it feels good to be able to do some serious damage. I grab an oversized camo and French toile jacket, the equivalent of two month's rent, then set light to the rest of the stupidly priced clothes, and it's so beautiful to watch. It's like a piece of performance art.

I duck down and crawl away through the legs of the dead people, and they don't even realise because they're too busy trying to get to the fire. All I need to do now is just—

Damn.

What an idiot.

I've lost my bearings.

I've been crawling away from the entrance, not towards it.

Maybe it's for the best. If I'm honest, I should probably hang around. I can't afford to go anywhere until I'm sure this is working.

Up ahead I see a staircase leading up to a galleried area I hadn't noticed before. It looks quiet up there, some kind of food court, so I get back down on my hands and knees and crawl again until I reach the steps. Wish I'd thought of this before. I don't think they're coordinated enough to be able to climb up after me. I'll be able to watch them from safety until I'm sure the fire's got a hold, then find another way out through the back of the building.

Now this is better. Now I can see everything. Wow. There are hundreds of them in here, and I can see the entrance and the dead people just keep on coming. They're really filling the place up.

It's crazy just how many there are. When I half close my eyes, it almost looks like it did when I came here before all of this happened, like they're just shoppers sheltering from the rain, queuing up to spend their hard-earned cash.

It's sad, really.

I keep telling myself what I'm doing is helping. I keep telling myself that what's happened to these people isn't fair, and that if I ended up like that, I'd want someone to end things for me, too. And it occurs to me, this might be all I do now. This might be how I spend the rest of my life. Imagine that. I'll get better at it, of course, because right now I'm making it up as I go along, but it feels good, in a world that otherwise feels really bad, to be able to help people like this.

I've been watching for a while, but it's not working like I'd planned. Shit. The fire looks like it's going out. That's not good.

No matter. I'll try again.

I hammer on the metalwork again every few seconds, just so they don't lose interest while I consider my options.

There's a Thai restaurant on this level of the building, the tables all set for meals that were never served. There's a trolley with a load of glass water decanters with wide necks. A photo from a history book comes to mind, the troubles in Belfast; I can use these to make firebombs. I fill a couple with acetone, shove strips of ripped up cloth napkins in their necks, set them alight and hurl them. The first one is pretty good. It hits the top of a stall and splashes fire over a handful of dead bodies, but the flames don't take. I reckon it's because they're still wet from the rain. The second one hits a metal strut and doesn't explode at all. Dammit. I need to get closer.

There's a huge steel supporting girder that spans the width of the building. If I get up on one of the taller cafe tables and really stretch, I think I can climb up onto it. I can creep across and drop the next couple of bottles down into the middle of the crowd. I make a few more cocktails, carefully put them in my rucksack, then put it on backwards so I can reach them easy. I drag one of the tables across, balance a chair on top of it (the girder is higher than I thought), carefully swing one leg up, lift... then start to shimmy across.

It's not the height that's bothering me up here, it's the noise. The rain's still hammering down outside, and the sound as it hits the glass panels in the roof is deafening, like someone's chucking gravel. I grip the metalwork tight and keep moving across until I'm right over the middle of the massive building, then I take one of the bottles out of my bag. It's not easy doing everything with one hand, but I manage it. I light the rag, drop the bottle, then watch as it explodes right beneath me. It hits the ground and soaks loads of them with fire. It's glorious.

And I do the same again with bottle number two, though I have to swap arms. I cling on for a couple of minutes to get my breath back and rest my muscles, and I look down at the mob below. The fire's still not catching like I hoped it would. I'm frustrated. I thought it would be easy, but this is a million times harder than blowing up a petrol station.

I'll chuck this third bottle down anyway then have a rest and a rethink. I need something more flammable than nail polish remover. I'm safe from them up here, so I can sit for a while and work things out, take my time. That's the one thing I have plenty of. Serves me right for trying to run before I could walk. I should have thought this through. I should have—

Wait.

What's that?

That's impossible. How can that be?

There's one of them up on the roof overhead. I can see it moving along outside, looking in through the glass. The corpse is rubbing a dirty patch clean, trying to work out what's going on. I haven't seen any of them show so much control before... are they changing again? Now it's banging on the window, like it's trying to break in.

Shit.

Oh, Jesus.

The glass shatters, but the figure doesn't fall. It's climbing down onto the gallery outside the restaurant, blocking my way out.

Is there another way I can get out of here?

What if more of them climb up from the ground floor?

Christ, I have to move. If I can get across to the opposite side of the building from here, then maybe I can—

Helen's arms were heavy with the effort of holding on, and in her sudden panic she lost her grip and fell.

In a room now filled with more than a thousand corpses, she somehow managed to miss them all, landing on top of one of the market stalls. She hit the roof with the back of her head and lost consciousness as her skull cracked against the metal framework. She slowly came around, and it was only when she tried to get up that she realised her left leg had snapped and was bent back under the rest of her at an impossible angle, and it was only at that moment that the pain started to register.

All her anger, all her hurt, all her frustration and fear exploded as a guttural scream that echoed throughout the building. Her defiant death-yell was all she had left, and she screamed until her throat was raw.

One slip. One fucking stupid slip was all it had taken.

She was stuck on top of the stall now, no way of moving, no way of getting down. Nothing to do but stare up at the glass ceiling, watch the rain pouring in through the broken pane and think about what might have been. What she'd just thrown away. She realised she was the same as the dead now. Helpless. Waiting. No longer in control of her own destiny. No longer in control of anything. She tried to focus on the pain to convince herself she was still alive, but she was as dead as the rest of them.

And the bastard that was the cause of all this was edging along the girder towards her. 'Don't panic,' he said. 'I've got you.'

WELCOME TO LONDON.
POPULATION SEVEN MILLION.
99.9% OF THEM DEAD.
THE SURVIVAL OF THE REST BALANCED ON A
KNIFE-EDGE.

I
DAY THIRTY-SIX

There must have been several hundred corpses on the other side of the window, and it felt like every last one of them was staring right at Vicky. It had been over a month since they'd died. She'd been terrified non-stop from the outset, but in the last hour things had become immeasurably worse. Until now the dead had been meandering, appearing vacant and directionless, reacting to occasional movements and noise. Inexplicably, today they had begun herding purposefully together in unprecedented numbers along The Strand. It felt like they were *hunting*, seeking out the last of the living, and, in the absence of anything else capable of conscious control in this decaying shell of a city, Vicky, Kath and Selena felt like easy targets. Vicky couldn't think of a worse place to be trapped at the end of the world than this sprawling, chaotic, overcrowded metropolis.

Kath hauled her rucksack onto her aching shoulders. 'What could have caused this?'

'Us,' Selena said. 'You've not worked that out yet, Kath? It's always us. I wish they'd just fuck off and leave us alone.'

'Language,' Vicky said.

'Whatever.'

'We've talked about this. It's not necessarily us, per se, it's more the fact there's nothing else left. This is different, though. There's something new going on out there. We haven't seen them acting like this before.'

'Different? How?' The teenager's voice was edgy, her panic barely contained.

'They're mostly heading in the same direction, for a start. We've never seen them do that. Before now they've always just drifted

19

along. It's like we've walked into the middle of a migration. There could be tens of thousands of them heading this way. There probably are.'

Kath moved a little closer, out of Selena's ear range. 'Careful what you tell her,' she whispered.

'She needs to hear this.'

'I know, but she's not in a good way this morning.'

'None of us are in a good way, Kath. Being in a *good way* went out the window when the rest of the world dropped dead then decided to get up again.'

'I know, love, but she's just a kid. Imagine everything we're both having to deal with – the loss, the fear, the disorientation – then chuck in a load of hormones and angst as well. She can't help it.'

Vicky sighed and leant her forehead against the cold glass. Outside, a woman, who might have been a similar age when she'd died, clattered into the front of the store. Vicky caught a glimpse of her own reflection, mapped almost perfectly onto the face of the corpse by chance. Where Vicky's complexion was relatively clear, the dead woman's skin sagged like an ill-fitting mask, slipping down and leaving drooping bags under her eyes. Her mouth was pulled out of shape like she'd had a stroke, and she ground her jaw continually, making her look like she was alternately chewing then groaning. A string of drool the colour of mud oozed down her chin. Her clothes were tattered and soiled, her decayed body misshapen, swollen in some places, hollowed out in others.

You look as bad as I feel, Vicky thought. She'd known nothing but loss and disorientation for more than a month now. Five weeks of running on adrenalin, scavenging for food, and snatching fractured moments of sleep. It was thirty-six days since the world she'd known had been stolen from her and replaced by this utter hell and right now, other than a heartbeat, Vicky could see little difference between the living and the dead. Like the millions of impossibly reanimated corpses roaming the streets without purpose, she too was barely even existing.

'We should make a move,' Kath said. 'There are more and more of them. The longer we leave it, the worse it's going to get.'

'I'm not going back out there,' Selena said, nervous.

'Kath's right. We can't stay here,' Vicky told her.

'Why not? There's food and space and—'

'And judging from the numbers out there today, if we wait much longer we won't have any choice. Lovely as it is, this place will be our tomb. Is that how you want to end your days, hiding in the corner of a bloody Tesco Metro store?'

'Go easy on her,' Kath hissed, trying not to let Selena hear.

'I'll go easy on her when we're safe,' Vicky replied, at full volume. 'We don't just need to get out of this bloody supermarket, we need to get out of London altogether.'

Selena edged closer to the front of the store. The sheer number of corpses outside was now blocking much of the available light. 'Why are they all coming this way?'

'It doesn't make sense,' Kath said. 'They're heading out of the city. Why would they be doing that?'

'They must be reacting to something,' Vicky said.

'Us?' Selena asked, panicked.

'I don't think they know we're here.'

'Good.'

'Not yet anyway. It's only a matter of time, though.'

'What else could it be?' Kath asked. 'Other people?'

'Maybe. But on the basis we've not seen anyone else alive for more than a month, I doubt that very much.'

'Surely we can't be the only ones. Common sense says there must be others.'

'Common sense?' Vicky said, laughing. 'Seriously?'

'Yes, seriously. We've spent the whole time hiding; they're probably all doing the same.'

'We've had this conversation a million times already, and now's not the time to have it again. Let's shift.'

'We could just stay here until they're gone,' Selena said.

'Yep, we could, but Kath's right. The risk is there's ten times as many that haven't got here yet. We need to get moving while we

21

still can.'

Kath looked straight into Selena's face, gently holding her chin so she couldn't turn away. 'It'll be alright, love.'

'You don't know that.'

'We've been okay so far, haven't we?'

'Yeah, but—'

'But nothing. Victoria's right. We're going to leave here in a minute, get ahead of the crowd, then keep heading out of London like we've been planning all along. Annalise and the others are waiting for us in Ledsey Cross, remember?'

Selena nodded. 'Yeah. You're right. Sorry, Kath.'

'You've nothing to be sorry about. This is hard for all of us, but I was just saying to Victoria that I think you've got it worst of all. I can't complain. I've had my time. And I might have seventy-three years to your seventeen, but I can still remember what it was like at your age. Even without all this madness, things can be bloody hard when you're a kid. Don't you let anyone tell you otherwise.'

Selena wiped her eyes dry with the back of her sleeve and half-sobbed, half-laughed. 'There's no one left to ask.'

'Hate to break this up,' Vicky said, 'but we really need to go.'

'Which way, Selena?' Kath asked. 'We need to try and avoid main roads if we can. Look for little alleyways and side-streets. There's less chance of them following us down there.'

Selena's face was illuminated by the light from her phone. The networks were long dead and the electricity had failed weeks ago, but she'd had enough about her to find various ways of keeping her phone going since day one by using a couple of solar powered charging bricks and occasionally plugging into abandoned cars. Digitally nimble, she'd also had the foresight to download offline maps of the local streets before the data had dried up. All that apart, she used the phone sparingly, eking out the time she had left with her digital self. The world she knew was gone, and though on some level she was beginning to accept that, she wasn't yet able to let go completely. The phone was the only shred of her pre-apocalypse life remaining. Its words and pictures, sounds and memories, that softly glowing light... right now they felt more precious than oxygen.

'If we can get out through a back door and come out on Savoy Street, there are loads of little roads we can follow.'

'Where to?' Kath asked.

Vicky looked over Selena's shoulder at the map as she scrolled. 'Go the other way,' she said. 'West, not east. We want to try and get ahead of them.'

'We need more of a plan that just heading west,' Kath said. 'It's alright for you two, but I can't keep running all day.'

'I know, Kath, I know.' Vicky continued to look at the map. 'Stop! There.'

'That's Trafalgar Square,' Selena said. 'Didn't you say keep away from main roads?'

'Yes, but that's a decent sized open space. If we can get ahead of the bulk of them and we reach Trafalgar Square, we should have a better chance of getting away.'

Kath wasn't convinced. 'How so?'

'More space means they should be spread out. It's the best idea I can come up with, anyway.'

'Then it'll have to do.'

The movement of the three women inside the shop was enough to attract the attention of several of the dead. One of the cadavers lifted a leaden arm and slapped a palm against the grubby window. The sudden noise alerted scores more of them, and within seconds the small supermarket was the focus of a rancid mob. They pawed and scratched and thumped and pushed to get inside. As Vicky ushered the other two through to the back of the store, corpses began thudding against the glass the way birds sometimes fly into windows. She might have thought it funny if she hadn't been so bloody frightened.

Stay calm. Stay focused. We can do this.

Getting anywhere took forever these days, but time wasn't an issue. They could hop from building to building the entire two hundred and fifty miles from London to Ledsey Cross, if they had to. No matter how many times they did it, though, and no matter how temporary their shelter might have been, leaving was always nerve-wracking.

The temperature and stench of the air outside was sobering, the lack of noise equally unsettling. In the past, with this many people in such close proximity, silence would have been impossible. The city soundtrack of traffic and people was long gone now, replaced by a constant dull, muted drone: the dragging of thousands of dead feet, the buzzing of flies... civilisation's death rattle.

Vicky looked left and right then stepped over the remains of a shop worker they'd had to evict from the store when they'd first broken in. Her blue check uniform shirt, heavily stained with rot, flapped around her emaciated frame.

Up the hill along Savoy Street to their right, they could see the dead continuing their unsteady march along The Strand in swollen numbers. A hundred metres or so down Savoy Street in the opposite direction was the Victoria Embankment and the Thames. Numbers were somewhat lower down there, but there were still far more of them around than they'd seen previously, and they were continuing to move west. 'Stay quiet, follow me,' Vicky whispered. Kath and Selena nodded, didn't speak.

Bunched tightly together, they crossed the road then went down Savoy Hill, another one of the similarly named, impossibly narrow, maze-like streets that could be found in many parts of London, where the growth of the city felt more organic than planned. These one lane roads and walkways made moving around the city more complicated; with tall buildings on either side, the view was limited to what was immediately ahead and behind with no way of knowing what was waiting around the next corner.

They'd been outside for only a couple of minutes, but Kath was already struggling. Vicky stopped and spoke directly into her ear to minimise the risk of drawing attention. 'How's your knee?'

'Knackered,' she said.

'We can go back if you want.'

'You know as well as I do, we can't. Keep going.'

Savoy Hill curved around to the left. They took a turning into Savoy Way, an even narrower strip of road which ran parallel with The Strand. Glimpsed through gaps, the slow-motion river of dead people moving along the major road they were avoiding appeared to be acting as a self-perpetuating distraction. There was enough collective movement at the top of the file to keep the hordes interested in shuffling along in fragile unison. Vicky, Kath and Selena disappeared into the shadows under a covered part of the road. Above them, ancient-looking protective netting had been strung between the buildings on either side, presumably to stop the even more ancient-looking pipework they could see from dropping onto unsuspecting pedestrians.

'The Savoy!' Kath cried. 'A theatre, swanky hotel, lovely restaurants... oh, we could have set ourselves up quite nicely here. I didn't realise we were so close; would have been better for my back than that floor last night.'

'We could stop here if you want,' Vicky suggested.

'For the last time, no. Just keep going. We'll never get anywhere if we keep stopping.'

Dead end. Savoy Way ended abruptly in a T-junction. Vicky looked at Selena who checked her phone then gestured left, down towards the river. 'We can get back onto Savoy Place if we go that way,' she said, and they started to move, spurred on by the shuffling sounds of a handful of bodies behind them. They'd been followed from the supermarket, albeit at a miserably slow pace.

They were closer to the many corpses on the Victoria Embankment than was comfortable now, but the embankment gardens, a wedge-shaped area of park bordered by black metal railings, kept the bulk of them at a distance. As she walked, Vicky recalled the details of the map she'd seen on Selena's phone. She remembered seeing Villiers Street along one side of Charing Cross Station, and there was a pedestrian underpass beneath the railway lines that would bring them out close to Trafalgar Square. What they did from there, however, was anyone's guess.

They'd dropped their guard slightly, fooled by the relative

inaccessibility of their current location with buildings on one side and the park railings on the other. Whether it was bad luck or otherwise, several of the dead that had been milling in the park saw the three of them and started to surge. They crashed through the undergrowth towards them, oblivious to their own physical limitations. There was never any danger – the fence stopped them getting anywhere near, and all they could do was stretch their gangrenous hands through the gaps in the railings – but their intent was unquestionable. 'They're definitely getting more aggressive,' Vicky said, standing just beyond their outstretched fingertips.

'No question,' Kath said. 'Didn't I tell you they were changing?'

'Can we go?' Selena said, clearly terrified, and now there was no way forward. The street ahead was blocked by building work that hadn't been visible until now, and though Selena and Vicky might have been able to climb over the construction site barrier and keep going, there was no way Kath could.

'You've got to be bloody kidding me,' she wheezed, more annoyed than afraid.

Vicky started looking for an alternative route. Should they break a window, try to get into and through the building to their left, or did they take their chances with the handful of cadavers approaching from the other end of Savoy Place? On the face of it, that seemed to be the most obvious option, but not with so many other corpses around. *Any day but today*, she thought.

Selena was staring at her phone again, looking for another solution.

'What's up, love?' Kath asked, struggling to read the confused expression on Selena's face. She showed her the map.

'There's another road.'

'Where?'

'Here. Look, Adam Street.'

'Let me see,' Vicky said, and she orientated herself with the map and tried to make sense of their surroundings. Selena was right, there did seem to be another road right next to them, but that was impossible. Hell of a time to find a glitch in the Matrix.

'Got it,' Selena announced, and she ran over to the corner of the next building along. 'Look. Steps. The other road's up there.'

'Seriously?' Vicky asked, marvelling at yet another example of unpredictable London's chaotic planning.

'Seriously,' she said, and she started to climb the steep steps zigzagging upwards. She waited at the top for Kath. Her dodgy knees struggled with the pace of their dash across town and the weight of her rucksack. Vicky frequently offered to help, but she was already carrying her own belongings and other shared provisions in a pack twice as heavy.

Adam Street became Adelphi Terrace which ran round into Robert Street, then they turned into John Adam Street. They were making quick, if indirect, progress now, but that ended abruptly at the next turning. Scores of corpses were flooding down Villiers Street towards them, accelerated by the downward slope of the road towards the Thames. Vicky saw that an open-top sightseeing bus was on its side where Villiers Street met The Strand. It had fallen in such a position that it was funnelling the creatures directly at them. She looked down towards the river and spotted the entrance to the underpass she'd been looking out for. She grabbed Selena's arm and dragged her from the shadows, reluctant. 'Down there,' she said. 'Get to the underpass.'

'But that's back down towards the river. You said—'

'Just move!'

She shoved Selena by the small of her back, pushing her out into the current of rot, then helped Kath. 'I'm alright,' the older woman hissed, clearly not alright at all. 'The slope will help. It's made this lot speed up, and they're dead. How much worse off can I be? I'm sure I'll be fine.'

Vicky nodded – there was no arguing with Kath – then stepped out into the river of dead. Her friend was right; the incline and the fact they were moving in the same direction as the corpses gave them an advantage. Selena had already made much progress. She was walking at speed now, barging through the bodies like an angry rush hour commuter.

But Christ, it was awful when they were forced to get so close to the undead like this. Their stench was magnified in such intimate proximity, and the sounds that came from inside them made Vicky's stomach flip. The dripping of their flesh. The swill and churn of partially liquified innards slopping around inside emptying chest cavities. The scrape and slide as they dragged their feet along the ground, not enough strength to lift and step.

Vicky kept hold of Kath's hand, the two of them walking in single file, not side by side. The move was well-rehearsed. One squeeze for slow down, two for speed up, and a sharp tug to tell Vicky to stop. Kath squeezed her hand twice, keen to catch up with Selena and get under cover. In haste, Vicky collided with the corpse directly in front, misjudging her step. She fell to the ground and just managed to let go of Kath before she was dragged down too. Another move from the survivors' playbook they'd developed over time: Kath kept going and didn't look back. Vicky scrambled to her feet, attracting much unwanted attention from the nearest cadavers. Trying not to panic, she grabbed hold of the closest one of them and lifted it up. They were surprisingly light, she'd found, with much of their weight having oozed and dripped away from their deteriorating frames as they'd wandered the streets over the weeks. Her nerves gave way to nausea as she felt the corpse's flesh slipping through her fingers like flayed eel skin, but she swallowed down her rising bile and swung the corpse around, chucking it into the path of those coming down the hill towards her. It wasn't much of an obstruction, but it was novel enough they didn't move to avoid it, which gave her the few seconds of space she needed. One domino went down and then another, then another and another, building a haphazard roadblock of the dearly departed, their brittle bones quickly piling high.

Vicky was so focused on reaching the underpass at Embankment Place that she almost missed Selena and Kath. They were waiting for her, hiding in the doorway of a branch of Starbucks. Selena stuck out a hand and grabbed her. 'Jesus,' Vicky said, heart pounding, and they carried on towards the underpass.

Kath was really struggling.

Everything sounded different under cover, and Kath's laboured breathing echoed off the walls. There were fewer decaying Londoners down here, and those that had found their way this far were disorientated by the darkness, their severely weakened vision limited all the more by the sudden turn to shadow. 'We can stop here. Let you get your breath,' Vicky said to her.

'How many times do I have to tell you? Just keep going,' Kath wheezed. 'I'll be fine.'

But it was clear that she wasn't going to make it if they didn't rest up soon. 'We're close to Trafalgar Square now. We'll cut through the buildings on the other side of the road and reassess.'

Vicky gestured for Selena to stay put with Kath. Before either of them could protest, she emerged from the other side of the underpass and walked up and across Craven Street. It was almost completely clear, only a handful of bodies. From there, she could still see the masses staggering along The Strand, their numbers undiminished.

She took from her pack a crowbar she'd picked up the day after everyone had died and immediately set about prising open an automatic door that was now anything but. The heavy metal tool had become indispensable. It got her into places that might otherwise have remained inaccessible and, when push came to shove, it made for a decent weapon too. She forced it into the metal seam between two panels of glass and grunted with effort as she tried to separate them.

Vicky was so focused on trying to get in, that she failed to notice the corpse inside trying to get out. Barely able to coordinate its movements, it tripped over its own feet and slammed against the door, deadweight. Greasy fingers groped at the glass and Vicky jumped back with surprise, landing in a heap on her backside in the middle of the street. She dropped the crowbar and it made an echoing, sonorous clang that let all the dead within earshot know where she was. She didn't stop and count, but she was aware of at least a dozen of them peeling away from the crowds on The

Strand and coming towards her. She got up fast and tried the door again, this time shoving the crowbar into the gap with all her strength to force the two sides of the door apart. They juddered open just enough for her to get between them and push.

She could hear many more bodies rattling around inside the building she'd opened up, but that was just too bad. She swiped the crowbar down and cracked the skull of the overly inquisitive fellow still trying to get out, then used her back and her legs to push the two parts of the door further apart. She gestured frantically to Kath and Selena. Once they were inside, she forced the door shut again.

Kath was in a bad way. 'You okay?' Vicky asked.

'I'd be a lot better if you'd stop asking me that.'

There were bodies outside the building now, looking in. Vicky and Selena held Kath's weight between them and took her deeper into the building. They stopped at a fire door at the end of an innocuous-looking grey corridor to work out their next move. The place wasn't what they'd expected to find. 'A gym?' Selena said, surprised. 'Here?'

'Good grief. Imagine the membership prices in central London,' Kath said, managing to force a grin. 'Used to cost me over fifty quid a month back home, and that was only a crappy leisure centre next to the local swimming pool.'

'Bit of a gym bunny were you, Kath?' Selena asked, laughing.

'You bet I was!'

Vicky peered through a narrow pane of safety glass, into the heart of the gym. She counted no more than twenty bodies out there. Some of them had been crushed or snapped or otherwise disabled by the equipment they'd been using when they died. She could see two of them unable to move, pinned by the weights they'd been lifting. One guy was on his back with a bar across his neck, a final, incomplete bench press having all but decapitated him. Another was caught up in the mechanism of a rowing machine, like some bizarre, badly malfunctioning cyborg. Though she'd allowed herself to become temporarily distracted by the gruesome sights in the next room, she was acutely aware there were many more in there that were still mobile.

'They're going to come for us as soon as we go through,' she warned the other two. 'I can see a door over to our right. We're going to head straight for that, okay?'

Kath and Selena both nodded.

The fire door stuck when Vicky tried to open it. She shoved hard and slipped through the gap, then dragged away another pile of human remains which had been causing the blockage. Vicky moved quickly and saw that there were actually two doors. She tried the wrong one first, almost walking into the middle of an open studio space where another bunch of people had died midway through an exercise class. For some reason they were gathered in a group in the diagonally opposite corner of the room – their limited attentions caught, perhaps, by the creaking of the building or the groaning of a pipe, or the scrabbling of hungry rats in the walls – but as soon as Vicky pushed the door open, they turned and came for her in a horrific avalanche of grasping, stiffened fingers and putrefying flesh. A host of Lycra-clad ghouls fought to be the first to get across the room, their horrific-looking, foul-smelling bodies distended by decay, swollen in all the wrong places and bulging from overtaxed bike shorts and sports bras. Vicky slammed this door and dragged Kath and Selena through the other before the dead could lunge, step, or Zumba their way anywhere near.

This time they found themselves in a glass-fronted reception area, empty save for the three of them and the unmoving corpse of a security guard who'd died at his station. Thankfully the door they'd just come through was substantial and the front of the building was secure. The windows muffled their noise and the dead crowds outside drifted past, oblivious.

It gave the three of them a chance to breathe.

'Where next?' Vicky asked Selena. 'That's Trafalgar Square out there, right?'

'Give me a sec,' she said, checking her phone.

There was a vending machine over in one corner. While she waited, Vicky used her crowbar to prise it open. She shoved energy drinks and bottles of water into her bag, then handed a bottle of each to Kath, who had collapsed into a chair. She looked at the energy drink with disgust. 'Do you have any idea how much sugar and caffeine there is in one of these?'

'Yes, and I also know that's exactly what you need. Now drink it.'

She watched Kath drinking. Her hands were shaking uncontrollably. Vicky wanted to believe it was just nerves, but she knew it wasn't. She managed half a bottle, then had to take a break. 'Do you think, Victoria, that we're going to be walking much further today?' she asked, ever polite.

'I'm sorry, Kath. I wish I could tell you otherwise, but I think we well might be.'

'Oh.'

'Rest up while we look for the best route.'

Vicky walked over to Selena, who was still scouring the map for options. 'This is Northumberland Avenue,' Selena said, nodding at the tree-lined road outside the gym. 'Up there will bring us out right in the middle of Trafalgar Square.'

'I still think this is our best chance of getting past them and keeping our direction north. We've just got to hope there'll be enough room to move...'

'You don't sound convinced,' Kath said.

'Just wondering if we're doing the right thing. I mean, look at all the places we're close to. Bloody hell, we could set ourselves up in Buckingham Palace if we want to.'

'Assuming Her Majesty has moved out.' Kath had a wicked smile on her ashen face. Her composure was returning.

'I'm being serious. You made the point about the Savoy back there... all these huge empty buildings, yet we're still risking our necks to get out of London.'

'We've talked about this endlessly, Victoria. It's the right thing to do. We agreed.'

32

'I know we did, but that was before—'

'Before what? Before I got old? I've got news for you, darling, I was old before all this happened. We all agreed, and you made a promise to me, remember? You promised me you'd get yourself and Selena to Ledsey Cross. This city is dead, Victoria. There's nothing for you here, but you know there are people waiting at Ledsey Cross.'

'I know.'

'So let's forget all about sightseeing and spending the night at the palace, and focus on getting out of here, okay?'

'Okay.'

Selena showed Vicky the map again. 'Straight across Trafalgar Square and we're back to narrow roads and loads of buildings again.'

'Good. Plenty of options.'

Vicky went to go back and check the vending machine again, but Selena caught her arm and stopped her. 'Do you think Kath's going to make it?' she whispered.

'I'll be fine,' Kath immediately called from across the reception space. 'My body may be knackered, but my hearing is pin-drop sharp, thank you very much.'

'There's no rush,' Vicky said. 'We can rest up for a while longer yet. Give more of those buggers out there time to drift away again.'

'I don't think that's going to happen, Vic,' Selena said, and she gestured outside. The congestion in Northumberland Avenue was worsening.

'It's just perspective,' Vicky said, doing her best to sound positive. 'It probably just looks like there's more of them.'

'No, there's *definitely* more of them.'

As if to underline the point, corpses began to hammer on the door they'd come through to get to the reception area. There must have been another entrance. The building was rapidly filling up. 'Damn things are like lemmings,' Vicky said.

'Like what?'

33

'Lemmings. You never heard of lemmings? Little rat-like things that throw themselves off cliffs. Mass suicide.'

'You serious?'

'That's a misconception, actually,' Kath said. 'They don't commit suicide, but they do follow each other. It's part of their migratory behaviour. They just happen to sometimes end up following each other into an ocean or off a cliff.'

'Thanks for that, David Attenborough.'

'You don't get to my age without picking up more than your fair share of useless facts. I'm a demon in a pub quiz. Now, shall we get going?'

'We can leave it a few more minutes yet.'

'I'd rather we got it over with, if you don't mind. We could try and get across Trafalgar Square to the National Gallery. I could spend weeks in that place.'

'Hang on, you're the one who was just telling us we need to keep moving.'

Kath smiled, then eased herself back up onto her feet. 'I do love a good art gallery, though.' She walked over to the window and looked out into the forest of swaying corpses. 'So, the plan is to go out into the middle of that lot, is it?'

'I'm afraid we don't have a lot of choice.'

'Lovely,' Kath said, though it was anything but. 'Just so we're clear.' Vicky was about to speak, but Kath got there first. 'And before you ask, yes I'm sure I can manage it. I don't have any choice. Like you said, all our options are pretty shitty.'

Crowbar in hand, Vicky ignored the main doors and went towards a fire escape, over to her left. She'd done enough breaking and entering over the last month to know that emergency exits were by far the best option for making a quick escape from a building as they were designed for getting out fast. This was her favourite type: mostly glass, with a vertical panic bolt that would only need one hard shove to open. *Christ*, she thought. Had her world really been reduced to such an extent that she now had a favourite type of fire escape?

One last look at the other two. 'Both ready?'

'Just do it,' Selena said.

They couldn't risk bursting out into the open. Instead, Vicky gently pushed the door open then waited. No matter that the power had been off for weeks, whenever she did this, she still tensed up in anticipation of triggering the alarm and letting every corpse in the capital know exactly where the three of them were. She held her breath – partly because of nerves, partly because of the stink – then relaxed slightly when nothing happened.

What Vicky could see of the horde on The Strand reminded her of the way crowds moved away after the end of a concert or football match. There were thousands of slothful figures, maybe even tens of thousands, dragging themselves *en masse* through the streets. None of the dead had noticed them yet, because the brightness of the sun and the shade from the trees had given them a little unexpected cover, lifeless eyes again struggling with the contrast. They needed to stick close to the buildings on this side of the road for as long as they could, she decided. Melting into the shadows was their usual game plan.

Vicky was about to move when Kath stopped her. 'Victoria, love, I'm having a bit of trouble with my rucksack. Would you hold it for a second?'

She swung her pack off her shoulders and Vicky took it from her. Then, while Vicky was distracted, Kath ran. She burst out onto Northumberland Avenue, immediately colliding with a trio of bunched up corpses, sending them flying, then hobbled away in completely the wrong direction, moving away from Trafalgar Square and down towards the Thames.

Both Vicky and Selena wanted to yell out at her, but the traumatic events of the last month had conditioned them to silence and the words were stuck in their throats. Before either of them could do anything, Kath turned back and shooed them away. 'Go!' she shouted. 'Get out of here! I've had enough. I gave it a good crack but I can't keep going. I'll make a bit of noise so you two have a chance.'

Selena went to run after her, but Vicky stopped her. If there was any argument to be had, it was a wasted one. Kath kept moving, all the time half-singing, half-crying, yelling nonsense and trying to fill the empty world with as much noise as she was able, for as long as she could.

But that wasn't long at all.

The dead were swarming over her already, scores of them converging. They grabbed at her with numb, gnarled hands and hooked their twisted fingers into her clothes and hair, dragging her down. Kath was old and tired and had barely any fight left, but she still had enough strength to take a final few steps with several of the foul, emaciated creatures clinging onto her. Far too soon there were many, many more, and she disappeared beneath them. Vicky watched, helpless, as her friend – her dear, strong, funny, supportive, lovely, selfless friend who'd kept her going since the rest of the world had died – drowned in rot.

Of all the loss she'd experienced since that Tuesday morning last month, nothing hurt like the pain of losing Kath. Selena felt the loss too, but panic kept her focused. She dragged Vicky towards Trafalgar Square, both of them knowing that the effect of Kath's sacrifice, if it had any effect at all, would be fleeting, and wasted if they didn't move immediately. Her screams had caught the attention of a large number of corpses, and their reactions had in turn attracted others, but now, barely a minute later, the scrum was over. Kath was gone and the dead were on their way back towards the crowds around Trafalgar Square. Nothing to see here.

Vicky was still carrying Kath's rucksack as well as her own. She didn't want to leave it behind. 'Just run,' she whispered to Selena. 'Bloody hard and bloody fast. Got it?'

'Got it,' she said, and they sprinted headlong into the masses.

Fuck.

Vicky knew almost immediately that she'd made a massive miscalculation. Their initial speed was enough to make some impact on the crowds, but nowhere near enough to get them through. She was just ahead now, holding Kath's pack in front of her like a riot shield, Selena following in her immediate wake. Although she shoved many corpses out of the way, there were many, many more of them still ahead. And here, near the base of Nelson's Column, there was another complication. The progress of the slow flow along The Strand had been interrupted by various obstructions – abandoned vehicles, safety barriers, the enormous bronze lion statues – and the dead were increasingly moving in unpredictable directions. Disoriented by the confusion all around her, Vicky almost ran straight into the plinth that the nearest lion statue sat upon. She pulled up just in time and saw that some disrespectful fucker had sprayed the statue with graffiti. A single word – MONUMENT – scrawled in yellow. Even now, after everything that had happened, the pointlessness of wanton damage like that really pissed her off.

Now it was Selena's turn to take the lead. She grabbed Vicky's arm and pulled her to safety up the high steps at the foot of Nelson's Column. From there they could see the National Gallery clearly with its stepped entrance, columns, domes, and turrets, but between them and the building was another few hundred figures that appeared even more tightly packed than the section they'd just managed to get through. The steepness of the steps on the other side and the walls around the square had combined to trap hundreds and hundreds of decaying locals and tourists together in a relatively small area. Even the fountains were full of dead flesh. Vicky and Selena's elevated position at the bottom of Nelson's Column was an island, and they were surrounded.

'What do we do now?' Selena asked.

'Keep running. We don't have any choice.'

'Yeah, but which way?'

Vicky looked around, trying to work out which nightmare scenario appeared the least suicidal, tracing the route of the staggering masses. The bulk of them were still coming up along The Strand, dragging themselves across Trafalgar Square and either becoming trapped there or managing by chance to keep moving along either Whitehall, The Mall, or Cockspur Street. From up here it looked like one of those bloody protest marches that seemed to be on the TV news every few weeks. But there were no banners today, and the vast crowds were almost universally, unnaturally, silent.

'We go back the way we came, I reckon.'

'You serious?'

'Yes. Listen, I know what Kath said and she was right, but it might be worth us paying a visit on the Queen. Just a stopover. That's The Mall over that way, isn't it?'

'Yep. Through Admiralty Arch.'

'We'll have a better chance if we're moving in the same direction as the masses.'

'Really?'

'You don't sound convinced.'

'That's 'cos I'm not.'

'Me neither, but other than spending the next few weeks camped up here on this bloody plinth, I don't see any better options.'

'I know.'

'Okay then, let's move.'

Vicky climbed down, still struggling with two rucksacks, and was immediately surrounded again. She was vaguely aware of Selena behind her, but the dead were so tightly packed that she couldn't look back and check. She tripped down the kerb then lost her footing and was shoved to one side by a sudden unexpected surge of bodies. She tried to compensate, to make sure she was still heading in the right direction for The Mall, but realised too late that the dead people directly ahead weren't moving. They were trapped, wedged between the wreck of a car on its side and the black cab that had driven into it. She tried to stop and turn around, but there were too many bodies behind, forcing her and Selena toward the blockage.

Boxed into a corner. They weren't going anywhere.

Selena was right behind her now. 'Scared,' she whispered.

'I know. Me too.'

Then came a noise neither of them was expecting to hear. It came from a couple hundred metres behind them, but was close enough to make a difference: a high-volume hiss of static and then, half a second later, 'The Marriage of Figaro' blasted out at an ear-splitting volume.

It stopped the dead in their lurching tracks.

Vicky felt the pressure from the masses behind her immediately start to lessen. They were being distracted by the sound and changing direction. In contrast to the vacuum-like silence of absolutely everything else, it was impossible to ignore. She was soon able to turn around, and, doing her best not to strut, mimicked the slow and clumsy movements of the dead. An army of corpses was surging towards the source of the music. Sufficiently pre-occupied, they didn't react when she grabbed Selena.

'What's going on?' Selena asked, but Vicky couldn't answer. For a second she wondered if the noise was something to do with Kath, but that was just wishful thinking. Kath would have needed to run several hundred metres through the dense crowds to get anywhere near this place, but she'd barely been able to walk.

'This is bad,' Vicky said.

'What are you on about?' Selena replied, confused. 'This is good. They're ignoring us.'

'For now, yes, but what effect do you think that noise is going to have? There will be tens of thousands more of those fucking things all heading this way now, and not just down The Strand, they'll be coming from everywhere. Even the ones that have already passed through here will come back. If we don't get out of here now, we never will.'

She was right.

The music was coming from a car on the far side of Trafalgar Square, near the junction with Duncannon Street. The space between them and the car had already become a chaotic mass of rot. Hundreds of corpses were homing in on the vehicle in an unstoppable slow-motion stampede, oblivious to the hordes that were already there.

39

'We could just break into another building,' Selena suggested. 'Hide out till they've gone.'

'Which part of this don't you understand? They're not going to go away. This place is going to be packed solid. They won't be able to escape, and neither will we.'

'You got a better idea then?'

'Same idea as before. Run!'

With Kath's rucksack held out in front of her again, Vicky tried to force her way through to The Mall. Selena followed, scared she was going to be left behind. Two small specks of life struggling to keep moving through a seething ocean of death.

'Head for the palace,' Vicky shouted, not pausing or looking back. Some of the closest of the dead snatched at her, but her strength was sufficient to keep pushing through.

To a point.

One of the corpses grabbed hold of Kath's bag and blocked her way forward. Vicky tried to snatch the rucksack away and keep moving, but the figure stood its ground. Dressed in ragged, loose-fitting clothing, the bearded man looked as bedraggled and worn as any of the thousands of corpses swarming all around them. It took Vicky several seconds before she realised he wasn't dead.

'Follow me,' he said.

2

The frontage of one of the buildings near to the end of Whitehall was covered with scaffolding which, in turn, was draped with a skin of white protective sheeting. The man nonchalantly jumped up, caught a crossbar, then pulled himself off the ground. Vicky didn't think she could match his athleticism, even though her life likely depended on it. He reached back down and told them to pass up their bags. Somewhat protected by the safety barriers and boarding that had been erected around the entrance to the building, they did as he asked. He then lay on his stomach and reached back down. 'Now you.' Selena grabbed his outstretched hand and used the soles of her boots on the wall to climb, then managed to reach an upright and pulled herself the rest of the way up. She crawled along the scaffold boards on her hands and knees while he helped Vicky, who collapsed exhausted once she finally reached safety. Breathless and broken, she buried her face in Kath's pack and sobbed.

'Sorry about your friend,' the man said. His soft Welsh accent took them both by surprise.

'Were you watching us?'

'No. Listening. I heard you. I think I heard your friend, actually. I'm Sam.'

'I'm Selena. This is Vicky.'

'Hi.'

'Hi.'

'We thought we were the only ones left,' Vicky said.

'You haven't seen anyone else?'

'Not a soul.'

'Everyone's keeping their heads down. There are a few more of us yet. What the hell were you doing out in the open? The streets are deadly around here today.'

'There was some kind of surge. Thousands of them. They forced us out of hiding.' She paused, trying to connect the dots. 'Wait... was all this anything to do with you? Our friend died because of—'

'Not guilty,' he said quickly. 'I was trying to work out why they were surging, as it happens.'

'And?'

'They were definitely reacting to something, but I can't work out what. Could have been anything. An explosion, a building could have collapsed... something like that. To be honest, I'm surprised the whole city hasn't gone up in flames yet. There must have been so much shit left running when they all died. I've seen a fair amount of damage in places, but nothing like I expected. Think of the number of gas appliances and...'

They were both staring at him. Self-conscious, he shut up.

Down at street level, the music was finally silenced.

'Was that you?' Selena asked.

'Yep.'

'How did you know where we were? How long were you watching?'

'I told you, I wasn't watching. I was listening.'

'So how did you know about Kath?'

'You're carrying an extra pack, that's how. And I think it was her I heard first. Which way did she go? Could she still be out there? Because I'm happy to go and look for her if you—'

'She's gone,' Vicky said, cutting across him. She held Kath's rucksack close, almost hugging it. 'She was tired, and she'd had enough. I think she thought she was slowing us down. She made enough noise to give us a chance of getting away.'

'She might still be out there,' Selena said, hopeful.

Vicky shook her head. 'She's gone.'

Sam peered out through a gap in the protective sheeting. 'Anyway, you were pretty easy to spot after that. I just watched the crowds and how they reacted. I knew roughly where I thought you were, then I saw you both pop up near the lion statues.' He nodded at Selena. 'Your red hoodie made you easy to spot. I could see you were trapped, so I set a car stereo playing on the other side of Trafalgar Square.'

'We weren't trapped. We'd have been okay,' she said.

'Whatever. You looked pretty trapped from where I was.'

He climbed up another level of the scaffolding, then walked along to the end of the building. They could hear his boots on the boards overhead. 'What do you reckon?' Selena asked, whispering again.

'Bit of an asshole if you ask me.'

'He seems alright.'

'Seems to have a bob on himself.'

'Does it matter? He's the first living person we've seen, and he says there are other people too. We have to stick with him for now, at least. Don't we?'

'Do we? Anyway, we haven't been invited yet.'

'Come on, Vic. Stop being difficult.'

'I'm not. I'm just being cautious. We've lost so much already. We don't know anything about him. He might be a psycho.'

Sam appeared on the other side of them, having climbed down another way. 'I'm not a psycho,' he said. 'And you are invited. The more the merrier. It's a bit of a trek back to base, though.'

He hadn't been joking.

Sam's group had stationed themselves in a hotel just off Fleet Street, only about a mile from Trafalgar Square, but given the amount of once-human traffic that had flooded along Fleet Street and on into The Strand today, it was necessary to avoid the most direct routes. Time no longer had the same certainty it used to, and a journey that would previously have taken less than half an hour, today took almost three hours. The winding route Sam led them along had been meticulously planned and committed to memory, designed to avoid the bulk of the street-level crowds. He took them through buildings and sometimes over roofs to avoid going around. He used passages, side-streets, and underpasses that they otherwise wouldn't have realised were there. His low-fi, low speed parkour route had been completely necessary, he'd told them, to ensure they stayed safe, but safe was absolutely the last thing either Vicky or Selena felt today.

The three of them were standing on the edge of the roof of a building which overlooked Fleet Street. They'd got up here by climbing onto a taxi, then getting onto the roof of the truck the taxi driver had stopped alongside. From there they'd entered the offices above a shop through an open first floor window then scaled a black metal fire escape up onto the roof. Straddling the gap between this building and the next was a makeshift bridge formed from two long metal ladders which had been lashed together and strapped down at either end.

'You're not serious,' Vicky said when Sam told them to cross. Until now they'd followed him without question, but things were getting ridiculous. 'Are you doing this on purpose? This some kind of stupid initiation stunt or something?'

Sam shook his head and grinned (which infuriated her). 'Believe me, crossing this gap is an infinitely safer option than trying to get in through the front door. You can see where we're based now, can't you?' He gestured towards a point around a hundred metres further down Fleet Street, where a swollen crowd of corpses had gathered. 'They know, you know.'

'What?' Selena asked.

'They know where we are. Don't ask me how, but they know.'

'Bullshit,' Vicky said.

'It isn't. The fact they're still there now kind of proves it. Thousands of dead people walked along Fleet Street and into The Strand today, yet they're still down there. I don't know if you've been seeing the same things I have recently, but there's so little happening in the world now, any kind of incident can get blown out of all proportion. We might find that all those thousands were reacting to something pretty insignificant in the scheme of things, and that it was their reactions to their reactions that blew things up out of control.'

'But you'd have expected those bodies down there to have followed the herd.'

'Exactly. They're becoming much more aware. It's as if they've worked out that what's happening here is more important than whatever's going on near Trafalgar Square.'

'Bollocks.'

'It isn't. Think about it logically.'

'Logically?' Vicky protested.

'Yes, logically. If there wasn't anything here worth hanging around for, that crowd would have been long gone. A lot of the ones we're looking at now have been here for days.'

'And you know that for certain, do you?'

'Of course. I make a habit of watching their behaviours.'

'Now that's just weird,' Selena said.

'Maybe, but I reckon it's important.'

'But what makes you think they're the same ones?' Vicky asked. 'They're all starting to look the same to me.'

'See the paint?'

Vicky swallowed her vertigo and looked down again. She saw that quite a few of the crowding corpses had been sprayed with fluorescent paint. A couple had bright crosses and spots painted on their backs, while others sported mops of crazy coloured hair. The luminescence was startlingly out of place.

'You've tagged them? That's a bit sick, ain't it?' Selena said. 'It's not their fault they're like that. You should have a bit of respect.'

'I think we're long past that now, don't you? As it happens, I afford those poor bastards more respect than most. I don't harm them, if I can help it, but I've seen people who make doing them in some kind of sick sport. It's just a bit of spray paint. If our positions were reversed, I'm sure they'd understand.'

'I don't get it,' Selena said, and she held onto a support and hung out so far over the edge of the building that it made Vicky's stomach flip.

'I've used different colours and different kinds of markings on different days and weeks. I try to keep a log of where I marked them and when so I can track how far they've moved and in which direction, but what happened today has screwed that up. A bright yellow makeover makes them easier to tell apart from a distance, so I don't need to get too close. That's how I know they're the same ones, and like I said, it's a real concern because the more control the dead begin to demonstrate, the bigger the problem they're going to become.'

'Can't see why it matters,' Selena said.

'It matters because if we can understand and anticipate what they're doing, then we've got a better chance of not being caught out by massive crowds of the fuckers like you two were today. And that's important, because we're stuck in the heart of London. I know there are plenty of people who stayed dead but, even taking them into account, we're still looking at potentially as many as four or five million corpses up on their feet and walking around. It's one thing trying to avoid them, but when you're looking at numbers like that... I'm beginning to think that locking ourselves away and waiting for it all to blow over just isn't going to cut it anymore.'

'That's still the safest option,' Vicky said.

'Is that what you've been doing? It didn't work out too well for you and your friend today, did it?'

'Screw you,' she snapped at him, annoyed.

'Jesus, get over yourself. Can't you see how important everything that's happened today might be? Tens of thousands of those damn things suddenly changed direction this morning, and there's nothing to say it won't happen again.'

'Could have been anything,' she shrugged.

'You're right, it could, but it was definitely *something*, and I don't know about you, but I'm not taking any chances.'

'I'm freezing. Can we argue about this inside?' Selena asked, tired of the standoff. Sam crossed the ladder bridge and, with a little hesitation and a lot less speed, she followed him over. Vicky didn't.

'It'll hold your weight no trouble,' Sam shouted back across the gap.

'I'm not questioning the sturdiness of your little bridge here,' she said, unimpressed. 'It's the drop down that bothers me.'

He shrugged. 'Suit yourself. Top few floors of the building you're standing on are empty, but I hope you've got a decent stash of food in your rucksack because there's not a lot left here. We cleared the place out early days.'

She still wasn't moving.

'Come on, Vic,' Selena said, teeth chattering with the cold.

'If you change your mind, the hotel's a couple of doors down. Avoid the main entrance for obvious reasons. There's a courtyard out back that's reasonably well protected.'

Apparently done with talking, Sam turned and walked away.

'I'll come back for you,' Selena said, and followed him inside through a service door. Vicky watched them go then forced herself to move. She took a breath and focussed on the narrow metal rungs, not the gaping chasms between them.

3

Vicky hated being in London. She'd always made a point of only coming into the city when she absolutely had to, and she couldn't get over the fact that the one night she'd had no choice but to come to town had turned out to be the last night on Earth for millions, possibly billions of people. Now she was trapped. She'd stayed over for an early hospital appointment because they'd wanted her there at the crack of dawn, and she'd wanted to be fresh and alert, not battered from the rush hour scrum. She hadn't slept a wink in the unfamiliar hotel bed; too nervous, gutful of worries and head filled with questions she didn't really want to hear the answers to. In the end, it hadn't made any difference. Next morning, all her existing uncertainties had been wiped away and replaced with new ones. Worse ones. She'd have given anything to have been safe at home in Luton when everything had happened.

'You okay, Vic?' Selena asked.

'Not really,' she said, and she wiped her eyes. She tried to convince herself she was crying with fatigue, but she wasn't sure. They were standing in the courtyard Sam had mentioned, a precious block of open space which was, as far as she could see, completely safe. All the visible access points were blocked by parked cars. There were other people out here, and they seemed so... *normal*. They were moving about freely, doing odd jobs, talking to each other, leaning against the wall and smoking... she hadn't experienced anything like this for over a month, and at times she'd thought she never would again. It was also the first time in a long time she could remember being able to turn a full three-sixty and not see a single dead body, moving or otherwise. It was almost overwhelming.

'Let's get you inside,' Sam said. 'I'll introduce you both to everyone, then find you somewhere to kip.'

He took them past a covered area where several people were sitting. Some were talking, some reading, others just staring into space. Most of them looked up and acknowledged the new arrivals, all of them seeming to say, *'we know how you're feeling and what you've been through, we've been there too,'* without actually saying anything at all. It was all Vicky could do to nod and smile back without completely losing her shit.

Inside, the building was colder and darker than she expected. Even now it never failed to take her by surprise whenever she walked into a place like this. She still expected warmth, light, movement and noise, but got nothing. There was a spacious lounge at the front of the hotel, tomb-like in its emptiness. Many of the ground floor windows had been covered to shut out the prying eyes of the undead masses on Fleet Street. The entire ground floor of the hotel was virtually empty. It made sense, Vicky decided. The quiet here was unnerving because it wasn't absolute. She could hear the door rattling as the dead outside clattered against it.

It was reassuring that these people were taking survival seriously and not just seeing out their time in as opulent surroundings as they could find. The temptation must have been there, because the hotel had certainly been a luxurious one. Sam took them past the entrance to an eerily soulless bar then through the reception area, past a huge front desk that might have been impressive, had it been lit up and not hidden in shadow.

'How many people are here?' Selena asked.

'Forty-eight, including you two.'

The number came as a shock. Until today, Vicky hadn't thought there were that many folks left alive anywhere.

They climbed a magnificent staircase which opened out onto a wide landing. Despite the scattered piles of supplies and bags of rubbish everywhere, it was still a welcoming place. 'Most stuff tends to happen around here,' Sam said. 'We use the kitchens if we have to, but we try and limit the noise downstairs for obvious reasons.'

'Will we have to do jobs?' Selena asked, suddenly sounding a lot younger than seventeen. 'I'm no good at cooking.'

'I'd be lying if I said everyone does their fair share, but it works best if people pull their weight. We've got some folk who do fuck all, others who just sit in their rooms and never come out, and the rest of us get stuff done. Funny thing is, most people actually like doing jobs. It's easier to cope with everything that's going on if you're distracted.'

'That why you were outside today?'

'That's exactly why.'

Sam stopped at the door to a large function room. There was a handful of people inside, but the contrast with the isolation of the last few weeks was such that, to Vicky, it seemed almost crowded. Selena went forward smiling, but Vicky couldn't quite step over the threshold. She cursed herself. *Get a bloody grip, woman.*

Sam showed Selena where to get some food, and introduced her to a short, thick-set woman who was the loudest voice in the room. The woman looked across, saw Vicky, and walked straight over. Without hesitation, she hugged her tight. Vicky wanted to hug her back, but instead just stood there.

'Just let it all go,' the woman said. 'I did when I first found this lot.'

'I can't, not yet.'

'Ah, there, now. Give it time. I'm Marianne.'

'Vicky.'

'Hungry?'

She shook her head.

'Cold?'

'Freezing,' Vicky said.

'Cup of tea?'

She smiled briefly, an unfamiliar tug. 'Yes, please.'

There was a large gas burner set up at the end of an expensive-looking boardroom table. Marianne lit the flame with a match and warmed her hands. 'Everything is such an effort now, don't you think?'

'You can say that again.'

'When this all kicked off, I was on my own in my office. Once I'd got my head straight and stopped screaming, I thought it made sense to stay there for a while. I'm on my own, and I didn't fancy trying to get out of London on foot. I was doing alright for myself for a while, I'm afraid my love of tea was my undoing.'

'How so?'

'I'd got myself all set up, you see, because I used to stay over at the office now and then if I was working late. I kept some bedding and a sofa ready, a small toilet bag, a change of pants and so on. I'd come in that morning planning on three nights, so I'd stocked up on food from Sainsburys on my way. It was bad enough when everyone dropped dead, but when those nasty bastards got up and started walking around outside, I thought I'd better stay put. When the electricity was cut off, I realised I was knackered. I went to make myself a cup of tea and couldn't. I had a kettle, a microwave and a toaster, and they were all fucking useless. That was the first time I sat and cried. Back to square one. And now, here we are, a month and a bit after the end of the world, millions of people dead, and I'm still getting angsty because I'm having to drink supermarket's own brand tea with long life milk. Middle-class problems, eh?'

Her comment made Vicky laugh involuntarily.

'That's better,' Marianne said. 'I don't know what you and your friend have been through, Vicky, but by the looks of things I'm guessing that you've had a particularly shitty day. I think you'd be happy with your tea if I made it with cold water and spat in it first.'

'I don't know about that, but yeah, it's been tough.'

'Want to talk about it?'

'Not just now.'

'Fair enough. Let me know if ever you do.'

Vicky just nodded, unable to respond with anything more.

Marianne put a plump hand on her shoulder. 'Sam mentioned... that you lost someone today. I'm sorry, love. It's strange, isn't it, how loss hurts so much more now. You never get used to the pain. I think we've all got so little left that when we—'

'I said not now,' Vicky snapped at her.

Marianne raised her hands in submission. 'You're right. I'm sorry. I talk too much. Bad habit. I was a lawyer, you see, and I used to spend all my time having to... and there I go again. I'll shut up now.'

'The day you shut up is the day I know the world truly has gone mad.'

Vicky looked around. The man who'd entered the room was large and confident, with cropped hair and sporting an impressive bushy black and grey beard. He wrapped an arm around Marianne and squeezed her affectionately, then shook Vicky's hand. 'David Shires,' he said. 'Good to meet you. Our Sam has a habit of picking up waifs and strays on his travels, and I'm glad he managed to find you two. You're the first new arrivals for a while. Sad to say, it doesn't look like there's many more of us left out there.'

4

David had apologised that all the biggest rooms had already been taken, but neither Vicky nor Selena cared. They were shown to adjacent rooms on another floor which were more than adequate. Truth be told, Vicky would have been happy sleeping on the carpet in one of the hallways. Her bed was almost too comfortable. She felt guilty lying there in comfort, propped up on her elbows with a panoramic view of dead London stretching out in front of her.

David and Marianne had both mentioned that they encouraged people not to shut themselves away. The group tried to prepare a rudimentary hot meal for between six and seven o'clock, then gathered together in the first-floor meeting rooms. Selena had been spark out in the room next door, but Vicky was too tired to sleep. When she heard voices drifting up the stairs and the noise of cutlery and crockery, she'd woken Selena and taken her down to join the party.

The food was decent and very welcome. It was simple dried pasta with some kind of sauce, an overdose of seasoning to take away the blandness, and it was the best thing Vicky had eaten in a long time. She'd had a hankering for fresh fruit and vegetables for weeks, but for now, a bowl of penne pasta hit the spot.

The majority of the group later gathered in a room across the landing from where they'd eaten. It was a comfortable, trendy-looking space that would have appeared far more contemporary had it not been lit by candles and battery-powered lamps. Most of them sat close to each other in one corner. It was on the same side of the hotel as her bedroom, Vicky realised, because the view across the city was similar. It was darker now, though, and that made outside appear increasingly foreboding. There was just enough light remaining to pick out the outlines of recognisable buildings, but the fact there was no depth, only silhouettes and shadows, stripped away all familiarity.

There was booze, though, which helped.

David Shires was sitting in the centre of the group, cradling a black spiced rum and Pepsi Max. 'Don't want you to get the idea we're some crazy cult or whatnot, but we've established something of a tradition. No pressure, no great long stories, but we do like to give new arrivals the opportunity to tell us who they are, how they got here, and what they've seen. It's never easy, we understand that, but it sometimes helps. Some folks find it cathartic. I know I did.'

Vicky cringed. A chap next to her sensed her unease. 'I'm Sanjay,' he said. 'Beat my story if you can. I drive buses. *Drove* buses, I guess I should say now. My sixty-three passengers all died while I was driving along Peckham High Street. I felt so bad, like it was my fault. I just kept going for a while. Pulled up at every bloody stop along the way before I got a grip. Hated myself for walking away and abandoning them.'

'I'd been at a lodge meeting on Great Queen Street the night before,' David said, picking up where Sanjay had left off. 'I was sitting in my hotel reception, waiting for a taxi to turn up to take me to Euston. I couldn't wait to get home. Needless to say, the cab never arrived.' A few chuckles sounded quietly.

Then silence. Vicky's turn. It was absolutely the last thing she wanted to do, but she knew she had to do it. These people had taken her and Selena in, had given them food and shelter and offered support... though she couldn't help thinking there'd be a twist in the final act. Her life had become a non-stop horror movie, so why should anything be different now? If she had anything left to bet with, and if money still had any value, she'd stake her final few quid on this being a group of closet cannibals or something equally perverse.

In contrast to Vicky, Selena was buoyed by the confidence of youth and the relief of being warm, well fed, in company, and not having to keep a constant lookout for corpses. 'I'm Selena. I'm seventeen. I come from Purfleet. I lived there with my mum and dad.'

'So, were you at home when it happened?' David asked.

'No, I'd come into town to get myself some clothes for college.'

'What were you studying?'

'Art and design. Fat lot of good any of that will do me now.'

An older guy sitting next to Selena dug her in the ribs. 'You never know. Sam likes to do a bit of painting from time to time.' He laughed alone at his own joke.

Sam was on the edge of the group, half-in and half-out of the light. 'Stop taking the piss. You can start having a go at me when you actually do something useful, Stan.'

David was keen for Selena's voice to be heard. 'So how did you and Vicky end up together?'

'I was with my friend Rochelle. We'd got the early train, so we stopped at Maccies for something to eat. There was supposed to be a few of us meeting up.

'We was sitting upstairs, killing time, and then it... it got Rochelle. She started choking. I just thought her food had gone down the wrong way or something, but then there was blood coming out of her mouth and she couldn't breathe. There was only us up there, and I was just trying to help her, you know? Chelle just went all limp and heavy; I'd never seen a dead body before, but I knew she'd died. And I was panicking and shouting out for someone to help and... and it was only then I realised everything else had gone quiet. No more voices, you know? Not a peep in the place.'

Vicky looked around at the other faces she could see, trying to gauge their reactions to Selena's story. It struck her that every single person in this room, along with everyone else she'd ever meet from now until the end of her time, would all have equally horrific tales of their own to share about the day the whole world died.

Selena carried on talking like she didn't want to stop. 'I was walking around on my own for ages, looking for other people

55

'cos I was thinking there was no way I was the only one left. It was hours later when I was going back to Victoria Station that I saw Kath. Stupid, really, but I wanted to go home, and I was still thinking I could get the train. This woman came running out of this coffee shop, waving her arms and screaming at me like some mad granny. I swear, I've never been so happy to see anyone; we hugged for, like, whole minutes. Then we found Vic a couple of hours later, and that was it until today.'

'What happened to Kath?' David asked.

'She died today,' Selena said, and that was enough.

Vicky hesitantly began her own version of the story. 'I was in a hotel, sitting in my room. Hadn't moved all day. Everywhere I looked there were dead bodies,' she shrugged, 'so I just stayed where I was.'

'Until you heard the two of us talking outside.'

'It was like hearing a foghorn. Sound travels when there's nothing else.'

'Yeah, and Kath never shut up, did she.'

'Kath was amazing. She was the best of the best. She did so much to keep us safe. She sacrificed herself so we'd have a chance. We wouldn't be here without her.'

'Sounds like you were lucky to have known her,' David said.

'She's the one who told us about Ledsey Cross,' Selena said, her voice now filled with more enthusiasm than the rest of the room combined.

'Ledsey Cross, what's that?'

'It's this community up north. It's where Kath was from.'

'Not exactly where she was from,' Vicky said, correcting her, 'but close. She had friends living there.'

'Still does,' Selena said. 'Her friend was texting her, even after everyone had died.'

'You serious?' Sam asked.

'Yeah. She showed us the messages on her phone.'

'Where is this place?'

'On the edge of the Yorkshire Dales,' Vicky told him.

'Hell of a distance to get to from here,' David said. 'I think we're going to struggle to get out of London, if I'm honest.'

'We were trying to get there. From what Kath told us, it sounds ideal. It's an eco-friendly village. Self-sufficient.'

'Sounds like a hippy commune,' Marianne said, laughing. 'Right up your street, Sam.'

'Piss off,' he said mildly.

'Our Sam's a bit of an eco-warrior,' David explained. 'Only now that pretty much the entire human race has been wiped out, you haven't got a lot left to protest about, have you, mate? The world became carbon neutral the minute everyone died.'

Sam looked less than impressed. 'Best thing that could've happened to the planet.'

'It does look amazing, though,' Vicky said, changing the focus. 'Kath said the village was designed and built from scratch a decade ago. Totally self-sustaining. It's got its own water supply, solar power, thermal heating, wind turbines, energy efficient buildings... It was supposed to be the first of many, but you know how these things go.'

'Probably didn't make enough money for the investors,' Sam grumbled. 'But the fact remains, it's still a couple of hundred miles from here at least. There's bound to be similar places a lot closer. I've been thinking we should head down to Kent, maybe, or the Isle of Wight. Things don't get much more self-contained than on an island.'

Stan, an older man who'd mocked Sam's spray painting, put his hands up to interrupt the conversation. 'Can you all just shut up a second. Did you not hear what this girl just said?' He nodded at Selena. 'She said her friend had messages from this place after everyone had died. You did say that, didn't you?'

'That's right,' Selena answered.

'But that's impossible.'

'It's true. There's people still alive there. Loads of them.'

Stan became far more animated. 'Crap. You can't just turn up here like this and start coming out with all this nonsense. Do you know how dangerous that is?'

Selena was offended. 'It's the truth, I swear. Kath's friend Annalise was still alive, and the two of them were texting right up until when the phone signal died. She said there's a whole group of people up there.'

'Bollocks.'

'Give her a break, Stan,' David said.

Stan crossed his arms defiantly and sat back in his seat. 'I don't believe a bloody word of it. And even if it was true, I still think we need to stay here in London. It's the capital city, for crying out loud. It's our best chance of staying in one piece.'

Sam took exception. 'You're wrong, as usual. You want to stay here because you're scared of having to go out there and get your hands dirty.'

'Quite happy to admit I'd rather not go outside, thank you very much,' Stan said, and he turned away from Sam, conversation over.

Selena wasn't finished. 'We don't care what you think, do we, Vic? There are other people at Ledsey Cross and we promised Kath we'd go there. We've got Kath's stuff. I can show you the messages on her phone if you want. I can show you her photos, and she made me save the map.'

Sam stood up. 'Look, I don't want to piss on anyone's parade here, but how many times do I have to say the same thing? We need to be realistic about what we can and can't do right now. With the number of bodies we're currently having to deal with out there, coupled with how unpredictable their behaviour is starting to become, we need to think very, very carefully about trying to go anywhere else until we're absolutely certain what we're going to find there. It's too much of a risk.'

'He's right,' David said. 'Much as I'd like to try and get home, I think getting out of the capital is pretty much a physical impossibility right now. Like Sam says, the dead are becoming more volatile. We need to wait until they're no longer a threat.'

'And how long's that likely to be?' Stan asked, back in the game.

'Probably six months or so.'

'Well, I'm going,' Selena said. The tone of her voice left no room for negotiation.

'Good luck with that. Send us a postcard when you get there, love,' Stan sniped.

Vicky leaned back and put her hands to her face. She felt more exhausted than ever. Noticing her new friend's distress, Marianne became keen to steer the conversation into safer waters. 'Did you work out what was going on out there today, Sam?'

'I've already told you what I know. There was a great flood of them heading west.'

'Heading towards something or going away from it?' Stan asked.

'Towards, of course.'

'Well, I don't know that, do I? I don't spend as much time messing with the bloody things as you do.'

'Maybe you should. You need to think about this stuff, we all do.'

'What does it matter, anyway? Bloody zombies.'

'Don't call them that,' David said. 'It's stupid.'

'But that's what they are.'

Sam shook his head in despair. 'Actually, no matter what you decide to call them, the direction they're moving in is important. Stan, you need to get your head out of your ass and wake up. They're not capable of thinking the way we do, and they don't react the same way either. You can't scare something that's already dead.'

'I know that...'

'So they're never going to be on the run from anything, they're only ever going to be heading *towards* things.'

'Such as?'

'I don't know. Light? Sound? Greater numbers? It's not easy being out there right now. By the time we realised they were moving down Fleet Street this morning, whatever it was that had caught their interest was already long gone. I was trying to get to the front of the herd, but that's when I spotted Vicky and Selena, so I focused on helping them instead.'

'But wouldn't we have heard it?' Marianne asked. 'Must have been something pretty substantial to have caught the attention of so many of them.'

'Not necessarily. You'd be surprised. The world's like a vacuum these days. There could be all kinds of stuff going on within a couple of miles of this place and we'd be none the wiser. The problem with hunkering down is you stop looking outwards.'

'But there are so few people left,' Vicky said. 'We hadn't seen anyone else until today.'

'I know, and that concerns me. Like I said, it could have been anything that triggered what we saw. It could have happened miles away, and it could have been something relatively minor that started a chain reaction. We've seen this before – a handful of them reacts, then more and more react to those reactions... you get the idea. I'm saying that even the smallest initial disturbances could end up being exponential.'

'Bollocks,' Stan said again. 'You read too much into everything. Like I keep saying, all we need to do is keep our heads down until they've rotted down to nothing.'

'Have you seen the crowd that's outside the front door of this place?' Vicky asked. Stan didn't answer.

'There's another reason why we shouldn't call them zombies,' Sam continued. 'Apart from the fact that Dave's right and it does sound stupid, we need to not fall into the trap of thinking that what we're dealing with here are the same things we used to watch on TV and in films. They're not trying to eat us or infect us... as far as we know, we all seem to be immune to whatever it was that did this to everyone else.'

'So that's alright, isn't it,' Stan said.

'Is it?'

'Yes. It means we're probably not going to end up like that.'

'You're probably right, but I can't believe you're still being so bloody blasé about it.'

'Or are you just paranoid?'

'Maybe I am, but there are two reasons for that.'

'Go on.'

'First, the dead are constantly changing. I'd say evolving, but that doesn't feel like the right word in the circumstances. I can't put my finger on it, and it makes no sense when I try to explain it, but the more time that passes since they died, the more self-control they're starting to show. We all saw it... they dropped dead, then got up again a couple of days later. Then they started to hear things and see things... it's like they're regaining more and more of what they lost.'

'Even by your standards that's mad,' Stan said.

'I know how it sounds, but I'm telling you, out there today, those bodies were a damn sight more dangerous than they have been previously.'

'We saw it too,' Vicky said.

'And chances are they'll be worse again tomorrow.'

The room fell uncomfortably quiet. Vicky pulled her knees up to her chest and focused on the lamplight. When they'd first gathered in this corner of the room, she'd found the familiarity and the closeness of everyone else reassuring. Now the only thing she was aware of was how dark the rest of the building, and the world beyond, was.

'I'm sorry,' Sam said. 'Didn't mean to freak everyone out.'

'These things need to be discussed,' David told him.

'On the plus side, Stan's right, they are decomposing. Honestly, it's gross out there right now. They're literally falling apart at the seams.'

Sam's attempt at reassurance fell on deaf ears. Vicky looked straight at him. 'You said there are two reasons why you're worried. What's the second one?'

He answered without hesitation. 'It's the fact there are so bloody many of them. The fact that for each one of us in here tonight, there are tens of thousands of corpses walking the streets. So, when you put those two things together, it starts to feel like a recipe for disaster. My advice is not to go getting a false sense of security because your bloody zombies or whatever the hell you want to call them don't appear to want to eat your brains. Just stay alert and stay switched on, because it's likely we'll only get one chance to fuck up.'

5

Vicky woke up with a start and jumped straight out of bed, fully dressed. She stepped into her boots and reached for her crowbar, then stood completely still and waited and listened. There it was again. She heard raised voices coming from another part of the hotel, then smashing glass.

She'd remembered where she was and what had happened in a heartbeat, a month on the run having made disorientation and quick starts the new norm. She went out into the corridor and checked Selena's room next door. Satisfied she was safely sleeping, Vicky pulled the door shut and carried on down the landing. She froze again when she heard more noise downstairs. Another smash, more muffled voices. *Christ.* Why weren't more people reacting? She realised it was likely because the hotel had been filled top down, and as recent arrivals, hers and Selena's rooms were on a lower floor to most others. She started to descend the main staircase, feeling increasingly nervous because the further down she went, the darker the building became. There was a glimmer of light coming from under a door on the far side of the reception area, and she could see slow shadows moving on the other side.

Weeks ago, when she, Selena and Kath had spent a couple of days hiding in a Victorian townhouse that had been converted into offices, the front door had been inadvertently left open. The three of them had been sleeping in a back room, and it was only when Vicky opened the connecting door next morning that she discovered the rest of the building was full of death, packed solid with bodies. Was she about to walk into something similar? Had the mass of corpses gathered in Fleet Street managed to break in?

She stopped when she was level with the reception desk. Yet

another smash. A definite scream. Were those the sounds of people panicking, trying to quieten each other for fear of riling the undead masses further? Vicky ducked into an alcove to compose herself and confirm her plan of attack: *find out exactly how much of the hotel has been compromised, then get back upstairs, get your stuff, get Selena, and get the hell out of here.*

Except it wasn't as simple as that anymore, was it? There were other people to think about now. They weren't her responsibility, but, at the same time, after waiting weeks to find other survivors, she couldn't just escape this place and leave the rest of them sleeping in their beds, could she? That would be inhuman.

Almost at the door now. Crowbar gripped tight. Ready to lash out, ready to run for cover, ready to do whatever was necessary. She opened the door before she could talk herself out of it.

'Who the fuck are you?'

Vicky just stood there, unable to answer, staring at the woman leaning over the bar, clearly drunk. She looked around the room and saw there were four others in here, three men and another woman, all the worse for wear. No dead bodies, not yet, anyway. No obvious signs of damage other than smashed glasses and drinks bottles.

'Sorry...' she stammered, 'I heard noises and I just thought...'

Another man appeared from around a corner, zipping up his trousers. 'Evening,' he said. It was Stan.

'You just gonna stand there gawping or are you coming in for a drink?' the woman who'd spoken first asked.

Vicky was struggling to string two words together. Stan helped himself to a bottle of beer from behind the bar and offered it to her. 'Sorry if we woke you up. No harm done. You're more than happy to come in and have a drink if you want.' He then turned to the others. 'Everyone, this is Vicky. She arrived today. I hadn't had chance to tell her about our little club.'

'Your club?'

'Just a few friends who'd rather not spend all our time hiding under tables, waiting for the end of the world to come.'

'Hang on, that was last month, wasn't it?' a bloke said, swigging wine from a bottle, laughing too loud at his own joke.

'Just because the world's gone to hell out there, doesn't mean we have to stop living inside, don't you think?' Stan continued. 'A lock-in while we're locked-up, if you like.'

'That's pathetic, Stan,' the drunk woman said.

'I thought the bodies had broken in,' Vicky said.

'Nothing but the warm type are welcome in here,' Stan told her. 'This building is a lot stronger than those scaremongers would have you believe. It'll take more than a few of those unfortunates outside to cause us a problem. Seriously, come in and join us. You're more than welcome.'

It didn't feel right. No, worse than that, it felt completely wrong.

'I'm good, thanks,' Vicky said, and she turned to leave and go back to bed. She was aware of a mumbled conversation going on behind her, then Stan ran after her and put a hand on her shoulder. She slumped, too tired for any grief.

'I'd be grateful if you didn't give the game away, Vicky. There are certain people here who'd not be best pleased if they found out we'd been helping ourselves to the contents of the wine cellar.'

'Do whatever you want, just don't cause me any problems, that's all I ask.'

Stan paused, checking that no one else was listening, then whispered to her as if he was sharing some great secret. 'You know who that is in there, don't you?' He nodded his chin back towards the bar.

'Which one?'

'Good looking lad with the wine just now?'

'Haven't got a clue.'

'Good grief, girl! Seriously? Bloody hell, that's Damien McAdams.'

'Damien McWho?'

'Plays for Arsenal. Scored a double in the FA cup quarter-final last year.'

'So?'

'So, do you have any idea how much he's worth?'

'Yes, same as the rest of us. Absolutely zero.' Vicky turned her back on Stan and went up to her room.

6
DAY FORTY

Outside in the hotel courtyard, David heard someone approaching. He turned around and saw it was Vicky. 'What brings you out so early?'

'Coming with you.'

'You really don't have to. You only just got here.'

'It's been almost a week. Anyway, I want to. Selena and I have been eating your food. It's only right I help replace it.'

'Like I said, you don't have to.'

'I know. And like I said, I want to.'

'Fair enough. I'll be honest, we've been putting this scavenger hunt off. Needs must, though.'

'Suits me. I'd rather stay occupied.'

'I'm with you on that. The quicker time passes, the sooner it'll be before I get home.'

'Where is home exactly?'

'Sixmilebridge.'

'And where's that?'

'Ireland. I definitely picked the wrong time to be visiting London.'

'You and me both.'

'I'll try and get back there as soon as I can. Don't know how, but I'll find a way. Gives me something to aim for.'

Vicky paused. Should she say anything, or would it be better just to keep her mouth shut? 'I don't know how much you've seen of what's left out there, but you do realise that—'

'I know the score,' he said, pre-empting what was coming next. 'I know there's very little chance of me ever getting home, and I know what I'm likely to find if I get there, but I've got to have something to hold onto, haven't I? So, in my head, my other half is back at home with the kids, and it's only a matter of time before I'm there with them.'

'Good to hear.'

'I've a young son, and I can see him now, waiting in the doorway for Daddy as I'm walking up the drive. I know it's stupid, but—'

'It's not stupid if it works for you,' she said, interrupting. 'Say hello to your family when you get there. Give your little boy a squeeze from me.'

Sam emerged from the building with two other people. Vicky had spoken to both of them over the course of the last couple of days. Charlotte, who preferred Charlie, was ex-police though she didn't look old enough. Gary Welch, in contrast, was a social worker who looked all of his forty-five years and then some. They were all done up like they were going for a hike, resplendent in outdoor gear which had been looted in bulk. 'What's she doing here?' Sam asked, looking at David, not Vicky.

'She's earning her keep,' Vicky said, annoyed. 'And she's got a name.'

Sam just shrugged and walked away.

'Ignore him, he's a prick,' Charlie said.

'I've noticed.'

'But a useful prick at times,' David added. 'And don't let him hear you call him that, Charlie. You'll break his heart. You know he's got a thing for you.'

Charlie screwed up her face. 'Oh, don't. He might well be one of the last men on Earth, but I'm not that desperate!'

Vicky laughed, something she hadn't done in a long time.

The main hotel building was roughly horseshoe shaped. They followed Sam diagonally across the courtyard then over a wall and into the grounds of a neighbouring building. From there, they walked through the offices of a law firm which had been cleared out, crossed a small car park, walked through an arched alleyway under another building, and into the grounds of a church. Sam waited at the side of the gothic building for the rest of them to catch up. He was about to carry on walking when Vicky stopped him.

'Can I ask, is there a plan?'

'Sorry, yeah. I was forgetting you haven't done this before.'

'So, are you going to share it?'

'Sure. One of the downsides of ending up stuck in the middle of London is that, apart from yuppies and rich kids, very few people actually lived here, and those who did often had money to burn. So, because there weren't many families, particularly around this area, there wasn't much need for decent supermarkets, hardware stores, that kind of thing. It makes everything that much harder for us to find.'

'But there are loads of little supermarkets, restaurants and corner shops and the like,' Gary added. 'Typically, we'll try and clear one out each trip.'

'And how do we transport it all back?'

'We find ourselves a vehicle while we're out.'

'Now that the dead are becoming more responsive, we need to seriously limit the noise we make,' David explained. 'We'll find a suitable store, then find a decent sized vehicle nearby. We strip the shelves, fill the van quietly, then drive it back.'

'Then what?'

'Park up somewhere near here, sit and wait until the crowds have died down. One of us will come back on foot and shift the vehicles blocking the entrance to the courtyard, then we'll drive the loot back to the hotel. These buildings are so tightly packed, the bulk of the dead usually can't get through. Usually.'

The crowds around the front of the hotel in Fleet Street remained, but many of the bodies that had continued west and clogged The Strand earlier in the week had gone. It was still terrifying, being out in the open like this, though. None of the small group were under any illusions – they all knew that if they put a foot wrong out here, made the wrong noise or the wrong move at the wrong time, the results would likely be catastrophic. Vicky found it increasingly difficult not being able to voice her fears out loud. There was no shouting for help if she got into trouble, no way of warning the others if she spotted something that would put them all in danger... She stuck to the rest of them like glue, remembering how it had felt when she'd been cut off and surrounded in Trafalgar Square, just her and Selena. She wished she'd known about these people sooner. Maybe things would have been different then. Maybe Kath would still be alive.

They'd agreed on a branch of Sainsbury's on High Holborn, about half a mile away. Charlie had worked the area in the past and knew it well. She remembered the supermarket as having a decent amount of pavement space outside, which would make loading up easier.

In smaller numbers like this, the dead were reassuringly easy to avoid. For the most part they appeared to pay each other little attention, with the slow, stumbling walk of their brethren going largely unnoticed. When there was any unexpected noise or flash of movement, however, the speed at which the corpses reacted was sobering. Any abrupt sound triggered an instinctive reaction in the nearest one or two, which spread to the next three or four or twenty, thirty or more. *Exponential*, that had been the word Sam had used to describe this behaviour previously, and that scared her. She remembered hearing people talk about exponential growth back in the early days of the coronavirus pandemic. *With exponential growth*, she remembered reading, *you don't know you've got a problem until you've got a problem. Then, tomorrow, you've got twice the problem. The same the next day, and the day after that, and the day after that...*

Funny how thinking about those halcyon days of lockdown now made her feel almost nostalgic. At least there'd been an element of control back then. As virulent as the pandemic had been, at least you'd been able to reduce your chances of infection by shutting yourself away, and that was what she'd had to do for months on end. But the motherfucker of a disease that had caused so much death in a single day in September had been firmly in control, and everyone's individual cards had been marked no matter what. No medication or masks or social distancing would have made a single iota of difference this time around. You got it or you didn't; you died on the spot or you were spared. For Vicky, the jury was still out on which was the best option.

They walked along The Strand, following in the decaying footsteps of thousands last week. It was bizarre how different it looked today, how empty. She wondered where the crowds had gone. Were they waiting around the next corner, or had they just kept walking?

The street names here reminded her of Monopoly and that, in turn, reminded her of how she'd spent last Christmas – *the* last Christmas, she now realised – with her brother and his kids. She'd enjoyed the few days she'd spent with them but Christ, she'd been glad to get home afterwards for some peace and quiet and headspace.

She'd tried to put a block on all memories of her pre-apocalypse life, finding it easier to stay focused on the present. But this lonely walk made it hard not to dwell on the past. If she went back to Harry and Leanne's house now, what would she find there? Would her brother and his perfect little family all be dead together, or would it be worse than that? Her absolute nightmare, the one image she found hardest to shut out, was the four of them locked in their house, dead but still mobile. Mum, dad, and two kids rotting together in some grotesque approximation of family life until there was barely anything left of them, until there was more flesh and blood spread around the rooms of their home than was left on their bones.

A tug on her arm brought her back to reality. Gary was indicating a change of direction. They turned right into Kingsway, altering course painfully slowly so as not to attract attention.

The shells of red double-decker London buses stood blocking up the streets like dinosaur remains, their husks now abandoned to the elements. When the group walked alongside one of them, the bodies of the passengers held captive inside stirred. Almost as one, several (it was impossible to tell exactly how many) hurled themselves against the windows. Gary jumped with surprise, ready to take evasive action, but Vicky had anticipated it and steadied him. She leant closer and said, 'no need to panic', and they kept walking. Behind them, more lumbering figures converged on the bus, reacting to the noise coming from inside. It could only have been a minute or two, but when Vicky looked back there was a crowd of more than thirty of them encircling the vehicle as if it was the only bus left running.

Kingsway was a wide road lined with well-established trees. Here they walked past cafés and stores which offered glimpses of a world they'd lost forever. It was the first time Vicky had been out in the open like this – not running, not panicking, not watching out for Selena and Kath – but the others appeared more used to it. They passed a branch of the Co-op, its doors busted open, and its shelves stripped bare. Charlie caught Vicky's eye and flashed a smug, self-satisfied grin. 'That was our doing,' her expression implied.

It was noticeable just how many of the dead had stayed dead and hadn't reanimated. Until now, Vicky's focus had always been on those who were mobile. After all, the undead presented the biggest threat. From here, it seemed as though the entire length of Kingsway had been carpeted with human remains. She stepped over one of them, a dead woman. Her clothing had been reduced to rags, flapping in the wind, and her brittle, straw-like hair was splayed around her skull, welded to the pavement with blood and other discharge. Her bony hand still gripped the handle of the shopping bag she'd been carrying like she didn't want to let go, and for some reason, Vicky found that disproportionately sad. Where had she been going when she'd died? Where had she just come from? What had she bought? Who was it for? Every single corpse had their own story, and to acknowledge that fact made the scale of the total loss almost unbearable. Being able to see it close up and in slow motion like this made Vicky feel immeasurably worse. The devastation was fractal-like. The large-scale damage was obvious – the vehicles that had crashed and the buildings that were ruined and burnt-out – but whenever she looked closer, all she saw was more and more devastation, ruin upon ruin upon ruin. Given the almost total lack of signs of life since early September, she assumed this was likely a global, extinction-level event that could be drilled down indefinitely without reaching the end of the hurting. At one end of the scale, she imagined whole continents and countries had been devastated, and within them, countless communities silenced. Within those communities, every family must have been wiped out. Every member of every one of those families was probably gone, and so, within each individual body, their organs would have decayed, their bones broken, their skin ruptured... Wherever Vicky looked, all she could see was pain on pain on pain on every conceivable level.

It was relatively easy to make progress when they were moving in the same general direction as the dead, but when they were coming head on it was harder to know how to react. Anticipation, Vicky quickly learnt, was key. A subtle change of direction several metres out was infinitely preferable to making last second movements, far easier to disguise. And the further they veered from the bodies coming at them, the better, because it was hard to conceal their disgust at the sight of these once-human monstrosities up close. Vicky was about to pass a particularly gross looking one, and it was all she could do not to empty the contents of her stomach over its feet. She didn't know what had happened to the poor sod that was tripping towards her, but her belly skin had been shredded, cut to ribbons. Maybe she'd fallen through a window or been caught on barbed wire or been savaged by dogs... she could probably have come up with a hundred ways to explain the lacerations that had allowed the dead woman's insides to slip out. Her chest cavity was pretty much hollow now, and what was left of her dried-up guts trailed behind her like a tattered bridal train. Vicky forced herself to look away and ignore the sounds and the stench.

The road layout here was unusual. Traffic coming from The

73

Strand merged via an underpass, and the railings on either side of the sloped section of road had formed a holding pen of sorts. As a result, a disproportionate number of dead bodies had congregated underground, and the collective echoing noise they made going nowhere in turn attracted more. It worked to the group's advantage, allowing them to keep moving largely unimpeded.

They walked past Starbucks and Costa and other similar places, and the Pavlovian memories made Vicky's stomach growl with hunger, so loud that she was genuinely worried the nearest corpses might react. She wasn't alone. Gary caught her eye and nodded towards a branch of Greggs. The expression on his face said it all: *I could murder a sausage roll.*

The supermarket was in sight now, the front door wedged open by a disembodied arm sticking halfway out. David forced his hands into the gap and tried to prise it open further, but it was stuck fast. Vicky saw that Gary had a lump hammer and, realising what he was about to do, she crossed the street, picked up a metal-framed traffic sign from a section of never-to-be completed roadworks, and chucked it like a frisbee at the glass frontage of a bank. It bounced off the toughened glass and hit the ground with a godawful clatter and crack, loud enough to distract almost all the corpses in the immediate vicinity. They changed direction virtually as one and swarmed towards the source of the noise.

Gary smacked the outer edge of the safety glass door twice with the hammer and, on the second strike, the entire pane shattered, immediately opaque with cracks. 'Jesus,' he said, surprised, and he hit the glass again, this time punching a hole through it. He moved the shaft of the hammer around to clear the frame, then stepped back so the others could get through. Sam paused before following them inside. 'Problem?' Vicky asked.

'Isn't there always?' he replied, and he gestured at the corpses near to the bank, who were now closing in on the supermarket. 'Look at the speed of the fuckers. They come at you so fast now.'

More commotion, inside the supermarket this time. In opening up the store, they'd inadvertently let loose a handful of trapped cadavers.

'Coming through,' David said, and the others stood to the side as he wrestled with a wretched, squirming figure. He groaned with disgust when he tightened his grip and her deteriorating flesh oozed between his fingers. He threw the dead woman out onto the street and went straight back in for another, sidestepping Charlie, who was grappling with one of them like she was a nightclub bouncer chucking out a belligerent drunk.

Gary and Vicky dragged a display unit across the shop, ready to secure the door and stop the approaching crowd getting in. Sam was still out there, trying unsuccessfully to draw them away. 'Get in here, we're clear,' Charlie yelled at him, and he turned and ran back. Once he was inside, Vicky and Gary shoved the display up against the door frame. Vicky felt corpses thudding against it on the other side, but she knew they couldn't get through, at least, she hoped they couldn't.

The interior of the store was dark, most of the glass blocked by rotting flesh pressed up tight. David returned from a recce of a rear storage area, allowing light to flood in from the other end of the shop floor. 'We're clear. No more of them here,' he said. 'Let's get to work.'

7

A van-sized stash of provisions had been harvested in no time at all. Pickings here were good. The store had received a delivery on the morning everyone died, and the staff hadn't had time to unpack it before they'd met their untimely demise.

Sam worked out that the loading doors were at the side of the building. He was disappointed, as he'd hoped for a decent covered driveway or other access point, but real estate in this part of London was at a premium, so it wasn't unexpected. When they were almost ready, he called David over. 'Make a noise up front. I'll slip out here and go get us some transport.'

The others were happy for Sam to take the lead. Gary obliged by repeatedly kicking and shoving the display unit blocking the front entrance, antagonising the crowd so that Sam could get away virtually unnoticed. The noise Gary made was such that Sam found himself with more freedom than he expected. He risked jogging up along Southampton Place, looking for the right vehicle to take.

It hadn't been six weeks yet, but Bloomsbury Square Garden was overgrown and unkempt. Hedges that had once been regularly trimmed into shape had grown wild as a result of heavy rainfall and late summer sun. It struck Sam just how quickly order had turned to disorder everywhere. What would this place look like next month? Or in six months? A year? He hoped he'd be long gone by then.

There'd never been any shortage of white vans on the streets of London, and now Sam could have his pick. At the box junction where Southampton Place met Bloomsbury Square, the traffic was permanently frozen, waiting for lights which were never again going to change. Those vehicles which had been heading west on the A401 had been held up on red and had queued for almost forty days now. Several drivers were mummified in their seats, held upright by their safety belts and baked by the sun. Others were far less passive. They began thrashing around when Sam approached. One smacked its head against the glass as he walked past, and the noise worried him. Fortunately, he could still hear the chaos around the supermarket – audible even from a couple of hundred metres away – and that was enough to ensure the focus remained elsewhere.

Buses, taxis, executive and performance cars, delivery vehicles, ordinary family runarounds... he found what he was looking for eight vehicles along. It was a long wheelbase Ford Transit van; plenty of room in the back for their stash and a couple of passengers. He was about to reach inside and drag the reanimated driver out by the scruff of his neck, but he stopped and checked himself when he clocked the livery on the side. It was a courier firm, so, had the driver finished his rounds, or was the back still piled high with deliveries? He'd been caught out in the early days when nerves and fear had made him do things with double the speed and half the concentration. He'd volunteered to fetch a van after a similar supermarket clearance but hadn't checked the back. When he'd turned up to collect the supplies and the other folks who'd ventured out, they'd first had to waste precious time emptying a load of tyres from the van, then had to wait several more hours for the dead to dissipate before loading up and heading home.

This time it wasn't so bad. The back of the van was locked, so he had to snatch the keys from the ignition first, ducking under the decaying driver's rotten, dripping arms. He opened up the backend and saw that it was about a quarter-full of boxes, which he immediately started to throw out. Old habits die hard – he stacked half a dozen of them at the roadside before realising he could just dump them in the street. The environmentalist in him felt guilty, but it didn't matter. In all probability, no one was ever going to drive along here again.

Already knackered, Sam grabbed the dead driver by the throat, reached across to undo his belt, then dragged him out. As a result of sitting in pretty much the exact same position for a month, wearing shorts and leaking from every orifice for all that time, he'd become stuck to the vinyl seat. When Sam pulled him free, strips of flesh tore away, and more of the dead man's liquified insides spilled out, gushing into the footwell. There was no time to find an alternative vehicle. Sam jumped into the sticky, slimy seat, and turned the key in the ignition.

Nothing.

Nothing again.

Nothing the third time he tried.

Fourth time the engine caught, and he floored it, swerving around the vehicle in front and mowing down the van driver, who'd just about managed to pick himself back up after being unceremoniously dumped. Sam raced back towards the supermarket and squealed to a halt as close to the back of the store as he could. David had been listening out for the engine. He immediately opened the loading doors then ran across and opened up the back of the van. He slipped through the gap as Sam reversed snug against the building, leaving no room for any corpses to get through.

But Christ, they were going absolutely nuts at the noise. He'd expected a reaction, but the ferocity, size, and speed of the pack now closing in on the van terrified Sam. He knew they were never going to be able to drive away with so many corpses jostling for position around it, and if these were anything like the crowd around the front of the hotel on Fleet Street, Sam doubted they'd just lose interest and drift away. He was going to have to divert their attention.

The others were flat out loading up the back of the van, but they still weren't going fast enough. Bodies were already crashing into the front. Five. Ten. Twenty. More and more... already enough of them to block the road.

Sam switched off the engine, left the keys hanging, and ran

around to the back. He pushed lethargic figures out of the way, then shot his arm through the narrow gap between the back of the van and the wall of the building and grabbed Charlie. 'Keys are in the ignition,' he said.

'You going walkabouts again are you, Sam?'

'Something like that. There are—' He stopped to deal with a group of three that lunged at him at the same time. 'There are bloody loads of them out here. I'll try and give you some space. Meet you back at the hotel later.'

And with that, he was gone.

Sam ran out into the middle of the yellow-hatched box junction where the A40 crossed Kingsway. Right in the centre of the road, two cars had crashed into each other when both drivers fell dead at the wheel. Sam climbed onto the roof of one of the cars and jumped up and down, denting the metal. 'Come on you fuckers!' he shouted, his voice bouncing off the buildings. 'I'm over here!' Another couple of jumps triggered the car's alarm, the repeated honking of the horn adding welcome volume to his cries.

How long could he risk waiting?

Many of the dead were moving away from the van and towards the crashed cars now. The quickness of their reactions was again disconcerting. He'd gotten used to their slothful movements, the way they seemed to rely more on gravity and momentum than any conscious effort to walk, leaning forward and dragging their feet behind them, but this was different. Previously, they'd appeared to be on a permanent two-second time delay, but their reactions were almost instant now. He hadn't realised how important that slight hesitation had been until it was no longer there. Every nerve and fibre screamed at him to run, but it was still too soon. There were too many of them that hadn't seen or heard him yet. He continued to jump up and down on the car, setting the alarm off again, shouting at the top of his voice and waving his arms like a frigging madman and all the time looking around, trying to suss out likely escape routes. *Just a few seconds longer*, he thought, watching hundreds of them swarm towards the intersection.

Time to move.

The crowds were thinnest on the opposite side of the junction to the supermarket, back towards Bloomsbury. Sam jumped down, dropped his shoulder, then ran at speed, bulldozing through any corpses that got in his way. Though their numbers now were a concern, a month of putrefaction had stripped away their bulk and individually they were easily dealt with. *They used to say the streets of this place were paved with gold*, he thought to himself, but from where he was standing, the streets of London were currently paved with what was left of the Londoners.

He had no real plan other than to keep running then find somewhere safe to sit things out for a couple of hours until he could go back to the hotel. Left and right turns came in quick succession, but he wasn't worried about getting lost. When the time came, all he'd need to do would be to head south until he reached the river, then get onto The Strand or Fleet Street. If he was too far east, he'd just use the dome of St Paul's Cathedral to orientate himself. For now he just had to keep moving, weaving through the bodies. Occasionally they came at him, but by the time they'd realised he was there, he'd gone again.

Their numbers thinned out surprisingly quickly. Almost too quickly. He'd only run a mile or so from where he'd left the others, but the street he was now pounding along was all but deserted. After being surrounded for so long, this sudden eerie emptiness unnerved him.

Sam took another sharp left into Doughty Mews, then pulled up and stopped when he realised that he was alone, no corpses here at all. It didn't feel right. There'd been so many flooding The Strand previously, so many around the front of the hotel, so many near the supermarket they'd been looting... It didn't make sense. He stopped in the middle of the empty street with his hands on his hips, panting. He could see a trapped corpse through the ground-floor window of a building he was in front of, and it reminded him that this was just an impression of emptiness, that behind the doors of many of the high-end flats in this road and every other there would be hundreds of the undead just waiting for release. So, was this sudden isolation a freak coincidence or a long-overdue lucky break? Neither option seemed probable.

And then he heard music.

It was faint at first. Tinny. Distant and echoing. So quiet and intermittent that he assumed he was imagining it and looked for other explanations. Was it the wind blowing through lifeless spaces, playing notes as it whistled through broken windows and open doors? Or was it the internal workings of his own body? His blood pumping through his veins? His heart beating at speed, accelerated by effort and adrenalin?

No. It was definitely music. And it was getting louder.

If there was one thing Sam had learnt about staying alive in this rotten, ghoul-filled world, it was to keep away from any kind of noise because the dead didn't. Now though, he knew he had to go against his instincts and head straight for the source. He started to move again, then changed direction. The music wasn't where it had originally been. It was moving too. It was clearer now – an ugly, repetitive, machine-like techno beat, the kind of music his dad would have moaned about, the kind of constant thumping bass that rattled windows.

Sam walked unopposed along Clerkenwell Road, a wider, busier road that, pre-apocalypse, would have been clogged with people and traffic. He could see a large number of bodies up ahead now, forty or fifty at least, and they were all moving in the same general direction, all following the distant machine-gun beat. Their preoccupation with the noise made it infinitely easier to move among them.

At the next junction, the dead Sam had been watching were absorbed into another vast mob of cadavers, all dragging themselves slowly north. Their numbers here were unimaginable. He wanted to run in the opposite direction but kept walking and allowed himself to be absorbed into the masses. The music was their focus, he told himself repeatedly. There were hundreds upon hundreds of them, stretching away further than he could see.

There was only one explanation for what was happening here: the dead were being deliberately drawn away from the centre of the city. The audacity of the operation put his amateurish attempts at corpse-wrangling to shame. He needed to see who was up front, but he couldn't speed up and risk the nearest creatures forgetting about the beat and turning on him instead. As uncomfortable as this slow-motion procession of the dead was, he knew he had to resist all temptation to run and keep gradually inching his way forward.

Sam was keen to find landmarks to help him keep track of roughly where he was, but it was difficult to look around without being noticed, and he'd found himself in a part of London which was unnervingly nondescript. Here he was, trapped in a city boasting more iconic landmarks per square mile than nearly anywhere else, yet this completely featureless street could have been anywhere in the UK. The irony was not lost on him. All he could see was ordinariness, and he struggled to find any way-post. But for now, finding his way back to the hotel was secondary to discovering who was leading this immense column of decaying flesh. Though they'd not heard any music last time, surely the purposeful movement he'd noted along Fleet Street and The Strand earlier in the week must have been the tail-end of a similarly coordinated action? Sam again struggled to regulate his speed as his mind raced, filling with possibilities. There were other people left alive, and they clearly had some kind of plan. Might the end of the world have not been the absolute end of everything after all?

The bodies in front of him veered over to the other side of the road, moving as a result of an obstruction in the carriageway. Sam continued to go with the flow and didn't anticipate, bunching up amongst a mass of foul-smelling cadavers that slowly shuffled around, pivoting awkwardly on inflexible, leaden legs. He was eventually jostled to the front where he saw that a truck had jack-knifed and was blocking the road, on its side with its cab at an unnatural angle to the trailer as if its neck had been broken. Sam saw there was a single word written in massive letters in bright yellow paint on the roof of the trailer: MONUMENT.

Sam scoffed. *Why the hell would anyone vandalise the roof of a truck? Who'd see it?*

The question rattled around his head for a second but was forgotten as he tried to negotiate the rear end of the truck without looking like he was negotiating it at all. Plenty of bodies had lost their footing here and had gone down, trampled underfoot by plenty more, and Sam did everything he could not to go the same way. He skidded in a patch of slippery offal and used another body to steady himself. Thankfully, his instinctive reaction went unnoticed, but in the process of staying upright he collided with other corpses and was covered with gore. He was used to the stink now. In some ways it helped. He was bedraggled, sweat-soaked, and drenched with decay, and when he adjusted his pace again and fell back in line, he realised he was probably indistinguishable from the rest of the pack.

The march to the music was strangely hypnotic, and the less he thought about what he was doing, the easier it was. He nearly broke ranks when the penny dropped about the graffiti on the roof of the truck. It had to have been painted *after* the crash, he realised with a smile. It had been painted *after the apocalypse*. But what did it mean? Something to do with the monument to the Great Fire of London?

Sam had become distracted and was in real danger of giving himself away. The harder he tried to stay focused, the harder it got. He was staring at the ghouls closest to him in the crowd now, repellent and tragic in equal measure, trying to work out the final chapters of their awful stories. The one immediately to his right was still dressed up like she'd been out all night and never made it to home. The material of her short, figure-hugging dress bulged with the distention of her stomach, then sagged where the fat had been eaten away from her stick-like legs. *Nice she had a final night out*, he thought, though it was desperately sad to see someone so young cut down in their prime. He couldn't dwell on her condition because there were thousands more like her in this queue alone. On his other side, the remains of a construction worker in badly stained high-vis gear, somehow still wearing his hard-hat. The corpse next to that one was naked from the waist down, the soles of its bare feet now worn down to the bone.

Unfocused, Sam caught up with the cadaver in front and trod on the back of its flapping shoe. The damn thing almost collapsed but he steadied it and kept moving forward. Those immediately behind then walked into him. The pace of the seething crowd was frustrating, never settling into anything resembling a steady rhythm. There were too many variables for them to stay constant: the state of their individual deterioration, the gradient of the section of road they were following, the movements of their neighbours, the human remains and other detritus which littered the ground... Sam tried to switch to autopilot again and go with the unsteady flow, but it was getting harder, and he could feel himself beginning to panic. He was in real danger of drowning in this sea of rot. From his current position, all he could see was the dead in every direction, and though he could still hear the grinding dance music, he was no closer to the source.

He'd drifted towards the centre of the column and so tried to get back over to the furthest edge where he thought it would be marginally safer. Right in front of him, the remains of an oversized man wearing sagging jogging bottoms and a stretched, badly stained hoodie tripped over his own feet and faceplanted into the pavement. Several other corpses fell over his bulk, none of them doing anything to stop themselves from going over. Sam managed to side-step the rotting mound of a man, then shimmied around a couple more stragglers without drawing attention to himself.

Way over to his right now, beyond the rest of the bodies, was a relatively empty side-street. Beyond that, another road which appeared to run parallel with this one. To stand any chance of getting close to the front of the queue he knew he'd need a burst of speed, and so he risked breaking away. He angled himself towards the fringes and kept moving across until he'd broken free from the bulk, then he went for it. He ran straight along the side-street, then left onto the parallel road, north for as far as he could, then left again and back out onto the main road. He slowed his speed and allowed the masses to reabsorb him.

Sam had made sufficient progress to be able to see the top of the line now. Jesus Christ. He hadn't expected that. There was a gap in front of the lead cadavers. Just ahead of them was a kid on a pushbike with an ancient-looking boombox strapped to the back, like something out of a museum. How the hell had they got hold of it, and why the hell were they risking everything like this? It made no sense.

Okay. Time to act.

Sam picked up his speed again, figuring he was close enough to the front now to take the risk. The dead were clearly focused on the cyclist up ahead, and if he needed to, he knew he could sprint the remaining distance before the herd had chance to react.

He was about to make his move when the cyclist made theirs.

She (he could see now it was a girl) twisted around in the saddle and switched off the boombox, silencing the music. She quickly faced forward again, crouched down low over her handlebars, then pedalled away at a speed Sam thought he'd struggle to match in a car, let alone on foot.

She was gone in seconds.

Nothing left now but Sam, the silence, and an impossible number of corpses that were no longer being distracted.

Fuck. Not good.

The dead immediately started to drift. No longer moving with any coordination, they wandered from the queue and began dragging themselves away in random directions. Corpses clattered into each other and caused hold-ups, while others appeared almost to fight their way through the crowds. Sam could see definite aggression building within the ranks of the undead now, an undeniable uptick in the voracity of their reactions, and he was stuck right in the middle of it all.

Time to make use of some of that life left to him.

Changing direction was a risk, but right now it felt no more dangerous than remaining a part of this increasingly chaotic crowd. A cadaver came at him from out of nowhere – a random collision which felt like an attack – and he grabbed hold of the creature's shoulders. Its head snapped back then lolled forward, butting him in the face.

Sam screamed with pain.

Their responses may have been suppressed by their physical limitations, but the viciousness of their reactions was unquestionable. The bizarre flash mob he'd been part of had collapsed into a feverish swarm, and he was surrounded. He tried to wade through them and get off the main road, but it was impossible. The harder he fought, the less progress he made. He was sinking, drowning in a riptide of decay. And then it occurred to him that going under the surface might be his only means of escape. Sam checked which way he was facing, then dropped to his knees and crawled away through an ever-shifting forest of legs.

By the time he'd reached the outskirts of the throng, Sam was struggling to keep moving. His hands and knees were raw. But there were fewer of them now, a little more space to breathe. He crawled around the back of a parked car and lay down in the road underneath it, exhausted.

How many dead bodies had been in the vast column that he'd been a part of? Ten, fifteen thousand, perhaps? Whatever the true number, he knew it was a drop in the ocean, just a fraction of London's total lifeless population. At moments like this the scale of the threat they were facing was sobering. No, he thought, curled up in a ball in the road and shaking with nerves, it wasn't sobering, it was absolutely fucking terrifying.

8

A couple of hours later, and Sam was still stuck under the car. It was pissing down with rain now, and though it made the conditions even more intolerable, the downpour provided him with a little unexpected cover. The noise confused the dead, and he was determined to capitalise on their disorientation. He was resigned to being stuck out here on his own tonight, but there had to be someplace better than sitting in the road with rainwater overflowing the gutter. He picked himself up, ready to work out his next move.

Moving in the same general direction as the dead had been one thing, but trying to move against them was a different matter altogether, and in the time that had passed, the hordes had become so diffuse that whichever way he turned there were corpses coming the other way. It was a confounding mosh without rhythm or intent. He'd only been back on his feet for a couple of seconds, and already they were coming for him *en masse*. One or two of them at a time he could avoid, but there were far too many of them around still. Speed and strength were his only weapons.

He ran further from the main road and into the backstreets, but even here it was like running into a solid wall of flesh. He sidestepped a woman whose face had caved in and sunk into her skull, then charged through the middle of another pack of them. He was constantly looking around for inspiration, but wherever he turned, all he could see were dead ends and reducing options. He could climb into the branches of a tree, but he'd just be stuck up there for hours as the crowd below him grew. It would be the same if he jumped up onto a car. He could try driving, but the streets were far too crowded, and he had visions of being trapped behind the wheel forever. Many of the houses here had basement flats, but once down there, he'd likely never get back out. He tried a couple of doors, but they were locked, and there wasn't time to try and force his way inside. The dead were brutish and relentless. They were everywhere, following his every move, individually weak but collectively strong. Their ferocity seemed to have increased even in the time he'd been out here today.

Another blind corner, another leap of faith. No choice but to keep going, but this time he caught a lucky break. It was quieter here, and he'd finally found a spot he thought he recognised. Granville Square. He was sure he'd been through here once before, summer before last when he'd been in London for a civil rights march. He'd got the train into Kings Cross and had got lost on the walk through to Hyde Park and had ended up here.

In the centre of Granville Square was a recreation area, which helped him. It blocked him from view, and it disrupted the flow of dead flesh through the square. A large number of them had stumbled through the gaps in the wrought iron railings and been unable to get out again. Now upwards of a hundred of them were trapped in a fenced-off children's playground, horrifically out of place.

Terraced houses boxed-in the area like a perimeter wall. Sam tried a few more doors, and virtually fell into a house when he finally found one that wasn't locked. The dead homeowner came at him and he grappled with her in the confines of the narrow, shadow-filled hallway. He reversed their positions and tried to shove her out onto the street. He'd have been successful had the woman not been bounced back into her home by a bunch of corpses surging into the building from the street. Fuckers weren't giving him an inch today.

The house was split into maisonettes, and that made the route through to the back of the building more complicated than it should have been. Unable to double-back, Sam instead burst through the nearest door into a lounge. He crashed into a crib and saw an infant lying on her back looking up at him, dead but constantly reaching and kicking, emaciated, her mouth stained with blackened leakage. For a few awful seconds he couldn't look away, and it was only the noise of the dead following him down the hallway that forced him to move. He wrenched a TV off the wall and threw it through a window, then pulled down a curtain and used it to knock out the remaining shards of glass.

In typical London style, the back garden of the house was a block-paved space about the size of an average bathtub. Sam climbed up onto a storage bin then onto the back wall. He waited up there for a second longer than he should have, needing to catch his breath. He was seriously flagging, and furious with himself for the cavalier way he'd approached the last few hours since leaving the others at the supermarket. He'd had no choice but to follow the music, but he'd fucked up big style. All that risk for no discernible gain. Fucking idiot. The increasing volatility of the dead world had caught him out; nothing was straightforward. No matter what he did or where he went, there was always something ready to knock him off course. The babe in the cradle had been the final straw. He'd tried to ignore it, tried not to look, but it was impossible. For someone so young and so innocent to be damned like that... the cruelty of this infection truly knew no bounds.

He knew he wasn't going to make it back to base tonight. He didn't have it in him. *Just find somewhere quiet and relatively safe. Scavenge some food and drink, get some sleep, start again in the morning.*

Across the street were several large, art deco-style apartment blocks, an upmarket development. Sam made a run for them, figuring he'd find a safe space up high somewhere. The nearest block was called Gwynne House, its name proudly emblazoned above its grand entrance door, but the door was locked, and there was no way he was going to get inside without making a lot of noise and wasting energy he didn't have.

He worked his way along a fence and around a corner into a driveway that ran between Gwynne House and the neighbouring block, avoiding groups of milling bodies. Here, he looked up and saw there were balconies on the non-street-facing side of the buildings, and that finally felt like a positive development. If he could find a way of getting up off ground level, he'd be home and dry.

But nothing was that simple today.

The apartment blocks surrounded a large communal garden area. The height of the imposing buildings on all sides and the driving rain and low cloud cover combined to reduce his visibility. In focusing on trying to find cover amongst the apartments, Sam didn't realise he'd gone full circle and was now heading back towards the bulk of the thousands of corpses that had been following the music. Since they'd been left to scatter, large numbers had drifted away in all directions, with a sizeable chunk moving towards the estate. They were reacting to his presence now, flowing in through the gaps between the blocks. Predictably, even more were following those.

Sam ran towards the nearest building but stopped and doubled-back because there was a pack of corpses gathered around the entrance. Jesus Christ, they were coming from all sides now.

He sprinted towards another one of the blocks, then stopped and ducked for cover when an arc of flame roared through the air directly overhead and exploded in a patch of space. The dumb dead gravitated towards it. Sam had visions of them all going up in flames, but the rain was too heavy, and the fire was quickly extinguished. Still, the brief burst of brightness had shifted the focus away from him momentarily. He scanned the area for another way out but was distracted by a loud crash from somewhere behind him. No fire this time, something being thrown from a balcony to distract a few more of the dead.

'Over here,' a voice shouted. Sam looked up and eventually spotted a flash of movement through the gloom. Hard to make out, he saw someone scurrying rat-like along a balcony towards a block of garages on the furthest side of the estate. He ran in the same direction, pushing through throngs of hideous figures that lashed out at him.

'Come on! Quick!' the kid shouted. And it definitely was a kid, he could tell by the size and speed. Sam lost sight of him for a second, then locked onto his position when another crude firebomb was lit and chucked into the crowd. Whatever propellant he was using, it was damned effective this time. Fire splashed up the legs and chest of the corpse that bore the brunt of the impact and the stupid thing staggered aimlessly from side to side, confused by its own conflagration. It crashed into another group of them like a pissed-up binge-drinker on a Saturday night, spreading flames instead of spraying vomit.

Ahead of Sam was a flight of concrete stairs he'd not noticed until now, access to the first-floor flats above the garage block. More of the dead were congregating around the bottom of the steps and he burrowed through, the kid frantically yelling directions at him. Sam was panting, absolutely done for. He reached the top of the steps and saw the boy hanging over a balcony, gesturing. 'Over here, mister! Come on! Quick!'

Sam would have happily bedded down where he was, finally off ground level and out of reach, but the kid had other ideas. He was making so much noise it would only be a matter of time before the corpses figured out where he was and started dragging themselves upwards. 'Keep your bloody voice down,' Sam said, half-shout, half-whisper.

'No time, mister. Over here! Now!'

Sam walked to the edge of the building then stopped when he realised he was going to have to jump to get onto the balcony. He peered down over a brick wall which had clearly been built to deter people from doing exactly what he was about to do. Below, all he could see was a mass of bobbing heads.

'Come on,' the kid shouted again. 'Quick!'

'Will you just shut the fuck up? You're putting me off,' Sam bellowed at him, and even from up here he could see the dead masses reacting to the volume of his voice. The kid had calmed down a little and had retreated further into the shadows. He'd probably gone a while without seeing anyone else alive, Sam decided. The boy's world view had likely been limited to the confines of this building.

Too tired to care anymore, Sam climbed onto the top of the wall, jumped across, and caught the balcony railings. For a few seconds longer he clung on, no energy to move. The kid was back again, trying to help him over. 'I'm fine,' he grunted, batting his overenthusiastic hands away. 'Give me some space.'

Sam followed the boy along the balcony and through an open door.

9

'What's your name, mate?'
'Omar.'
'I'm Sam. This your place?'
'Yep.'
'You here on your own?'
'Yep.'
Sam looked at him. 'How old are you?'
'Sixteen.'
'Try again. How old are you?'
'Fifteen.'
'Getting closer.'
'Okay, twelve.'
'And is this really your place?'
'It is now.'
Sam walked through a spacious, well-appointed lounge and looked down into the overcrowded street below. 'Look, Omar, you and I will get along a lot better if you stop bullshitting and tell me the truth.'
Omar said nothing.
'Thanks for your help back there, by the way.'
'No probs,' he mumbled.
'What was in the firebombs?'
'Just stuff I found in the flats. Something in a bottle from under a kitchen sink.'
'I thought I smelled booze out there.'
'Yeah. I chucked some Jack Daniels. Shoved a sock in the end and lit it.'
'Nice.'
'Seen it done in a film.'

'Shame. I could do with a drink.'

'I've got loads more. Keeping some for me, though.'

'Mate, drop the act. I'm impressed enough that you helped me out there. Hell, I'm impressed you're still alive.'

'Didn't do anything clever, just didn't die.'

Sam laughed. 'Yeah, that's about right. Can't argue with that. I guess that's something we've both got in common, isn't it? We both managed to not die.'

'You nearly did out there.'

'Tell me about it. I'd have been screwed if you hadn't seen me when you did.'

Omar shifted on the spot awkwardly. 'Tell you the truth, I been watching you for a while now. Just didn't know what to do. I seen you on the street outside but I couldn't shout in case they heard me.'

'No worries. I get that. I reckon we're both making this up as we go along.'

'Yeah. Need a wee, back in a sec,' he said, belying his age, and he disappeared to the bathroom. Sam watched him scurry away. The kid looked nervous. Scared. Small.

'So, if this is your place now, whose was it before?' Sam asked when he returned.

'Dunno. There was no one here.'

'And why were you here, exactly? You had the whole city to choose from, so why pick this flat? I've seen some massive mansions, and there are some awesome penthouses at the top of really fancy buildings. You could have set yourself up anywhere.'

'I like it here,' he said.

'So, thinking this through logically... I reckon you stayed here because you're local. Do you live somewhere close?'

'Yeah.'

'Somewhere on this estate?'

Omar didn't say anything, he just bit his lip, then nodded.

'With someone else?'

He nodded again. Standing in front of him, looking up with

wide, questioning eyes, Omar's years fell away.

'Was it your mum and dad?' he asked.

'Just Mum.'

'And I guess she's...'

'She started walking around when the rest of them did. I wanted to stay with her but...'

'It's okay, mate. There's nothing you could have done. There's nothing anyone could have done.'

'But she was dead.'

'She *is* dead. They all are. There aren't many of us left that are still breathing.'

'You're not on your own then?'

'No. There are others.'

'Where?'

'Nowhere near here, I'm afraid. I managed to get myself lost.'

'Good job I was looking out for you, eh?'

'Yeah, good job, Omar. I owe you.'

'Was that you playing the music? Crazy, that was.'

'Not me, but that's why I'm here. There was a girl on a bike... I was trying to work out what she was doing.'

'I heard it before. Couple of times this week.'

'Have you seen her?'

'Nope, just heard her. What d'you reckon she's doing?'

'Trying to shift the bodies away from wherever it is she's staying, I guess.'

'What, and dump them all here?'

'Yeah, well if you didn't know about her, chances are she doesn't know about you. Hey, Omar, you got any food? I'm starving. I've had a shitty day.'

'In the kitchen, help yourself,' Omar said with a casual nod of the head, and he sat down on a plush sofa and pulled his knees up to his chest, almost disappearing.

Sam wandered around the apartment. He had to hand it to the lad, he'd picked a decent spot to hole-up, and he'd made a half-decent job of keeping himself safe too. It looked like he'd looted many of the neighbouring apartments, judging from the piles of stash he'd accumulated. There was a definite edge of juvenility to his hoarding: a pile of comic books, several games consoles and a spare TV, enough pairs of trainers for an entire football team... 'What's with all the footwear?' he asked.

'Limited editions,' Omar answered from the sofa. 'Worth loads, they are.'

'Hate to break it to you, mate, but everything's a limited edition now.'

He could see the top of Omar's head from where he was standing. Poor little bugger. Four foot nothing, barely any meat on his bones, tousled mob of dirty hair sticking up at all angles... but he reminded himself again, the boy had done well to keep himself safe and alive, not to mention rescuing him just now. He had a put-on arrogance about him that Sam found endearing and annoying in equal measure. There was no way he'd found all those shoes just lying around. He must have worked his way around the estate, wrenching them off the feet of dead kids before they'd risen. Sam made a mental note to look out for deceased teenagers walking around in socks when he left here. No, when *they* left here. There was no way he was going to leave the boy behind.

The kitchen was disappointingly sparse, but that was only to be expected. With no fridge or freezer, no power or gas, the odds of Omar maintaining a balanced diet had been slim. Sam found evidence of plenty of junk food and cans of drink, but there was more rubbish now than food. He piled a tray with the few edible things he could find and took it through to the next room.

'You want anything, Omar?'

Omar shook his head. 'Not hungry.'

'Funny, isn't it. When everyone's going on at you to eat healthy, all you want is crisps and chocolate and crap. You go off junk pretty quick when it's all you've got, don't you think?'

'Whatever.'

Omar was staring straight ahead, looking out of the window into the swirling sky. He wiped a tear away with the back of his hand and Sam pretended he hadn't noticed.

'We've been staying in this plush hotel,' he said. 'We've got gas burners set up so we can do hot food. The menu's pretty limited, but it's better than nothing. And hot drinks, too. Christ, I could murder a cup of tea.'

He waited for a response, but the kid stayed silent.

'Look, mate, I'm going to need to get back to the others. You coming with me?'

'I want to stay here...'

'Why? I get that this is your manor, but there's no reason for you to stay here now. I don't reckon things are going to get any easier for a long time, and nice as this place is, you're going to struggle. Your mum would want you to go and find other people and keep yourself safe, don't you think?'

'Guess so.'

'So, come with me. We'll stay here tonight, give the mob outside chance to chill, then head back. We'll fix you up with your own room.'

'Is it far?'

'Just off Fleet Street. You know Fleet Street?'

He shrugged. 'Dunno. I haven't been out properly since everybody...'

When Omar's unfinished sentences faded away to nothing, Sam knew it was because he couldn't bring himself to say those final few words. They hurt too much. Sam understood completely. Christ, coming to terms with the loss of everything, the loss of everyone, without any warning or explanation was hard enough for him to handle at thirty-three. How the hell was a kid like this supposed to cope?

'Look, I can't tell you what happened, mate,' Sam said. 'It's best to be honest and upfront with you, so I will. I don't have any answers. No one does. I mean, we could come up with a hundred different explanations between us if we tried, but they'd probably all be wrong. I don't think we'll ever know what caused this.'

'So how can we put it right?'

'We can't. We have to find a new right. We're just little people, you and me. If there's anyone who does know what happened, my guess is they're either a million miles from here or hidden in a bunker somewhere. Or, most likely, they're dead too. I think this was just one of those things.'

Omar almost laughed. Almost. 'One of those things... that's what Mum used to say when I lost at football. You're talking about the frigging apocalypse, the end of the frigging world!'

'But it's not really, is it?'

'It is from where I'm sitting.'

'Then that's another reason to come with me. Get a new perspective.'

Omar remained on the sofa. He nodded towards the window. 'Bit shitty out there though, eh?'

Sam smiled. 'That's one way of putting it.'

Omar was beginning to rediscover his cockiness. He sat up straight and fished a packet of crisps out from the pile on the tray. 'What's up with them things out there today anyway? They're acting proper riled, and not just 'cos of that music. Before they was just wandering around, all sleepy like. It's like they're still waking up.'

'I know. Weird, isn't it.'

'I mean, I watched *The Walking Dead* before it got shit, and I seen that *Dawn of the Dead* once and loads of other zombie stuff, but they was never like this.'

'You can say that again, mate.'

'Where you're from, are they all trying to eat your brains and that?'

'No brain eating that I've seen.'

'What then? Why are they up and about? Why they all getting so vexed?'

'All good questions. But I'm sorry, I still can't give you any answers. They're a bit more than vexed though, I can tell you that much. From what I've seen, the longer this goes on, the worse they're getting.'

'That's stupid. Makes no sense. They're already dead, so how can it get any worse?'

'A couple of weeks ago they weren't interested in us, now it's like they want to tear us apart. Who knows what they're going to be like next week or the week after that...'

'And what about us?'

'What about us?'

'Are we gonna end up like them?'

Sam had pondered that question before, and his gut reaction was again to admit to Omar that he honestly didn't know. But being so brutally honest didn't seem right or fair. 'I reckon we'll be okay. If it didn't get us when it got everyone else, why should it get us now?'

'That's what I thought,' Omar said, and he returned his attention to his crisps, then threw the barely touched packet back onto the tray. 'Don't even like prawn cocktail,' he grumbled. Sam picked up the packet and polished them off.

'Can't afford to waste anything now, mate. There's only a finite number of packets of prawn cocktail crisps left in the world.'

'You what?'

'Doesn't matter.'

'You talk a lot of shit.'

'Thanks. And you swear a lot for a little dude.'

'Little dude? What the fu—'

'Okay, that'll do.'

Omar shook his head. 'You don't talk right. Where you from, anyway? You got a proper dodgy accent.'

Sam laughed. 'Treorchy.'

'Where's that?'

'Wales. Midway between Cardiff and Swansea. You know where I mean?'

'No.'

'Doesn't matter. Maybe you could give me some elocution lessons if you end up coming with me.'

'What you on about?'

'Never mind. Come back to the hotel with me, Omar. Okay?'

'You sound like a right perv asking that.'

'Grow up. You know what I mean. Fact is, you're just a kid and in all good conscience I can't leave you here on your own.'

'But I should stay...'

'There's no point. You know it as well as I do. I'm sorry, Omar, your mum's gone. Same as my mum. And my dad. And my two sisters, I reckon. You're not going to be doing anyone any favours hanging around this place.'

'You going back to Wales?'

'Not a lot of point really.'

'But if that's where your family is then—'

'Then there's even less point. Hard as it is to accept, I think we all have to work on the assumption that most, if not all of the people we used to give a shit about, are dead. That's why I'm going to stick with my friends at the hotel, and that's why you're coming with me.'

Nothing.

Sam took Omar's lack of response as unspoken acceptance and agreement. He was surprised. He'd expected more of a fight.

'That's sorted then. We'll go first thing. Try and get on the road before sunrise.'

'Why not tonight?'

'Too many of them outside still. A lot should have drifted off by morning, and it'll be easier for us to move around if it's still half-dark. Their eyesight's not so good, I don't think.'

'I need to get some things from home first.'

'Are you sure? You really want to do that?'

'Yes.'

'What kind of things?'

'Clothes, mostly.'

'We can pick stuff up on the way. We can get you whatever you need.'

'Yeah, but I want *my* stuff.'

'Just because it was yours? For sentimental reasons? Seriously, mate, you're going to have to start thinking differently about things now. We all are.'

'But I just—'

'If you're thinking about going back to say goodbye to your mum, then don't. I understand, but don't do it. There's no point. Your mum's dead, Omar. I know that's harsh, and I know it's not what you want to hear, but that's how it is. You go back to your apartment and you'll be scarred for life, because what you see there won't be the mum you knew, won't even be the one you left behind. Instead, just think about the last night you had with her before the world went to shite, and cling onto that.'

'I was grounded. She had a right go at me.'

'Doesn't matter. Hold onto that memory, mate, and don't let it go. Look, I know we've only just met, and I know you saved my skin out there and I'd be buggered if you hadn't, but trust me, I know what I'm talking about. Leave here with me tomorrow morning and never look back.'

'No way are we getting in there,' Omar said, and Sam had to admit, he was probably right. The situation at the hotel had deteriorated substantially since he'd last been there. The two of them were standing on the roof next to the ladder-bridge. The sun had only just begun to rise, but Sam wished it would bugger off and sink back below the horizon again, because the lighter it got, the more trouble he could see. The unwelcome undead crowds in Fleet Street had grown in number disproportionately. There were so many now that, along with the numerous abandoned vehicles and other obstructions, they'd formed a dam of sorts which stretched the width of the road. It had prevented the bodies already outside the building from going anywhere else, whilst also trapping others that happened to end up here. *What's the opposite of a flash-mob?* he asked himself, because that was what he was looking at. *A squatters' convention?* Those dead fuckers had staked their claim. They weren't going anywhere.

'What now then?' Omar asked, impatient. He was cold and scared but was doing what he could not to let it show.

'Hold on, kid. I'm thinking.'

'Are they even still here, your mates?'

'Yes.' He pointed at the hotel. 'See? Over there. Top floor windows.'

Even from a distance they could see movement. Reflections in the glass. Frightened faces reacting to the chaos in Fleet Street.

'They're stuck, ain't they? Trapped.'

'It would appear so.'

'We should go then.'

'Go where exactly?'

'Back home.'

'Not happening. There are other ways to get in beside the front door.'

'With all them dead people outside? No way. Too risky.'

'What do you suggest then? We just abandon them all?'

'We could.'

'You've got a lot to learn, mate.'

'I just don't get why we have to risk our necks?'

'Because it's not just about us, is it. I happen to give a shit about the people in that hotel. Some of them, anyway.'

'Lame.'

'Well that's how it is.'

'Whatever.'

'I guess we could just wait up here until you develop a conscience or at least grow out of your current annoying little kid phase.'

'What you on about?'

'Nothing. Follow me.'

'Wait on. Can't we give it a bit longer? I've walked miles this morning.'

'We walked about *a* mile, that's all. Honestly, Omar, if you put as much energy into moving as you do moaning, this would be a lot easier on both of us.'

Omar ignored him and casually crossed the ladder bridge, unfazed by the deadly drop on either side, then waited for Sam to show him where to go next.

They stopped again on their way down the staircase of the next empty building. 'Fuck,' Sam said under his breath. He pressed his face against the window. The area around the back of the hotel looked as busy as the road out front.

'We're never gonna get through that lot,' Omar said, unhelpfully. 'There's millions of them.'

'Maybe a thousand. Not that many.'

'Too many for us, though.'

'No, I think we'll be okay. Just shut up for a minute and let me think.'

Omar didn't shut up, but Sam blocked out his chatter as he tried to work out what might have happened in the time he'd been away. From their current position he could see portions of the winding route they'd need to use to get back inside the hotel that appeared clear. He was hopeful the others had made it back yesterday with the supplies. The increased size and volatility of the insipid crowds was likely a reaction to the van returning and being unloaded. He had to hope that was what the case, anyway.

'Are you even listening to me?' Omar said, annoyed.

'No, but you need to listen to me. See that church down there?'

'What about it?'

'We can get to the hotel from there.'

'So how do we get to the church?'

'That's the problem. There's an easy enough route, but there are a hell of a lot of dead bodies in the way. I think we can do it. You just need to follow me and remember my golden rule.'

'What's that?'

'Keep your fucking mouth shut. I'm serious. We've got away with it so far, but when we're down there, we can't take risks. The dead are relatively dumb, but there are loads and loads of them. It's not like on your estate where you could see all the entrances and exits, it's like a maze down there. We could probably outrun a few of them, but there are so many corners and hiding places that we could end up the main attraction in a crowd of hundreds if we're not careful. And if they slow us down enough, we'll drown.'

'Drown?'

'That's the way I think of it. We'll drown in rotting flesh.'

'Shit, man, that's gross.'

'I know. That's why I need to know you understand. I'm not messing around here. We only get one chance at this.'

'I get it.'

'Do you? Do you really?'

'Yes! Stop going on at me, man.'

'No, I won't. I'll keep on at you until we're safe. Then you can find someone else to annoy.'

'Whatever.'

'Will you stop saying whatever.'

'Whatever.'

'Jerk. Right, we're going, but there's one more thing you need to hear first.'

'What's that?'

'It's simple. I'll look out for you and I'll keep you safe, but if you do anything stupid, you're on your own. Likewise, if you fall behind or go off course or anything like that, there won't be much I can do to help. Got it?'

'Got it,' he said, sounding less than convinced.

'I mean it, Omar, this is serious. You could die out there. We both could.'

'I get it,' he mumbled, and this time Sam sensed that he finally understood the gravity of the moment.

'Good. And the opposite's true as well. If I get into trouble and I tell you to go on alone, you do it. Okay?'

'Okay.'

'You remember what the hotel looks like, don't you? Just get yourself there and tell them you were with me. Right?'

'Right.'

'Okay, let's do it. Match my speed and my route.'

Omar nodded. He looked terrified. *Good*, Sam thought.

The air down at ground level was rank with the stench of death, far stronger than it had been here yesterday. It was an indication of just how many corpses were now in close proximity. He glanced back at Omar. The kid looked tiny, stripped of all his cockiness. When Sam moved on, he felt Omar grab hold of the back of his coat.

It struck Sam just how very different everything looked from a distance. What had appeared to be a relatively sensible route to the church from their viewpoint up high now looked like an obstacle course of epic proportions and insurmountable risk. He peered around a corner and his heart sank. He'd intended getting there via a vacant building he'd used several times previously, but in the hundred-or-so metres between their current position and the entrance to that building there was nothing but death.

There had been roadworks on this narrow road, and it had been blocked by traffic waiting at temporary (now permanent) lights, so they'd never used it as anything more than a cut-through. The bodies here had increased in number, and the close confines and stationary vehicles had acted like a valve, preventing them from getting away. Corpses had flowed like a semi-solid liquid into every nook and cranny, blocking themselves in. Sam turned around to face Omar. He'd been hard on him, but it was necessary. He just hoped he hadn't overdone it and traumatised the kid. He pulled him close and whispered, 'We can do this, bud.'

Sam could see the roof of a blue security van intermittently through the throng. He led Omar through the crowds, then lifted him onto the front of the van. Omar scrambled up the windscreen and onto the roof. Sam followed, but was dragged back when a corpse in the wrong place at the right moment swung a leaden arm and grabbed him. Sam caught its fist, twisted its arm around its back and then, ignoring the popping of dried-up sinews and cartilage, forced it down onto its knees and used it as a step-up. He stood alongside Omar on the roof of the van and gestured a hopping motion with his hand, car to car to car. But Omar wasn't watching. He was frozen to the spot, moving only his eyes, looking down into the sea of grotesque faces now staring up at them from all sides.

'Go!' Sam said, and he pushed him towards the back of the van. Omar pulled up, but Sam leapt over another glut of dead flesh and landed on the bonnet of a police car. He lost his footing, the soles of his boots wet with blood, but was able to grab the rack of lights on the roof and stop himself falling. The whole car rocked precariously. He'd left huge dents in the bodywork. The noise sounded cataclysmic.

Omar was still on the van. Sam gestured for him to jump. He took a run up (for what it was worth), then pulled up again. They couldn't afford to hang around. Sam turned his back on him, ready to jump over to the next vehicle, but stopped when he heard the kid call out. 'Wait!' he screamed, frantic, and he came flying across. Sam caught him.

'You okay?'

Omar nodded.

'Good,' Sam said, and he shoved him forward again. They clambered over the roof of the police car together, then stepped across a narrow strip of corpse-free space onto the front of a Mini. The vehicles were getting progressively smaller. From towering over the heads of the dead on the security van, they were now level with their chins and all Omar could see were those fucking horrible faces glaring at him. Clumsy hands flailed at Sam's boots and he stomped and kicked them away, almost losing his balance in the process. This time it was Omar's turn to catch him. 'Cheers,' he said.

The gap between the Mini and the next car was too big and too crowded to even consider jumping. Sam knew he'd struggle to make it, so Omar didn't stand a chance. But this had been a calculated risk all along, because of the roadworks. There was a flatbed truck parked up at the side of the road, but from the spot where Sam had scoped out their escape, he hadn't been able to see whether there was any space in the back. There wasn't. Not enough, anyway. The flatbed was loaded up with a tarpaulin-covered mound of hardened bitumen.

'Wait here,' Sam whispered.

'What else am I going to do?' Omar said, gesturing at the dead all around them. Sam took his increasing antagonism as a positive sign.

He shoved a couple of awkwardly placed corpses away, then threw himself across the gap onto the truck. He over-jumped his intended landing spot and hit the rubble in the back with a painful slap. His face stinging, operating purely on instinct, he used the oily tarp to pull himself up. He wiped blood from his nose on the back of his sleeve, then turned back to Omar. 'Easy. Your turn.'

'Fuck that,' Omar said, looking at the state of him.

'Suit yourself,' Sam replied, and as soon as he went to carry on without him, Omar hurled himself across the gulf. The boy hit the side of the truck with a godawful thump and dropped down, just managing to cling on with outstretched fingers. Dead hands clawed at him and he kicked and thrashed furiously, terrified of going under. Sam grabbed him by the scruff of his neck and pulled him up, still kicking and thrashing, then dropped him onto the summit of the bitumen pile. 'You okay?'

Omar couldn't speak.

'We need to keep going. Are you okay, Omar?'

He nodded but didn't get up. Instead, he began scrubbing at his trainers. They'd been clean and white when he'd put them on first thing but were now black with blood and grime.

'Omar, now!'

The two of them jumped again, this time onto the back of a sedan car, and held onto each other for support, just about managing to remain upright. The car was rocked by scores more surging bodies, frantic to get at the leaping pair. Sam pointed up ahead.

'See that doorway? The green one?'

'Yeah.'

'That's where we're going. Five more cars, then we make a run for it the rest of the way, okay? We've done the hard part. The cars here are tight. We can pretty much step from one to the other.'

He started off, listening out for Omar's noise behind. The kid grunted and yelped, continually cursing. Considering his size, he made a hell of noise whenever he took off or landed, probably the most entertainment the dead had seen since their reawakening.

When Sam thudded onto the bonnet of car number three, he set off the alarm. Its lights flashed and its horn wailed but he kept moving. When he jumped over onto car number four and looked around to check on Omar, the kid had gone.

'Omar!'

The dead didn't react to his voice, drowned out by the blaring alarm. They were gravitating towards it as he'd known they would, oblivious to everything else. He tried to look beyond them for any sign of Omar, but he'd disappeared completely. Sam had warned him to stay close, had told him that he'd be on his own if they got separated... but he'd known all along that was a bluff. When it came to it, he couldn't just keep going without him.

As quickly as it had started, the car alarm stopped.

It took a couple of seconds for the dead to react, their senses on a slight delay. A few of them noticed him, but most didn't. He was used to being the sole focus of undead attention and it was jarring to see the backs of their heads rather than their ghastly faces. He knew the only explanation was that something more interesting was happening nearby.

It could only be Omar.

There was a commotion over by the flatbed truck. Without hesitation, Sam jumped back onto the previous car and bounced up and down on the roof until he'd retriggered the alarm, then dropped down into the crowd.

He was disorientated. Deep amongst the dead he couldn't make out anything other than their crisscrossing and blind collisions. Individually featureless and unremarkable, down here and close-up it was hard to see where one ended and the next began. But then, in a razor-thin gap that briefly opened up between one corpse and the next, he saw Omar crawling away on his hands and knees. Sam charged towards him like a snowplough.

Omar was a couple of metres and a million miles away. He changed direction when he crawled into one of the abandoned cars and couldn't keep going. Sam tried to intercept but the dead blocked his way, an impasse formed purely by chance. He was pushed back into a safety barrier by the weight of the crowd pressing against him. When he looked at his feet, he saw that the ground was literally about to disappear. A trench had been dug along the pavement. Less than half a metre wide, it was a couple of metres long and deep enough that it would cause serious damage if he ended up falling in. When the dead surged again, he jumped back over the ugly scar in the ground and the dumb dead collapsed into it. As the first few dropped down, he saw Omar again. Sam grabbed one of the safety barriers and charged towards him, holding it out in front of him like a shield then using it to create a little defensible space around the kid. He was sobbing. Terrified.

'It's okay, mate,' Sam said. 'I've got you. Stay close.'

And he ran into the crowd again, the safety barrier carving a clear channel, a machete through brush, all the way through to the green door. They burst into the empty building and Omar slumped against the wall and covered his head as the dead began to batter against the windows.

'Keep going,' Sam said, dragging him back onto his feet. 'We're almost there.'

They left the building through a rear exit which led them to the grounds of the church. Sam looked around, sensing that Omar was holding back. He could tell by his face that something was wrong.

'Watch out!' Omar yelled. Sam braced for more violence, but relaxed when he saw who it was.

'Where the hell have you been?' David Shires asked.

Once they were inside the church and the doors were shut, it felt like the outside world no longer existed. The thickness of the ancient walls and the lofty space within them was like a firebreak, holding back the endless chaos outside. Sam was so relieved he could hardly speak. He was too exhausted to explain why he hadn't returned last night or to ask why David, Vicky, Gary and a couple of the others were here in the church rather than the hotel. He could see Stan, as well as Damien McAdam, his footballer mate.

'So?' David pressed.

'So what?'

'So where did you go?'

'Found something strange. Thought I'd check it out. This is Omar, by the way. Poor little shite was home alone.'

'I saved his ass,' Omar announced.

'Cocky little bugger,' David smirked.

'You're both right, as it happens,' Sam told him. He sat down on a pew, exhausted. It looked like the others had been stuck in the church for some time. To the best of his knowledge, they'd hardly used the place before. With the hotel in spitting distance, there'd been no need. But he could see beds made out of prayer cushions, altar cloths that had been used as sheets... 'What's happened here?'

'Believe me, I've been asking myself the same thing all night,' Stan said, sounding as pissed off as he looked. 'It's not through choice, I'll tell you that much.'

'Well, that's a given,' Sam replied quickly, looking directly at Stan and Damien. 'It's a struggle to get you two lazy bastards out of the bar at the best of times. There's not one bit of me thinks you're out here because you volunteered your services. Did you think you'd be able to save a few souls out here, Stan?'

'Fuck you, hippy,' Damien grumbled.

'We hit problems as soon as we got back here with the van,' Vicky explained, trying to get the conversation back on track. 'We were—'

'Is Charlie okay?' Sam interrupted.

'She's fine,' Gary said, limping over. 'In better shape than me, anyway. I knackered my ankle when we—' He stopped talking abruptly and stared. 'Omar Gahnem? Jeez, is that really you? What are you doing here?'

'Oh shit, man, not you,' Omar said. He glared at Sam. 'You never told me he was here.' He stormed over to the other side of the church and hid behind a pillar where no one could see him.

'What's all that about?' Sam asked, confused.

'Me and Omar have history,' Gary said, and he laughed and shook his head. 'Bloody hell, what are the chances? Of all the people... I was his caseworker for a while, if you can believe that. Right little reprobate he was.'

'He still is,' Sam said. 'He looks thrilled to see you again.'

'I'm the last person he'll have wanted to see.'

'Do you mind if we get back to the point?' Vicky asked, unimpressed.

'Sorry. Go on,' Sam said.

'Have you seen the state of Fleet Street this morning? In the time we were away yesterday, loads more bodies turned up; it was like a dam burst somewhere. Obviously, we weren't to know until we arrived. We had to wait for hours for the dead to calm down outside the supermarket.'

'Your little party piece after you got the van was a nice try,' David said, 'but it hardly had any impact. They weren't fooled, and there were loads of them about.'

Vicky continued. 'Judging from the state of you two, I'm sure you've realised that the streets are pretty bloody congested around here now. We managed to get the van reasonably close, but couldn't get through to the hotel courtyard. So, we were having to transport everything through by hand. We had a human chain going, all hands to the pump. Even theirs.' She gestured at Damien and Stan.

'No need to be quite so antagonistic, Vicky,' Stan said, annoyed. 'We all helped, didn't we?'

'After a little persuading. Anyway, it was just one of those things. We'd managed to hold them back, but the dead broke through when we weren't expecting it. They cut straight through the lines. Most of us were able to get back to the hotel, but we were cut off. We had the stuff we were carrying, so we had a bit of food. We decided to sleep here last night and wait till morning to try and work out how we were going to get back inside.'

'When we heard that car alarm, we thought the cavalry had arrived to save us,' Damien said.

Sam shook his head. 'No such luck. It's vile out there today.'

David agreed. 'I know, and if we're not careful we'll compromise the hotel and end up cutting ourselves permanently off from the rest of the world.'

'Jeez, I'm gone for one day and it all goes to hell,' Sam said, sarcastic.

'Jerk. You're so far up your own arse,' Damien grumbled. He lay flat out on a pew and stared up at the church's arched ceiling. Sam ignored him.

'And everything's just been fine and dandy with you, I take it?' Vicky said, equally unimpressed. 'You said you found something strange?'

'Another flood of bodies, for starters.'

'Same as the one that caused all our problems?'

'Bigger.'

'And did you find out where they were heading?'

'They weren't heading anywhere. They were being led away.'

'Who by?' Stan asked.

Sam hesitated. 'You're not going to believe this. By a girl on a pushbike with a CD player strapped to the back.'

'Bullshit,' Gary said.

'It's not. There's part of me wishes I could come up with a more logical explanation, but that's what I saw. I got to the front of the queue just at the wrong time. She'd done whatever she set out to, switched off her music and disappeared. Left me stuck in the middle of thousands of corpses, nothing else for them to fixate on but me.'

'Nice.'

'That's when I saved him,' Omar said, wandering back over to pick at the scraps of food the others had left.

'So, this girl on a bike, was she working alone?' David asked.

'I seriously doubt it. She was taking too much of a risk to have been flying solo. And why would you want to get rid of thousands of bodies at a time if you're on your own? It's not like you'd need the space.'

'Sounds crazy,' Vicky agreed. 'But if there was ever a time and place you could forgive people for losing their marbles, this is it.'

Sam wasn't finished. 'There's something big going on here. If the kid I saw was working with the same people who sent the dead down Fleet Street the other day, and I can't imagine she wasn't, then there's got to be a method to the madness. If I had a map to hand, I'd trace her route, maybe backtrack what I saw at Fleet Street, and try and work out where they might have been coming from.'

'Let me get this straight,' Stan said, unconvinced. 'Are you seriously suggesting there's someone casually cycling around London like some bloody Pied Piper, trying to tempt the living dead away from their own backyard and into ours? Christ, I've heard it all now.'

'I'm not suggesting there's anything casual about it, and I don't think they even know we're here, but yes that's about it. I'm all ears if you can come up with a better explanation.'

Vicky and David looked at each other. 'Are you thinking what I'm thinking?' David asked. She nodded. He turned back to Sam. 'When we were on our way back, we ended up driving down

Holborn. I didn't think anything of it at the time, but someone had spray-painted the word "Monument" on the side of a couple of buildings. Vicky said she'd seen the same thing in Trafalgar Square.'

'Just before you found me and Selena. Someone had sprayed it on the base of one of the lion statues by Nelson's Column.'

'I've seen it too,' Sam told them. 'It was just before I got into trouble near Omar's place. Tell you the truth, I hadn't given it too much thought since, haven't had the chance. It was written on the roof of a jack-knifed lorry.'

'Has to mean *the* Monument, doesn't it?' Gary said. The monument to the Great Fire of London.'

'It's down by the Tower of London and Tower Bridge. Very close to the Tower, in fact,' Stan said. 'I know the area well. Spent a lot of time around there, I have.'

Damien sat up. 'You're jumping to a lot of conclusions here, aren't you? I saw some graffiti in a public toilet that said, "your sister's a slut". I mean, okay, but which sister? My eldest? Or Sister Mary Agnes who cracked my hand with her bloody ruler? There's graffiti and street art all over London.'

Sam sighed. 'You're missing the point.'

'Enlighten me.'

'The graffiti I saw was on the roof of a lorry. Just let that sink in for a second, will you. What's the point of putting graffiti where no one's going to see it?'

'So?'

'So, that means it was written after the event.'

'What event?'

'Holy fuck. *The* event. The one where everyone but us dropped down dead, remember? It makes sense. There's someone based near *the* Monument who is systematically clearing the dead away from their domain. I don't know London that well, but I know where Tower Bridge is, and it's not a stretch to think that both of the hordes of bodies we've seen this week could have emanated from around there.'

'This is all well and good,' Stan said, 'but what does it matter? There are almost fifty of us here.'

'No,' Gary said, 'there are seven of us here. Everyone else is in the hotel, and who knows how much longer they'll be able to stay there? I don't know what everyone else thinks, but I reckon it'll be worth checking to see if there is anything happening around the Monument. Even if it's just some lone crazy with a bike and a boombox, it's probably worth a punt. I mean, the Tower of London's a bloody fortress... that's got to be a better long-term option for us than the hotel, and like I said, I think we're going to need another option before long.'

'I still say getting out of London is the best long-term solution for all of us,' Vicky said, 'but short-term I'd be more than happy to hole-up in a castle until we can leave the city for good.'

'So let's do it,' David said. 'Today. Now.'

'And how are we supposed to get there?' Stan asked.

'Hire yourself a paddle boat,' Damien said, the tone of his voice making his intentions clear. He was going nowhere.

'He's right. The river probably is the easiest option,' Sam agreed. 'I'm sure we can find a boat and get it going. More chance of that than getting anywhere fast on the roads.'

'Agreed,' Vicky said.

'Someone should stay here,' Gary suggested. 'Maybe try and get back into the hotel when things calm down a bit, let the rest of them know.'

'I'll do it,' Stan said, immediately volunteering.

'No,' Vicky said. 'You just told us you know the area. You're coming with us. Gary, you stay. Give your ankle a rest.'

'Makes sense,' David agreed. 'Me, Stan, Vicky and Sam will go. Omar, you stay here and keep an eye on Damien.'

'And I'll keep an eye on Omar,' Gary said.

12

Sam, David, Stan and Vicky raced across a large public garden, down towards Victoria Embankment. A wave of dead bodies followed them across the grassy expanse, hundreds chasing in a slow-motion pursuit. Stan, who until yesterday hadn't left the hotel since he'd first arrived there, and who was furious with himself for somehow getting embroiled in this ridiculous, risk-filled journey, panicked when he realised they were running out of lawn. The area was boxed in by ubiquitous looking black metal railings, at least two metres high. There were more bodies loitering on the other side, and he didn't appear to understand the correlation between his very vocal panic levels and their piqued interest. Sam went over the railings first, followed by Vicky, leaving David to make sure Stan followed. 'Pull yourself together or we'll leave you out here on your own,' David threatened him once they were all on the other side.

In the moments after the world had come to an abrupt end last month, a bus had mounted the kerb here and smashed into the low wall on the river side of the road. More cars had crashed a little further east, and between the two well-spaced wrecks, an unexpected bubble of space had been preserved. There were several small piers here within a relatively short distance, and alongside one of them they found a little fishing boat trapped like driftwood against the hull of a much larger vessel. David, who'd had some limited experience in a similar-sized craft back home in Ireland, was able to get it started.

Stan had been uncharacteristically quiet since David had admonished him, but once they were safely on the water and on their way down river, he regained his composure and talked incessantly about the horrors he'd witnessed since leaving the hotel, and how he was sure that no matter how long he lived, he'd never be able to block those images from his mind. Vicky just looked at him. There was so much she could say, but what was the point? It was all she could do not to push him overboard and be done with it.

The water was deceptive. It looked calm, but there were ebbs, flows and currents to contend with. David didn't complain because concentrating on steering the boat meant that he didn't have to acknowledge the rest of the world. Some of the time everything appeared reassuringly normal, but the illusion was always fleeting, and nightmarish sights were never far from view. A black cab had hit the wall of the Embankment, shooting the driver halfway through the windscreen where he lay still, rotting. It had come to rest at an angle that afforded the wan corpses a way of climbing up onto the stonework, reacting to the boat's engine noise, which was disproportionately loud against the silence of everything else. The dead inevitably ended up in the river, and whilst it sounded comical, the reality was anything but. They thrashed in the water. Some sank beneath the green and brown-tinged ripples, while others remained afloat, buoyed up by noxious, decay-brewed gases that had inflated their bellies. At times the river appeared to be full of movement. Cadavers nudged against the hull of the boat almost continually. Some had obviously been in the water for weeks. Vicky watched one bob past. Its face was white and bloated, doughy and round. Its eyes flickered and the corners of its mouth twitched like it was talking to her, whispering: *pull me out pull me out pull me out...*

Despite all the open space around them, on the water it was hard not to feel impossibly claustrophobic. 'Even after all this time, I still can't get my head around the scale of it,' David said. 'Everything's ruined.'

Vicky agreed. She'd been living (if this could even be called living) among the wreckage of this world for more than forty days, but until now she'd only ever had to look at a small fraction of it at a time. Today, though, it was as if they were being forced to take a guided tour of the apocalypse. Perhaps it was because their location was so well known that everything looked so bad? Everywhere she turned, she saw picture postcard views that had been devastated, everything irredeemably scarred.

'It's neverending, that's what gets me,' Stan said. 'I've seen some things in my time, but never anything like this.'

David agreed. 'I know what you mean. I used to work security back home. This one time they had me keeping guard on a bunch of industrial units that had caught fire. I remember being on my own, looking up at these burnt-out shells of buildings, thinking that this must be what the end of the world looks like. But then I got back in my car and drove home to the missus and kids, and everything felt normal again. That's what gets to me. That's what we've lost, what we'll never get back. There is no normal anymore, nowhere safe to go home to. It's like you said, there's never going to be any let up from this.'

Vicky thought about Ledsey Cross, the self-sufficient eco-village that Kath had enthused about incessantly. It felt about as far from here as the planet Mars, and she thought she probably had just as much chance of getting to Yorkshire as she did another planet. It all felt impossible. It all felt hopeless.

The October morning was cold, foggy, and relentlessly grey. The mist, although not particularly heavy, did enough to blur the edges of everything, making distant details hard to discern. She thought that was a good thing, initially, protecting them from things they didn't need to see. But the longer they were on the water, the more unsettling everything began to feel. Rather than shield them from more ruination, the fog instead just gave the dead more places to hide.

'What the hell is that?' David slowed the boat as a dark shape appeared through the mist. It was hard to work out what it was at first, not least because it had reared up so unexpectedly.

'It's another boat,' Stan said. 'No surprise, really. Busy stretch of water, this. Must have capsized and got stuck.'

He was right. They were looking at the upturned hull of a

vessel much larger than the boat in which they were travelling. From what they could see, its bow was wedged against the north bank. David turned to starboard, drifting a little way out from the wreck, then sailed along its length to navigate past. But when they rounded the stern, they saw the capsized boat was only a small part of a much bigger problem. Here, over the course of days and weeks, more and more wreckage had become trapped and entangled. From their current position, it looked like the entire width of the river had been blocked. There were other boats tangled up in the debris, huge piles of driftwood and waste and even occasional land vehicles that must have ploughed off bridges or down banks. And as they were travelling downriver, they realised the first boat they'd seen was likely only the latest addition, not the cause of all the chaos.

'Stuff like this used to happen all the time, just not in the Thames,' Sam said. 'There's a massive island in the Pacific made of floating garbage, apparently.'

'Never mind that,' Stan said, 'are we going to get through?'

'Other than turning around, I don't see we have much of an option.'

David gave the engine a nudge and let the bow gently push through the enormous accumulation of flotsam and jetsam. The deeper they sailed into the mess and the closer they looked, the more bodies they saw. There were hundreds and hundreds of them filling the gaps between other pieces of wreckage, initially hard to make out because they were as drained of colour as everything else. It would have been easier to deal with had the dead not begun to move. They reacted to the noise and the rippling of the water when the boat came near, and the movements of a few quickly spread to many more. Within minutes, the surface of the river appeared almost to be boiling, such was the ferocity of the combined reactions of so many partially submerged corpses.

In the back of the boat, Sam found two metal punt-poles. He handed one to Vicky and between them they began pushing debris away on either side so that David could continue to prod the bow through.

The cause of the dam on the water was a Thames Clipper – a water taxi which had hit one of the remaining columns of the old Blackfriars Railway Bridge then become entangled with another vessel that had crashed into the newer bridge adjacent. As David and the others approached the wreck, they saw that many of its dead passengers were still onboard and were reacting to the engine noise. David steered towards the south bank to try and keep the maximum distance from them.

Until now, they'd not ventured anywhere near the other bank of the Thames. But like everywhere else, the footpaths and roads on the south of the river were heavily congested. 'Why here?' Stan asked, looking up at the endless undead crowds.

'Topography,' Sam said. 'Both banks slope down towards the river. It's easy for the dead to get down towards the water, not so easy for them to go back the other way.'

The strips of pavement alongside the Thames were often clogged with tourists, and they looked as busy as ever today. The haze of the foggy autumnal filter made the crowds of shuffling shapes appear familiar, commonplace. They congregated in groups, bunched up by the lay of the land, and reacted disproportionately to any stimulation. As they travelled downriver, a ripple of lethargic movement followed along both banks like an extension of the boat's wake. David wanted to open up the throttle and race away, but he knew the safest way forward was to continue at this steady, infuriatingly glacial, pace.

'When we get close you should try and coast in. No noise at all, okay?' Sam suggested, and he agreed.

13

L ondon Bridge. Not far now. They'd lost track of how many
 hours they'd been on the water, but the journey felt like it had
taken forever. David cut the engine, and the silence served only to
amplify the tension they all felt. The current carried them towards
Tower Millennium Pier, and the lack of noise, coupled with the
persistent mist, made this part of the world feel disconnected
from everything else.

Sam leant over the port side of the boat and caught the pier
with the tip of the outstretched punt-pole. He wedged the end
of the pole into a gap in the railings, and that caused the bow of
the boat to veer towards the bank. As soon as he could he caught
hold of the railings and guided the vessel along the launch. David
jumped out and tied up the boat (after a fashion).

There were bodies coming, three in total, stumbling out of
the mist and down the ramp towards them. 'Here we go,' said
David. Beside him, Vicky took her crowbar from her belt, ready
to defend herself.

And then the approaching figures stopped.

One of them turned to say something to one of the others, who
then sprinted away, back the way they'd just come. They were
pointing and gesturing and... and it was clear that these people
were alive!

'That's a good sign,' Stan said, a massive understatement.

David agreed. 'You can say that again, but don't let's get ahead
of ourselves. Okay, so they're alive, but don't forget, these are
the jokers who send kids out on bikes to deal with thousands of
corpses at a time.'

The two-remaining people – a man and a woman – continued
to approach the group of four. The others hadn't moved an inch

since stepping onto dry land. Soon there was only a couple of meters between them, and the two sides regarded each other in silence. It was beginning to feel awkward, then the woman spoke. 'Hi,' she said. 'I'm sorry... it's been so long I've forgotten what to say when I meet new people. I'm Lynette.'

'Good to meet you,' Vicky said.

'We'd have given you a proper welcome if we'd known you were coming.'

'We didn't know we were coming until this morning,' David said. 'Pleased to meet you, Lynette. I'm David, this is Sam, Vicky and—'

Stan barged to the front, crowding the others out. 'I'm Alec, Alec Stanley,' he said with more enthusiasm than he'd ever shown previously. 'Just call me Stan.'

'Well, it's lovely to have you all here,' Lynette said. 'Come on, come on, let's get inside. It's bitter out here this morning. Jonah will look after your boat. Dominic will be keen to say hello.'

They left Lynette's colleague properly securing the boat, then walked with her away from the river. The mist was much reduced further from the Thames, and a little faint sunshine threatened to break through the cloud. 'That's a good omen,' Stan whispered to Vicky.

'It's just a coincidence,' she said, unimpressed.

David and Sam held back slightly. 'What are you thinking?' David asked.

'I'm thinking, *that's the bloody Tower of London*,' he replied, looking at the grey stone walls over to their right. 'I saw a TV programme about it not long ago. You think it's just some old ruin, but there's a lot more to it than that. There are houses and all kinds of other spaces in there. Did you know there was even a pub for the Beefeaters?'

'Seriously?'

'Seriously. Mad, isn't it. Perfect place to set yourself up to survive all this, don't you think?'

'Absolutely. Honestly, Sam, I'm struggling to stop my imagination running away with itself. Just wait till these folks find out there are so many of us. This could be a real turning point for us and them, you know.'

They were surprised when Lynette kept going past the entrance to the Tower, instead following a narrow, block-paved path adjacent to a modern-looking building. It had a branch of Starbucks on the corner which Vicky looked at longingly. She would have killed for a coffee. Or something stronger.

'There are no bodies,' she noticed.

Lynette corrected her. 'Oh, there are plenty of bodies, believe me. We've got them held back at a distance.'

'And don't we know it,' Sam said. 'The reason there are fewer of them here is because you sent most of them our way.'

'But they wouldn't have had any idea we were there,' Stan said, immediately jumping to Lynette's group's defence. 'Anyway, they left us messages, didn't they? The graffiti? We wouldn't have known where to come if they hadn't left their location spray-painted around London.'

Vicky corrected him. 'No one left *us* a message, Stan. They left *a* message.'

'Oh, stop being so bloody cynical, will you.'

'No, not yet. Not until I know exactly what's going on here. I'm not taking any chances.'

'Honestly, there's nothing to worry about,' Lynette said, and even that casual comment sent Vicky's mind racing. She was aware she was thinking negatively, but her world had been flipped on its head more than once recently, and she was tired of constantly fighting to keep her head above water. *Better to plan for the worst and be surprised*, she thought, *than to be optimistic and end up let down and crushed*. Again.

But it was hard to contain her enthusiasm, though, because the more of this place Vicky saw, the more she was impressed. On their right was an open area in front of the Tower, where a huge number of vehicles had been parked up in rows. She counted more than fifty. And still there were no dead bodies immediately visible.

She couldn't remember the last time she'd seen such a large space that was clear of corpses. In fact, she realised, she hadn't seen a single one since getting out of the boat.

Up ahead, Stan had monopolised Lynette and was chewing the poor woman's ear off. He stopped walking abruptly and just stared at her. 'How many?' he asked, unable to believe what he'd just been told.

'There are about three hundred of us here,' Lynette said, loud enough for Sam, David and Vicky to all hear. 'I guess one of the few advantages of being stuck right in the middle of the city is there was always a good chance of finding other people left alive. There isn't anywhere else in the country where so many people worked in such a relatively small geographic area. I worked at City Hall, just across the river, so I'm used to the crowds. I used to hate how busy and fast-paced London was, but I'm so glad I went into the office that day.'

'Three hundred,' Stan repeated, shaking his head with disbelief. 'Three hundred people!'

'Give or take,' Lynette shrugged, and started walking again. She turned left towards a vast, corporate-looking building: two huge wedge-shaped blocks, connected by an enormous glass atrium. 'This is Tower Place. We use it as a hub.'

They followed her inside. Vicky thought it a shame that with the Tower of London on their doorstep, All Hallows by the Tower church opposite, and all manner of other historic buildings in the immediate vicinity, they'd chosen to base themselves in a functional yet soulless office block, larger in scale, perhaps, but otherwise little different to thousands of similar buildings she'd seen elsewhere. They were surrounded by so much beauty, so much important architecture, yet they'd locked themselves away in a metal and glass box like this. 'Take that disapproving look off your face,' David whispered to her. 'You're allowed to be happy, you know. This is a good day.'

'Yeah, I know,' she said, and she managed half a smile. She reminded herself that week or so ago, she'd have been overjoyed to find even one other person left alive. Today they'd found hundreds.

Lynette led them up a staircase and through a once-busy office space. The desks were all empty now, stripped of computers and phones, all obsolete technology removed. It was quiet like a library, though they occasionally heard voices elsewhere. There was a conference room with opaque glass walls, and they could see the shapes of other people inside. The sound was muffled, and even though she couldn't hear the words being spoken, Vicky thought the tone, volume and rhythm made it sound less like a discussion, more a business meeting.

They were taken over to the far side of the room where a girl was sitting on her own at a desk next to the window, taking advantage of the daylight. 'This is Georgie,' Lynette said, introducing her. 'She's our records clerk. She'll get you all booked in.'

Georgie took four handwritten forms from a pile and handed them around. There was a series of standard questions for completion: name, date of birth, place of birth, blood type, known allergies, skills and qualifications, work history, religious affiliations... whole lives reduced to single sides of A4 paper.

'No, wait,' Sam said, handing his form back. 'I think you've got the wrong end of the stick. We're not staying.'

'I don't understand,' Lynette said, confused.

'We came to see if there was anyone here,' David explained. 'We saw your graffiti. We've got a group of people in a hotel back along the river.'

'How many?'

'About fifty.'

'I'm sorry,' Lynette said. 'My fault. I just assumed. In that case you really do need to speak to Dom. He should be out of his meeting soon. Can I get you a coffee while you're waiting?'

'Yes, please,' Stan said without hesitation, and Lynette nodded politely then disappeared.

Vicky was struggling to take it all in. 'I don't know about you lot, but I feel like I've just gone back in time a few months and

I'm waiting for a job interview. Coffee? Meetings? Christ, what are these people, apocalypse deniers?'

'Don't worry, it's not like you think,' Georgie said.

'And what exactly do you think I think?' Vicky asked, her abruptness appearing to take Georgie by surprise.

'I'm sorry...' she stammered, 'I didn't mean anything by it. It's just that,' she took a breath. 'I guess some of the other people we had join us had seen too many horror films. When they saw what Dom was trying to do, and how much progress we've made here, they immediately assumed we were cannibals or fascists, I think.'

'And you're neither?'

She laughed. 'No, we're definitely not. I was a vegan, actually.'

'Don't know which is worse,' Stan grumbled, all too predictably.

Sam was not impressed. 'Fuck's sake, Stan, do you not think it's time to drop the clichés and stereotypes?'

'Being vegan was all the trend though, wasn't it?'

'Yes, but we don't have the luxury of trends anymore. There aren't enough of us.'

'Anyway,' Georgie said, 'we eat what we can get now. It's that or starve. We're a pretty civilised bunch, all things considered. Pretty dull, actually. I mean, look at me. There's this wild, dystopian world out there, and I'm still sitting in an office, shuffling paperwork like nothing's changed. I'm not complaining, though. The inanity of it's pretty comforting, if I'm honest.'

Vicky admired the fact she was so candid. She thought it augured well. Maybe these people really had found a way to distance themselves from what was left of the world to such an extent that they could waste their days with meetings, making coffee, and doing paperwork. Part of her was jealous. It had been a long time since she'd felt anywhere near as relaxed as Georgie appeared.

There was movement from the conference room. The door opened and a stream of people poured out. Enough had clearly been said in the meeting, because no one was talking now. Lynette reappeared with a thermos flask and went into the room after the last person had left.

'Why do I feel like I'm waiting to see the headmaster?' Stan asked.

'Dom's okay,' Georgie told him. 'Nothing like you'd expect.'

Less than a minute later a man emerged from the conference room and came striding over towards them. 'Bloody hellfire,' Stan said. 'It's him.'

Vicky had been staring out of the window at the empty, corpse-free space below. 'It's who?' she asked, and she turned around to see. 'Oh, Jesus Christ. A frigging politician. That's all we need.'

They might not all have immediately remembered his name, but his face and his manner were instantly familiar. 'Good to see you all,' he said, overconfident. 'I'm Dominic Grove.'

'You don't have to introduce yourself. I know who you are,' Stan said. 'Good lord. What a turn up.'

Dominic greeted each of them in turn, then gestured for the group to follow him into the conference room. Once again, Vicky felt like she'd been hurled backwards to a time she'd thought was long gone. The room was dominated by a long wooden conference table, around which a number of comfortable executive-style chairs had been arranged. The seats were still warm, the air tinged with the smell of cooped up bodies from the meeting just ended. 'Come in, come in,' he said, enthusiastically. 'Sit down, please. Let me get you some coffee.' He poured drinks from the Thermos flask and handed them around, then sat at the head of the table, piles of papers spread out in front of him. 'It's good to see you here. Lynette says there are quite a few of you.'

'Just under fifty,' David said.

'That's amazing. I mean, I've always believed there had to be other groups in the city that we hadn't yet found, or that hadn't yet found us. I assumed anyone else left alive was sheltering, but if I'm honest, I was starting to lose hope. I can't remember when we last had anyone turn up here. I take it you saw the graffiti?'

'We did,' David said, and he was about to speak again when Vicky cut across him.

'Are you the ones who've been sending tidal waves of dead

bodies across town?'

'Yes, it was us, we find that—'

'My friend died because of that little trick. Was that what you were trying to do? Flush out the remaining survivors?'

The anger in her voice was barely contained. Dominic didn't appear at all fazed by her aggression. Stan, however, was almost embarrassed. 'There's no need for that, Vicky. We're all on the same side, you know.'

Dominic shook his head. 'No, of course that wasn't the plan. I didn't realise we'd caused a problem for anyone. I understand your anger, though, and I'm sorry about your friend.'

The apology came too quickly, too easily for her liking.

'Fuck me,' Sam said, 'a politician apologising. I've seen dead bodies walking, but a politician who apologises? Christ, I've heard it all now.'

'Ex-politician,' Dominic said, correcting him. 'You're not wrong, though. Being an arrogant gobshite was pretty much a pre-requisite for the job. Glad not to have to deal with all that nonsense anymore, if I'm honest. No, I'm not a politician now, same as none of you are what you used to be either. We're past all that.'

'You sure? Because I don't think I could handle politics on top of everything else right now.'

'I'm sure.'

Dominic handed round a packet of biscuits.

'This is all very civilised,' Stan said.

'Now that's the key word I wanted to hear,' Dominic said. 'Let me tell you a bit about what we're trying to do here, and do feel free to tell me to shut up at any time, because I have a habit of rattling on, and building this place has become something of an obsession. Actually, that's not quite right. It's not the place I'm obsessive over, it's the people in it. Did you know there are over three hundred of us?'

'Yes,' David said, 'Lynette told us. And you're the boss man?'

'I'm absolutely not. Not like that. You know my background,

though. I said I was an ex-politician, but I've been in and around politics too long just to shut up and fade into the background. I'm not in charge, not by any stretch of the imagination, I'm just part of the team. I'm using my experience to help shape things and get things done, and it would be wrong of me not to. We're all still reeling from what's happened to the world, and we all need to contribute to build something from the ruins. We've got people who were in construction, people who know how to cook, people who can keep vehicles on the road, a couple of doctors, counsellors... my job was about pulling stuff together and making things happen, so that's what I'm doing.'

David was tired of the spin already. 'That sounds like a very long-winded way of telling us you are the boss after all.'

Dominic just smiled at him, didn't react. 'Can I show you what we've done here before you pass judgement?'

'Yes, please,' Vicky said, also weary of the posturing.

He jumped up and dragged a flipboard closer to the table, flicking through the sheets until he found what he was looking for. 'Now you'll have to excuse the fact this is all hand-drawn. Normally the planning department would have mocked everything up on computer, but the planning department are all dead, and the computers don't work.' He paused to laugh at his own joke, then continued when no one else reacted. 'If we're ever able to get a steady power supply running, then maybe we'll dust the computers off and start using them again. Can't see that happening for a while, though. For now, they're all sitting in a spare room somewhere.'

He found the right page and angled it towards the table. On it was a crudely drawn map of the immediate vicinity. The Thames was shown in blue at the bottom, and a large area of the city had been bordered in red ink. The Tower of London, the Monument to the Great Fire of London, and the building they were currently in were all marked inside the red line.

'You've cleared all that area already?' Stan asked, surprised.

'Not quite, but we've made a good start.' Dominic picked up

a marker pen and used it to point to the map, slipping straight into Corporate Presenter Mode. 'We started with the Monument and cleared the area around it in the first day or so before the dead began to walk. We figured it was symbolic and practical. We had a light up there to try and get people to come here, but that died when the power was cut off. There were about thirty of us here back then, I think. We had folks walking the streets, shouting for other survivors. Then the dead picked themselves up off the pavements, and it all went to shit again. First we put barriers in place to keep them out, then we blocked Tower Bridge and London Bridge. There may well be other people still alive on the South bank, but for now we've chosen to stay on this side of the water.'

'It looked pretty corpse-heavy over there from what we saw today,' Sam said. 'I was saying to the others, it's the geography of London that causes them to drift down towards the water.'

'Totally agree. For now, we've put pretty substantial roadblocks across both bridges, but they can be moved if the situation changes. If anything, though, I imagine we'll be strengthening the barricades or maybe even destroying the bridges altogether. That's all a long way off, of course. I'd love for us to be able to raise Tower Bridge, but chances of us being able to do that are very remote.'

Lynette shook her head. 'I'm sorry, I still can't get used to having conversations like this. I have to pinch myself every time I walk around the Tower. Doesn't feel right for us to be doing what we're doing with these landmarks, but I know we don't have any choice.'

'I wasn't that far from this area when it first happened,' David said, ruing missed opportunities. 'Just looking in the wrong direction at the wrong time, I guess. If I'd walked down a different street that morning, maybe I'd have found you sooner.'

'Frustrating, isn't it? Distances are deceptive now, don't you think? A mile seems far longer than it did, and even the smallest decisions can have huge implications. I wouldn't be surprised if there are hundreds more people still out there, frightened and alone.'

'Don't count on it,' Sam said. 'I've spent more time out there than most, and I've hardly seen anyone.'

'Well, I hope there are others. I hope we're not it. For what it's worth, I can imagine lots of folks dug in and hid when this all started, and they probably won't show their faces until the dead are less of a threat.'

'Whenever that is, and that's assuming they're still alive.'

'Like I said, I hope that's the case, because the more people we find, the more strength we have. More people will mean more experience, more knowledge, and more hope. We can certainly cope with the numbers. We've planned everything we've done here on the basis of expanding our population. We'll have room for everyone, no matter who they are or where they're from.'

Vicky winced. Dominic's last comment sounded contrived and over-rehearsed, designed to win votes. She looked around the table but couldn't see anyone else ready to raise objections. Sam looked pissed off, of course, but it was obvious that bloody treehugger had a problem with any kind of authority.

'So, once the bodies were up and mobile, we knew we had to act fast to secure the area. That's been our main focus so far, and the faster and more aggressive the dead have become, the quicker we've had to move.'

'You've noticed that too?' Sam asked.

'Christ, yes. We've been studying their behaviour so we can try and get ahead of the game and anticipate the problems they'll cause us next. They're getting worse by the day. Orla – she's the behavioural psychologist we've got studying them – is becoming increasingly concerned. She thinks we're on the verge of a rapid downward spiral.'

Stan interrupted. 'A psychologist? Are you serious? They're dead, and you've got a shrink trying to work them out?'

'I know how it sounds. I needed some convincing myself when she first approached me. When you think about it, though, it makes sense. Behavioural psychology is the study of the connection between someone's mind and their behaviour, and that's exactly what she's looking at. Why are they doing what they're doing? What makes them do it? How are those behaviours changing? Again, I know how crazy this all sounds, but it makes about as much sense as anything right now. We're talking about walking corpses, for Christ's sake; who would you have studying them? Fact is, there's some kind of spark still driving them on, whether it's primordial instinct or conscious thought... Orla's trying to understand the extent to which they might develop.'

'Right up your street,' Stan said to Sam. 'Sam's always messing with those damn things. If he's not studying them, he's spray-painting crosses on their backs and the like.'

'I'm trying to track and understand their movements,' Sam explained.

'Oh, that's easy,' Dominic said. 'They move towards us. We're the only thing left that interests them. That's why they're becoming such a major pain in the arse. Seriously, you and Orla should talk.'

'Happy to.'

Dominic returned to his map. 'So, our original plan was to reclaim this entire section of the city, from the Monument right across into Wapping. There's a lot of green space and residential buildings in Wapping, by London standards anyway, and that's where we eventually envisage most people setting up home. To the south, the river protects us. To the north, though, things get more complicated. We're using the overground train line as a boundary for much of the way. Pretty much all of the track from Fenchurch Street station right across to Limehouse is elevated, so we're planning to use that as a border wall. It's just been a question of blocking all the roads and walkways beneath it. We've not needed to do anything with Fenchurch Street station itself. If there are any corpses left up there, they're likely being held back by the ticket barriers, believe it or not. Also, there was a derailment. They can't get through.'

'You make it all sound easy,' Vicky said.

Lynette became animated. 'Oh, it's absolutely not. Dom has a habit of downplaying things sometimes. It's taken a lot of hard work to get this far, and we've only scratched the surface.'

'Guilty as charged,' Dominic agreed. 'It's a bad habit, a definite holdover from my political days. No, I'm under no illusions here. What we're doing is proving to be anything but easy. It's like they say, it looks good on paper.' He gestured at the map again, drawing an imaginary line above the railway track border he'd just told them about. 'What we're currently doing is trying to push the dead further back and put another barrier in place, another layer of security. It'll keep them at more of a distance from us, which means they're less likely to hear us and thus less likely to react. We've shifted our focus these last few days. Better to put a double-barrier here and secure the area we're already using before we try and make any more inroads into taking back Wapping.'

'Dom,' Lynette said. 'Take a breath.'

He laughed. 'Sorry. Thank God Lynette's here. She keeps me in check. Another bad ex-political habit I have is talking a lot but not listening. I haven't even asked how your group's doing.'

'We're nowhere near as well organised as you are here,' David admitted. 'We're based in a hotel off Fleet Street. We were doing okay until—'

'Until you sent around ten thousand bodies marching our way,' Sam said, cutting across him. David ignored his unhelpful interjection and continued.

'Actually, I was going to say until the dead started to become more tenacious. We went on a supply run yesterday, and when we got back to the hotel it was surrounded. We managed to get a lot of stuff and most of our people to safety, but then the bodies surged. A few of us got separated from the rest, and that's how we ended up here.'

'This lot saw your graffiti around town,' Stan explained. 'We decided to come and check you out.'

Vicky shook her head. Stan's demeanour had completely

changed. Gone was the gibbering wreck they'd had to put up with first thing.

David continued. 'So, the bottom line is, right now we're a little bit fucked. The hotel is prone, far from ideal. Short of trying your tactic and drawing them away, I don't know what we're going to do.'

'We're very fortunate. We have a couple of youngsters who are tough as nails. They go out on bikes and make enough noise to attract thousands of them.'

'I know. I saw one of them,' Sam said. 'A girl with a boombox.'

'That's Ash. She's lovely,' Lynette said. 'A real asset. She's eighteen but she looks about thirteen, a proper little dynamo. Maybe she could go back with you and work her magic? It can take a while, but she's incredibly effective.'

'There's an obvious alternative,' Dominic said. 'Look, I hope I'm not being too presumptuous, but from where I'm standing the answer looks pretty simple. Come here and join us. We've got plenty of space and, if I'm honest, we need as much help as we can get. You certainly sound like you do.'

'It's not our decision to make,' Vicky said. 'We need to go back and talk to the others.'

'Of course. I wouldn't expect anything else.'

'Well, I know we've not been here long, but I'm all in favour,' Stan said.

'Why does that not surprise me?' David asked.

'Just think about this sensibly. You can see how much they've achieved here and what they've got planned. Now look at the state we're in. Personally, I think it's a no-brainer.'

'It does seem to make sense,' David admitted.

'It's a positive for all of us,' Dominic said. 'Win-win.'

'There is a problem that I'm not hearing anyone talking about,' Sam said.

'And what's that?'

'I keep hearing people say how lucky they were to be in the middle of London when this all kicked off, but I actually think we're in the absolute worst place possible. Yes, there was always going to be more chance of us finding other survivors initially, but there are so many corpses here... we're massively outnumbered. And it's not just the immediate threat they pose. What about disease? Rodent infestations? Infrastructure risks... Not to mention we can't grow a damned potato around here, much less enough to feed three hundred people or more. If we were anywhere else, we might have a fighting chance, but not here.'

'We can mitigate all those risks.'

'Maybe, but there are other factors you need to think about.'

'Such as?'

'The fact this city is so old, for a start. London is impractical for our purposes. If we want to build a future, we're going to need housing and farmland, not prime retail and office space. Pastures, not penthouses. We'll need room to roam, not mile after mile of stupidly narrow roads clogged up with rusting traffic.'

'I appreciate what you're saying,' Dominic said, 'and I agree with much of it. As I was saying, those risks can be mitigated by putting maximum distance between us and the dead.'

'But as *I* was saying, what about food? We've been out day after day stripping bare bloody metro supermarkets that were only ever stocked up to keep office workers supplied with lunchtime meal deals and doughnuts and cakes for when someone on their team got a new job. There's so much more potential for survival out there in the real world. London's always been built on bullshit, disconnected from the reality everyone else has to deal with.'

'I didn't think your accent was local,' Lynnette said.

'He's right, though,' Vicky said, looking at Lynette, then at Dominic. 'I've only been with this group for a little while, but I've been stuck in the city since day one and I agree. To stand any chance, we need to get the hell out of London as soon as we can.'

'Oh, here we go. She's going to start going on about that bloody fantasy commune up north again,' Stan said, talking as if Vicky wasn't there.

'It's not a fantasy, you stupid little man.'

'I'm a bit lost here...' Dominic said.

'The friend I mentioned who died when you sent ten thousand corpses our way?'

'Go on.'

'She knew of a place up in Yorkshire that's self-sustainable, and we were planning to try to get there. She'd been talking to someone she knew. There's a community.'

'Sorry to break it to you, but your friend's friend is most likely dead too. From what we've been able to ascertain, at the very least the whole country seems to have been affected by this, if not the entire—'

'No, you're wrong. Listen to me. Kath spoke to her friend *after* everyone died. It's called Ledsey Cross, and there's a whole bunch of people like us up there. So, we need to forget about London and start making plans to—'

Vicky was abruptly silenced by the tolling of a bell outside. Lynette got up and moved to the door. 'Breach bell. Follow me,' she said, nervous.

The ringing continued, constant and unnerving.

14

Lynette took them outside where scores of people were already moving towards the Tower. 'It's probably nothing to worry about,' she explained as they walked. 'Just a precaution. There's a crew working under the railway. Most likely a few of the dead have managed to get through.'

Stan and Vicky followed her and were absorbed into the crowds. Sam held David back. 'I think we should see this.'

They continued past the entrance to the Tower and were all but ignored, most people too focused on preserving their own safety to give a damn about anyone else's, particularly a couple of strangers. It was easy to work out where the breach was. A group of people ran past, and it was clear they meant business. Most wore protective gear like they'd just come off a building site, and all of them were tooled-up, carrying knives and axes and bludgeons of various sizes.

Sam and David followed the pack, holding back so they didn't get caught up in any trouble, but staying close enough so they could see what was happening. They moved quickly along a road that ran parallel with the elevated train track Dominic had talked about. David had to admit, using the track looked like it had been a smart move. It was a part of old London, grubby and industrial, dominating its surroundings rather than blending in, forcing the rest of the world to conform. Roads and footpaths wound beneath it under bridges and arches, all of which had been blocked up. They'd mostly used vehicles parked side-by-side, preventing anything from getting through.

Almost anything.

The breach had occurred another fifty metres or so along the track. Here, a once busy road junction was again a hive of frantic activity. Even though there were people all over the place, and despite the sudden mass of dead figures that had managed to get into the compound, it was easy to piece together what had happened. Sam and David climbed up onto the edge of a half-filled skip to get a better view. 'That's where they're coming in,' Sam said, pointing at the slenderest of gaps between two vehicles.

'Doesn't look big enough for anything to get through,' David said.

'They're not as meaty as they used to be.'

Sam screwed up his face in disgust as another corpse began to force itself through. It reached out its arm, grasping at thin air, looking for something to hold on to but finding nothing. Then its head and neck appeared, then the torso, then the rest of the creature broke through. The deteriorating flesh of its chest had torn open as it squeezed through the narrow gap, and its innards sloshed over the tarmac.

'That's disgusting,' David said.

'I know, right. See what I mean? They've rotted away so much they can get into places they couldn't have reached before.'

David could see the heads of many more cadavers behind. 'They're being forced through under pressure. Looks like there are thousands of them out there. I don't necessarily think they're trying to get in, I think it's just happening naturally. Like a hernia.'

'Nice way of putting it, but there's nothing natural about this.'

All the creatures that had so far made it into the compound appeared similarly emaciated. Flesh had been pared from bone. The contents of their chest cavities had been emptied. Over time their bodies had changed and become more malleable, semi-solid. Sam watched another one come through and its suit jacket, as damp and mouldy as the dank flesh it covered, fell away from its shrunken frame, now several sizes too big. The next corpse was naked. A flap of flesh just above its hip became snagged on a car wing mirror, and a whole sheet of skin was torn away from its back as it was forced through the gap.

There was a guy standing on the roof of a car shouting orders.

He was a big, burly bastard, barking instructions at the workers in protective gear who were mopping up the dead, gesticulating wildly at them with tree-trunk arms. Sam thought he sounded Polish. It was hard to make out much of what he was saying above the chaos of everything else, but the gist of his words was clear: deal with the dead, and deal with them fast.

The men and women scattered around the junction showed no mercy, taking great pleasure in hacking down those corpses unfortunate enough to have made it through. One lethargic looking figure dragged itself towards a woman who was holding a hand axe. She waited for it to come closer, working out the angle of its unsteady, lopsided attack, then swung at it when it lurched into range. She buried the head of the axe in its neck, then hacked at it again and again with savage fury. The corpse offered no resistance and was unresponsive after the first few strikes, but she didn't stop until it lay in several bloody chunks around her feet. With an almost maniacal grin on her blood-streaked face, she looked around for her next victim.

Sam found the one-sided sounds of battle disturbing. It was like a stereo soundtrack with one channel muted; he could hear the grunts of effort of the fighters, the clatter of their weapons, the shouted orders and instructions... but the dead remained impossibly mute throughout. Presumably, they felt no pain; in any case they soaked up their punishment without complaint. Not a whimper.

A car horn sounded from the road behind them.

Boss guy was signalling to the driver, pointing out exactly where he wanted the vehicle placed. The fighters and workers scattered, leaving the road relatively clear, just a solitary corpse left standing and one other dragging itself along the ground. The driver accelerated then braked hard and skidded in the blood and gore, slamming into the other vehicles side-on, and wiping out both the remaining bodies. One more had almost squeezed through the gap but was now stuck, pinned between the newly parked car on one side and the seething crowd of dead flesh on the other.

When the engine stopped there was silence, an eerie calm. A clean-up squad appeared within minutes. Body parts were collected up in wheelbarrows then carted down to the Thames and dumped. Water was brought up from the river and the worst of the semi-human muck was washed off the street. Two rings of the bell in the Tower in quick succession indicated that all was well, and the rest of the people began to emerge, returning to whatever it was they'd been doing before being interrupted by the incursion and subsequent massacre.

'Do you know what's missing?' Sam asked as they began to walk back towards the Tower.

'What?'

'Panic. No one's screaming and shouting, apart from the bloke giving the orders. They're calm and well-coordinated. They've each got jobs to do and they're doing it. When you think how shitty everything is, it's pretty bloody remarkable.'

'You're sold, then?'

'I wouldn't go that far. Gives you something to think about, though.'

They found the others outside Tower Place with Dominic. He'd been looking for them. 'Glad you got to see that. We're getting pretty good at this, don't you think?'

David nodded. 'I'm impressed. Seriously.'

'I'd love to show you more of what we've been doing here. I think it's important. I've often wondered what people in your position might think when you first walk into this place.'

'Too good to be true, that's what I think,' Vicky said.

'And I completely understand that. If I'd been out there having to deal with the hell you've endured day after day, I'd probably feel the same way, and you're right to be cautious. We're very fortunate here. Things have come together well. We've worked hard for it, though, and I intend for us to continue to do that. On the other hand, I've seen the same movies you have. You're expecting us to be members of a cult or some such shite. Maybe you think we sacrifice virgins to the god of the dead to keep us safe? Well, I promise you now, you can forget all that crap. We're just a bunch of people who happen to have survived when everyone else died, and we're determined to keep surviving. There's no ulterior motive, no grand plan for rebuilding society, not yet anyway. Whether this is a new beginning, a reboot of what we had before, or just a way of making the time we have left a little easier and more comfortable, is a question none of us are looking to answer right now. To be honest, I'm just happy to count my blessings and take each day as it comes, and I'd be pleased if you'd go back to the rest of your group and invite them all to come and be a part of this.'

'We'll do that,' David said.

'But not today,' Dominic said. He looked up into the grey clouds swirling overhead. 'It'll be dark soon. I don't think you should risk it on the river if you don't have the light. Stay here tonight and travel back in the morning.'

15

Despite Dominic's assurances, Vicky still thought the Monument group's set-up felt uncomfortably cult-like, but as the night wore on, she began to relax. A few cans of beer and a good meal made all the difference.

It was no surprise the food was good. Phillipa Rochester had, until a month or so ago, cooked in a Michelin-starred restaurant in the city. She now worked from the kitchen of a cleared-out hotel diagonally opposite the Tower of London. Phillipa's number two was Steven Armitage, who'd previously worked as a chef in the Royal Logistics Corps. They made a hell of a team. Phillipa assembled the menu from whatever supplies were available, while Steve scaled it up for mass consumption. Despite having a high-end kitchen at their disposal, the absence of gas, electricity and running water meant the whole operation was a makeshift affair, but that didn't matter. Phillipa could, to quote Dominic, 'season the shit out of anything' and, even if the food was limited and basic, the alcohol was not. In what had been such a tourist and business-centric part of town, you couldn't turn a corner without finding a pub or cocktail bar. The group had a quartermaster who kept an eye on stock levels. Booze was one thing they couldn't afford to run out of but, for the time being at least, there was still a plentiful supply.

Dominic had given them a guided tour of the compound from west to east, starting with the area around the Monument itself. There were blockades across Cannon Street, Arthur Street and Lower Thames Street, Eastcheap and the A10, and also across London Bridge to the south. Dominic took them up to Monument tube station and explained how it had an underground footpath linking it to Bank Station out in the wilderness, which had given the group a way of accessing the outside world in relative safety. Darren Adams, a twenty-five-year veteran of Transport for London who still proudly wore his TfL tabard every day, guarded the entrances and exits to both stations. Metal grilles controlled the flow of corpses, preventing those who'd died during their final commute from straying anywhere other than the platforms and tracks they'd landed at almost two months ago.

The Monument to the Great Fire of London itself had seemed a useful asset when the group had first settled here, but that usefulness had been limited. Standing over sixty metres tall, with a viewing platform at the top of its three-hundred-plus steps, it appeared to be an ideal lookout post. In reality, though, the rest of London had grown in height and density around it since it had been constructed in the late seventeenth century, rendering it redundant. Buildings blocked the views of the streets on all sides. It was good for looking far out into the distance, but less useful when it came to spotting threats which were closer to home. As a focal point, though, as a memorial to massive death, destruction and rebuilding, it was undeniably fitting.

The group's initial focus had been the immediate area around the Tower of London, and apart from a cursory check for dead bodies and any useful supplies, most of the buildings between the Monument and the Tower remained empty and unused. Tower Place had unquestionably become the hub. It was where most people met, where much of the non-food supplies were stored, where records were kept, and where key decisions were made. As the new arrivals had already discovered, the Tower itself was a precious bolthole; an eleventh century stronghold they could retreat to whenever the shit threatened to hit the fan.

All Hallows by the Tower (the oldest church in London, according to Lynette) was in use. A lady by the name of Audrey Adebayo based herself there, offering spiritual support to those who wanted it. Elsewhere, a handful of shops had been repurposed as makeshift marketplaces. There was no need for trade, just volunteers recycling scavenged clothing and other odds and ends.

Vicky thought it looked like a way of keeping people occupied more than anything. She watched them with jealousy. Their days were taken up washing and sorting spare clothing. She'd been too busy trying to stay alive to give any thought to what she was wearing, let alone anyone else.

The accommodation was spectacular. They'd walked past and barely even noticed it when they'd first arrived; just another modernistic, odd-shaped block among so many others. Yet the importance of this building, nestled between Tower Place and the Thames, was clear. It housed more than one hundred and fifty spacious apartments that had, up until the apocalypse, been fully serviced and available to rent. From individual studios all the way up to vast penthouses, this building offered more to the group than any of the hotels that had, by chance, been enclosed within the hastily defined perimeter of their base. People stayed here in twos and threes – sometimes more in the larger apartments – living in relative comfort. With doors that could be closed and curtains that could be drawn, the individual flats offered safe spaces in which people could start trying to come to terms with what was left of their lives.

At the other end of the compound, the eastern edge of the territory the group had so far claimed, all the roads and footpaths had been abruptly truncated with yet more vehicles. Dominic pointed out a hotel they'd been getting ready to clear out (which, he told them, would double the amount of accommodation they had available). He also showed them St Katherine's Docks, an impressive-looking marina at the very edge of their secured space, that he had great plans for.

Finally, Dominic showed them the work that had been done under the railway and did his best to reassure them that the breach they'd witnessed earlier was a rare occurrence. Most of the time, the dead were held back safely. It would be less of an issue, he explained, when work on the second barrier was complete and there was a truly sizeable chunk of space between the living and the dead. When he took them up onto the tracks, using a metal staircase that had been removed from the outside of a building and bolted into place, the importance of the work was made clear. On the other side of the line was a crowd of dead bodies of such a size that their numbers were almost inconceivable. They filled every street and passageway for miles into the distance. From above Leman Street, the point at which Vicky, David, Sam and Stan were standing, the lifeless hordes appeared endless.

They ended up where they'd begun, back in the conference room with Dominic and several others from around the top table. The gruff, no-nonsense Pole they'd seen earlier marshalling activity around the barrier breach was introduced as Piotr, in charge of the construction, maintenance, and security of the perimeter boundary. Next to him was Ruth, his second-in-command, an ex-debt collector who dwarfed him. Then Orla, the behavioural psychologist, and next to her was Liz Hunter. Liz had worked as a surgeon at the nearby Royal London Hospital. Now, alongside a stuffy retired GP in his late sixties who still insisted on being addressed as Dr Ahmad (and who hadn't emerged to greet the new arrivals), she provided medical care for the group. Next to Liz was Mihai Ardelean, who was the quartermaster, then there was Lynette. Vicky had struggled to work out exactly what her role was at first. Often, she gave the impression of being a pandering PA to Dominic, but the more Vicky saw of her, the more she began to question which one of them was actually in charge. Lynette kept Dominic on track and stopped him wasting people's time with his bullshit and spin.

The room was illuminated by a series of burnt-down church candles placed along the length of the table. Although not particularly bright, the light was sufficient so that no one could hide.

'It's not just as simple as saying we'll drive everyone over here,' David said. 'If the others decide that they want to come – and that'll have to be a democratic, majority-led decision – then we'll need a plan.'

'Fuck democracy,' Piotr said. 'We don't have time for that anymore. Those who want to come here, come. Those who don't, rot.'

'You're a proper charmer, aren't you? Quite the diplomat,' Stan said, peering at him over the rim of his glasses, then pushing them back up the bridge of his nose. 'Did you ever think of going into politics? You're a natural.'

Piotr shrugged. 'Democracy, diplomacy... all counts for nothing now.'

Ruth backed him up. 'Right now, it all has to be about action, not words. People need to contribute and take responsibility.'

'But not everyone can,' Orla said. 'We've got people with PTSD who find it hard to even leave their rooms. You can't expect them to contribute just yet.'

'We've all been dealt a shitty hand. We can't keep pandering just 'cos someone's feeling a bit down...'

'Fuck's sake, what if you broke your leg and you ended up bed-bound?'

'That's different.'

'Is it? Just because someone looks alright, it doesn't mean they are, and—'

'This kind of bullshit makes me think it's not worth our while coming here,' Vicky said, and the rest of the people around the table just looked at her. 'Everything's changed, don't you get it?' She pointed at Piotr. 'Who made you the judge? You don't know who's sick and who isn't. You don't know who's struggling. For all we know, you might be the one crying yourself to sleep every night.'

He exploded at her. 'You don't get to come here and talk to me like that.'

'And you don't get to decide who's worth saving and who isn't.'

'Come on, folks,' Dominic said, gesturing for everyone to calm down. 'We've talked about this and, to be frank, now's not the time to go over it again. We're ready to accommodate everyone who wants to be here. What David's group does is their business,

Piotr, and how they make decisions is their business too. I think David's original question was more about the practicalities of getting people here safely, and we need to work together to do that.'

'Can't you just get a bigger boat?' Lynette asked.

David shook his head. 'Not an option. The river's full of wreckage in places. We hit a ton of debris today and it took us an age to get through. Also, I was making it up as I went along. I'm not sure I could sail anything bigger.'

'If it was up to me, I'd stay off the water unless it's absolutely the only available option,' Dr Liz said. 'It's one thing bringing a handful of people here in a little tug, but anything else should be an absolute last resort. Sounds risky as hell, particularly if you don't know what you're doing. No offence, David.'

'None taken.'

'The roads are clogged out there,' Vicky protested. 'I don't see how else we're going to be able to avoid the dead.'

'In terms of getting over here, I'm afraid we can't offer much help,' Dominic said. 'We've got limited geographic knowledge.'

'Also, you've spent the last few days sending thousands of bodies our way,' Sam unhelpfully reminded him.

Piotr sighed heavily. 'Just get yourselves to Bank station, send someone through on foot, we'll open up a hole in the barriers and get you and your stuff through.'

'Sounds easy,' Vicky said, knowing it was anything but.

'We'll do what we can to help,' Dominic explained. 'I mentioned earlier that we're going to be pushing back the dead and creating a buffer between us. We can accelerate our plans. We'll send the runners out again and try to send more of them north. If we send different runners out from different locations, it should take some of the pressure off your route. Stay close to the river, and we'll try and draw them away.'

'Sounds good,' David said. 'As much as any of this sounds good, that is. We're going to need a bit of time to get back and get everyone ready.'

'How long?'

'I don't know... a couple of days. What day is it today? I've lost track.'

Lynette gestured to a calendar on the wall of the boardroom. 'Sunday October thirteenth. Georgie changes that calendar for us every day, otherwise we'd completely forget.'

Dominic looked across at Piotr. 'Get here on Wednesday,' Piotr said. 'That gives us enough time.'

'How does that sound?' Dominic asked.

David looked at Vicky, Stan and Sam. No one objected. 'Why not. Let's do it.'

16

DAY FORTY-TWO

Piotr rounded up the troops as soon as the sun came up, and his crew was ready to get to business before the others were anywhere near ready to head back up the river. Late last night they'd agreed on an exchange of personnel. Orla volunteered to travel back to the hotel, figuring she might be able to help persuade the other group to leave and vouch for everything they were being asked to leave for. When it came to picking a volunteer to stay behind with the Monument group, Stan had managed to come up with all manner of reasons why he should be the one to stop, and he met with no resistance.

The morning was as misty as the day before. Stan stood on the pier with Lynette and watched the boat vanish into the grey haze that clung to the surface of the water. The sound of its motor hung in the air a little longer, but a minute later it was gone, leaving the gentle lapping of the water against the pier as the only noise.

It was an illusion, but at that moment the world felt calm and serene. He couldn't hear any trouble, couldn't see any trouble, didn't have to be on the lookout for meandering corpses ... For a few precious seconds Stan thought it felt like the base around the Monument was the last place on Earth.

Darren Adams was on duty, same as he was every morning. He met her in the entrance to Monument underground station and walked her through to Bank. 'Morning, Ashleigh. You ready for this?'

'How many times do I have to tell you, Darren, it's Ash.'

'Sorry, Ash. So, are you ready?'

'I'm ready.'

'And you know where you're going?'

'Up towards the far end of Commercial Street, Dom said.'

'I thought Mark was going that way.'

'Mark's gone east, out towards Limehouse.'

'Ah, right. And you're sure you know how to get there?'

'Yep. There ain't a part of London I didn't deliver to before all this. Anyway, what are you, my dad?'

'I'll tell you this much, you wouldn't be going out there at all if you were my daughter.'

'Good job I'm not then.'

He laughed. She always made him laugh. 'Go on, get out of here. Be safe and I'll see you later.'

'Thanks, Daz.'

'It's Darren, not Daz.'

'Whatever,' she said, grinning at him.

Darren pulled open the metal grille at the entrance to Bank station then stepped back into the shadows. Ash gently nudged her front wheel forward, tentatively edging out onto the daylight, then stood completely still and waited for Darren to slide the grille to shut behind her and for the nearest few cadavers to lose interest in the noise. She used those precious seconds of stillness to focus and plot a course through the madness up ahead, but there were so many corpses moving in so many different directions this morning that it was difficult to pick a way through.

The importance of this station to the group could not be overstated. It was a lifeline, allowing them to leave the confines of their precious base with relative ease, and although the exit was only a few hundred metres beyond the perimeter of the compound, it was distance enough. The fact that Bank Station was at the junction of several major routes was an added bonus. It gave Ash options. She waited for a gap in the crowds to appear, then kicked off and pedalled hard.

She could turn the bike on a coin. A burst of speed, then she'd brake hard and make an unexpected change of direction. Bunny-hopping down steps. Cutting through the narrowest of alleyways, along slender strips of pathways, balancing on the tops of walls. Ash danced around the dead with alternating grace then force, lifting herself out of her saddle and leaning over to avoid one corpse, then sticking out her foot and taking out the legs of another on the opposite side without batting an eyelid. Before they realised she was anywhere near them, she was gone again.

She finally found herself in a little more space and rode at speed along Princes Street before swerving into Moorgate. The wider roads gave her plenty of options. She used the remains of the last ever morning rush hour as cover, ducking down behind the rusting vehicles, weaving through the gaps between the cars, trucks, taxis, vans and buses that had all ground to a halt on the morning of the first Tuesday in September.

Ash preferred to navigate by train station. She'd lived, loved, and biked around London all her life, and she used overground stations to navigate the way ancient mariners had used the stars. That was what she told herself, anyway, and what was wrong with a little romanticism? It helped to think of this as some great quest rather than face up to the truth, which was that she was out here (again) risking her neck (again) for potentially very little reward (again). But despite the danger, being out here was preferable to being stuck in the compound with everyone else. Out here she was free.

She turned right when she reached Moorgate Station, cycling towards Liverpool Street Station. Then she rode down Middlesex Street, heading south again until she reached Whitechapel High Street. Ahead of her now was the crossroads where Leman Street finished and Commercial Street began. Perfect.

The bodies were fewer in number out here because the bulk of them had gone south towards the compound, attracted by the noises made by the group. She was out here to make a louder noise and tempt the dead away. She hoped she'd judged the distance right, but there was no way of knowing for sure. *About half a kilometre from base.* From experience, she thought that should just about do it.

Ash stopped the bike at the centre of the crossroads then pushed away an unsteady corpse who'd staggered too close. The dead woman tripped over the kerb and ended up on her bony backside, so weak and poorly coordinated that she was unable to pick herself up again. Another one of the dumb fuckers tripped over her outstretched legs, and between the two of them they managed to cause enough of a temporary distraction to allow Ash to get on with the task at hand. She focused on her breathing and readied herself, knowing that everything would change once she pressed the button; everything always did. Cycling in and around the dead was about to become a thousand times more challenging, and she actually enjoyed it. In large part it was because of the music. It took the edge off her fear and gave her something else to focus on, and a rhythm to her movement.

Ash swung her backpack off her shoulders. She flicked through the CDs she carried along with a bottle of water, a can of Red Bull and a mountain of batteries. It was definitely a retro day today. She had a re-release of the first ever *'Now That's What I Call Music'* compilation from the eighties, salvaged from home in a last-minute memory grab before she'd left her house for the final time. It was one of Dad's that he'd played to death when she was a kid. Even just reading the track names and artists made her feel good. This was definitely going to hit the spot. The nostalgia of the tracks would keep her safe and warm out here on her own.

Ready.

Do it.

She cranked up the volume of the boombox, skipped to track four disc one, and pressed play.

Heaven 17. 'Temptation.' Fucking love it.

Dad used to listen to this band on repeat. She knew the song like she knew her own heartbeat. The moody, swirling synthesiser opening immediately made the nearest of the dead swivel to attention. When the vocals kicked in more of them began to pivot around, soon a crowd was coming towards her.

Back in the saddle again, face-forward. She could sense them getting closer, could almost feel their fingers on her back. She fought against her instinct, knowing that a little hesitation now could make all the difference.

Twenty seconds in, and the music exploded full-on. Ash started to ride and allowed herself a quick glance back. *Result.* A whole fucking pack of them was on the march after her.

Third time she'd done this recently, and it never ceased to both thrill and scare the hell out of her in equal measure. Pace was the key to success, and when she realised she'd pulled too far ahead, she simply looped back around and drove deep through the front of the crowd, whipping them into a relative frenzy. She repeated the manoeuvre a couple more times to make sure she'd got a critical mass building behind, then moved off again.

It took an age for the ripple of movement away from the compound to become a flow, then something resembling the beginnings of an exodus. When he was satisfied that enough of the dead were heading north towards Commercial Street, Piotr gave the word, and the clean-up operation began.

The plan of attack had been agreed upon last night as Piotr and his crew had sat cracking beers, hidden away from everyone else in their equipment store (a sliver of a car park on dead land between Royal Mail Street and the train tracks). Dominic left him alone, trusting him to do what needed to be done. Piotr was up on the bridge over Mansell Street now, the next road down from Leman Street, yelling orders in a voice loud enough to be heard for miles across dead London. Dominic watched him from a distance, admiring his skill. He had to hand it to Piotr, he certainly knew what he was doing.

Dominic turned his attention to the dead immediately below him. It was almost comical how they blundered into each other like confused tourists trying to navigate the footpath chaos of London. Many were trying to go north, following the vast numbers already traipsing away under the spell of distant New Wave music, but it was concerning to see so many others that remained focused on trying to get into the compound. And there were others, he noticed, that seemed to be caught in two minds, neither here nor there. *But that's impossible*, he thought. *That kind of indecision would imply that they were capable of conscious decision-making and that, given that their brains are rapidly reducing to a gruel swishing around their empty skulls, is completely fucking ridiculous.* He decided it was more likely they were being distracted by the music, then distracted by the noises coming from the compound, their attention ping-ponging between whichever of the two was loudest at the time.

Here, the blockade Piotr had built under the railway tracks was moveable, giving them a way to get heavy machinery in and out of the compound at speed. A cloud of oily black exhaust fumes belched up into the air, and an old backhoe loader they'd acquired trundled out into the open. It had seen many better days on many better sites, but that didn't matter. As long as it kept running and shifting, that was all anyone cared about. It had a tractor cab with a loader-style bucket on the front and an articulated arm with a digger bucket on the back. Most people referred to it as "the digger," but whatever they called it and whatever it was used for, the dead didn't stand a chance when they came up against it.

'Move up,' Piotr yelled, cupping his hands around his mouth to make his loud voice even louder. 'Now! Move yourselves!'

Eight drivers followed the digger out and instantly overtook it, racing out from inside the compound in a rough formation and obliterating swathes of bodies. They carved bloody furrows through the crowds, then parked up in pre-agreed locations. Five of them blocked Mansell Street just past the junction with Portsoken Street, preventing more of the dead from getting through. The other three vehicles blocked Prescot Street, which was off to the right and much closer to the compound.

Thousands of bodies had been stopped from getting closer to the compound, and hundreds more had been trapped in the area that had been sealed off. Now it was the turn of the backhoe loader to join the fray. Kevin, the guy who usually drove it, had been working in demolition for longer than most other survivors had been alive. He'd cleared all manner of sites in all manner of places, but until now had never demolished a mass of human flesh.

A growing crowd of people on the railway tracks watched in awe as Kevin dropped the bucket at the front of the digger and started scooping up the dead. The way he scythed through them was beautiful and grotesque at the same time, inspiring and nauseating in equal measure. Their increasingly corrupted bodies deteriorated almost instantly the moment the mechanical monster made contact, dropping limbs and the occasional head from the bucket. Kevin had confessed to feeling an undeniable exhilaration in his task. He knew that the moment he drove out into the open, he'd be the sole focus for the ire of hundreds and hundreds of those vile creatures, but it didn't matter because as long as he was safe in his cab, he was invincible. He drove deeper into the scattering crowd, leaving a trail of bloody devastation in his wake. From his elevated position, their numbers were almost incomprehensible. The digger's bucket clipped the corner of an upturned car, but it didn't matter. The impact sent the useless vehicle spinning on its roof, and that in turn wiped out another swathe of corpses. He scooped what was left of them into huge bloody heaps, ready for burning.

Piotr had spotters waiting at key locations. The first was positioned on the railway, overlooking a Travelodge. She signalled to her boss once the digger had made it far enough along the A1211, Goodman's Yard, and on her mark, Piotr dispatched another phalanx of drivers who followed the route the digger had taken. Kevin steered towards the buildings on one side, then used the full width of the street to turn around and come back the other way. The other drivers wove around him, then formed up in a line, blocking the road completely.

Stage one complete.

Kevin drove the digger round and around the section of street which had been sealed off and reclaimed, terminating as many cadavers as he could get to. One of the car drivers climbed up onto the roof of his vehicle and waved his arms in the air to get the attention of Piotr's spotter. He booted a corpse in the face that staggered a little too close for comfort then gave the spotter the thumbs up. She acknowledged him then ran over to Piotr to pass on the message.

'All secure,' she said, breathless.

'Good. Worked like clockwork. We could clear the whole of London by the end of the year at this rate,' Piotr said.

He crossed the many sets of tracks to get to the other side of the bridge and looked back into the compound. There was a group of more than thirty people waiting, ready for him to give the order. They wore protective gear and carried all manner of improvised weapons.

'All yours,' Piotr shouted down to them. 'Get out there and get the area cleaned up. Get rid of anything that used to be human, then clear out the buildings and bring back anything useful. Stay in pairs, take no unnecessary risks. Good hunting!'

17

The morning had evaporated. Ash had been pedalling for hours. That was what it felt like, anyway. Dominic and Piotr hadn't given her a timescale to work to, but she thought she must be close to being done now. She'd heard the controlled carnage unfolding back at base and had continued to corral the dead with her own noise to stop them becoming distracted and drifting back the wrong way.

She'd skipped a handful of tracks and had listened to others two or three times over, but now she'd almost reached the end of 'Now That's What I Call Music' and it was time to head home. She glanced back over her shoulder to check the size of the crowd still following her. Numbers were academic, really. From here it looked like the dead went on forever, a single, never-ending mass of rotted humanity. Thousands and thousands of them, one of her. And whenever she thought she'd seen the last of them, more appeared. It was only to be expected, given that London had always been hideously overpopulated. It didn't bother her, though. Her speed and strength always gave her plenty of an advantage.

Time to call it a day.

Ash didn't ride in straight lines for too long if she could help it. She'd found that it paid to go up and down a few side-roads and deviate from the main routes. She was starting to feel the effort in her legs. It was exhausting work, as demanding mentally as it was physically. Being on a constant high alert was draining, and she couldn't wait to get back and relax in her apartment with a drink and some food. She was most looking forward to curling up in bed later and drowning in one of the staggering pile of books she'd scavenged on her solo trips out in the wilds.

As she neared Spitalfields Market, she was almost knocked off her bike by a trio of bodies that came at her unexpectedly from around the back of a truck. She elbowed the closest of them in the face as it lunged for her and it collapsed, taking the others out with it. No great shakes, nothing to worry about, but it unsettled her all the same. She was getting tired and losing focus. Best to get back before she made a more serious mistake.

Ash had her route home mapped out. She'd take a left soon and keep going until she reached the A10, then go south past the Gherkin as if she was heading toward Fenchurch Street Station. Then she'd head west to Bank Station where Darren Adams would inevitably be watching out for her like an over-protective parent.

One last push.

She switched off the boombox, and the dead began to drift. Ash pedalled hard to get some distance on them, then slowed down, confused. The ground here was littered with chunks of flesh. This wasn't vehicle damage or anything like that. An untold number of corpses had been intentionally hacked and slashed to pieces, and it was recent, too. Rivers of red-black blood ran into the gutters.

She was too busy looking side to side to see what was directly in front of her. Everything needed a double take these days because nothing looked like it used to. There was no order anymore, everything random and shambolic. Problems didn't manifest themselves as problems until you were right on top of them, and Ash didn't spot the blockade stretched across the full width of Commercial Street until she couldn't go any further forward. She skidded to a halt and looked back at the dead masses still following her. She didn't have long before they'd catch up and box her in.

Was this something to do with Piotr? She didn't recall hearing him say anything about having been this far north in a while... it must have been something him and Dom had cooked up to strengthen the group's defences, though why they'd done it so far from the Monument, she had no idea. She was at a crossroads. She saw that Lamb Street on her left and Hanbury Street on her right were both blocked too. She was going to have to ride back into the bodies and try and find a way of—

Distracted, Ash didn't see what was coming until it was too late.

18

David, Vicky, Sam and Orla eventually made it back the church where they'd left Gary, Damien and Omar yesterday. The building was empty, but a note had been pinned on the door. The others had returned to the hotel. Charlie had managed to get to them and had left a crudely drawn map which showed the returners the route she'd taken. It was a long, convoluted, and physically challenging way around, that culminated in another unsteady ladder bridge spanning the gap between a roof garden on top of one of the neighbouring buildings and a previously unused room in the hotel. As she crawled across the ladder, exhausted, Vicky looked down and watched an endless number of corpses swarming around the hotel. And when she got inside and was able to look out over Fleet Street, she saw that their numbers had continued to swell since she and the others had been away. It was hard to see the edge of the crowds now, and though the numbers were nothing like those they'd seen around the Monument base, here there were no blockades to protect them. She shuddered at the idea of the doors and windows downstairs giving way and the dead flooding inside. She had no doubt that leaving this place was the only sensible option. She'd drag Selena out kicking and screaming if she had to.

Gary had told the others about the Monument, but few people had believed the trip downriver was going to be worthwhile. The arrival of a new face and the absence of Stan was met with genuine surprise. Sam and David in particular were greeted like returning heroes. Orla had expected people to be cautious of her, but not of Vicky. The two of them were loitering outside the first-floor lounge, waiting for the rest of the group to assemble. 'Have you not been with these people long?' Orla asked her.

'No, why?'

'Because they've been looking at us both like we're a pair of fucking aliens.'

'I hadn't noticed. Not too bothered, if I'm honest.'

Orla just nodded. She leant against the wall and looked at Vicky but didn't say anything. Vicky felt the pressure.

'I'm shit at small talk, if that's what you're waiting for.'

Orla laughed. 'No, I'm good, thanks.'

'What then? Why are you staring? I don't have any words of wisdom or positive vibes to share, if it's that you're after.'

'It isn't.'

'What then?'

'You'll think I'm stupid.'

'Go on.'

'I'm worried about you. Something's not right.'

'Everything's not right at the moment. Anyway, you don't even know me.'

'True, but I know about people.'

'I'm fine.'

Orla scoffed. 'None of us are fine.'

'Okay, then I'm not fine. Honestly, love, butt out.'

'Something you said in the boardroom last night about knowing who's sick and who isn't...'

'Did you not hear me? I said butt out.'

'Okay. I'm sorry. But if ever you want to talk—'

'I don't.'

'—if you want to talk at any time then let me know.'

Vicky was about to tell Orla to mind her own fucking business but was saved by the arrival of the last few stragglers.

It was standing room only in the lounge, virtually everyone there. They listened in almost total silence as David talked about Dominic Grove and the three hundred or so people living in the well-stocked, well-organised, and well-defended base around the Tower of London. 'What they've achieved there is a world apart from what we have here.'

As she looked around at the gathered faces, it struck Vicky just how right his words were. There was an undeniable gulf between the appearance of the people here and those at the Monument. It hadn't occurred to her before, but seeing Orla standing alongside them, among all this shabbiness, the comparison was stark. For her, it sealed the deal. 'Can I say something?' she asked, and David stopped so she could talk. 'Look, I know you've not known me for long, but hear me out. Everyone I've spoken to since Selena and I got here has been through as shitty a time as I have. We're all beaten. We're all broken. We're starving, and we're scared and we're barely holding our shit together. Look at Orla, though. She's different.'

Orla herself appeared confused. 'Am I?'

'Yes. Christ, just look at you. You look... *normal*. Me, I've lost a shedload of weight since all this happened. I'm scraggy as hell. I've been wearing Lycra leggings for the last month and a half and they're *baggy*, for Christ's sake. I think it's a combination of not enough food, and then being too bloody nervous to eat when I have managed to find something.' She looked at Orla again. 'No offence, love, and please don't take this the wrong way, but you look pretty well-fed. Compared to most of us, anyway. Your clothes still fit, you're not as gaunt in the face as I am, you're clean... you look like we used to. When we first arrived at your place, I felt like I'd just crawled out from under a rock.'

'I don't see the relevance,' Marianne said from across the room. 'We've got more important things to focus on these days than looking the part.'

Vicky shook her head. 'You're missing the point. The people at the Monument are living. All we're doing here is just about managing to exist. I think there's safety in numbers. I vote we leave here and join them.'

'Even when there's a jumped-up little prick like Dominic Grove calling the shots?' Marianne said, distinctly unimpressed. 'Do you know anything about him, other than what you've seen on TV? He's a vile, two-faced toad who'd sell his mother for a bag of beans. I've had clients who suffered as a direct result of some of the government policies he voted in favour of. Have any of you read any of the reports into the way he helped his mates get access to—'

'I have, as it happens,' Orla interrupted. 'I know exactly what he's capable of, and I know precisely where his priorities used to lie.'

'Then you should be asking to come here and stay with us, not trying to get us to go with you.'

'Did you not hear me? Where his priorities *used* to lie. For the record, I actually agree with you – if we'd met under different circumstances, Dom and I would have had absolutely nothing in common. You're jumping to conclusions about the way we're doing things back at the Monument, and you're wrong. Dom's not calling the shots. Sure, he can talk the talk and he absolutely loves the sound of his own voice, but he's helping us to make collective decisions, he's not making them for us. It's an important distinction.'

'Well I don't buy it.'

David sighed and dropped his head. 'Oh, come on, Marianne, get your head out of your ass. The world's changed. I thought you of all people would realise that.'

'Don't patronise me, David.'

'I'm not. Look, if we get there and you don't like what Dominic's saying, then don't listen to him. What's he going to do, lobby against you? Pass a frigging law? Take you to court or cut your benefits? Seriously, come on.'

'Staying here makes no sense at all,' Vicky said. 'There are more of the dead out on Fleet Street than ever, and all that's separating them from us are the walls of this building. It's hard to put into words until you've seen it, but the space they have back there... the protection... Selena, Kath and I were on the run for weeks until Sam found us, and it was only when I got settled here and I could walk around this place without worrying about bloody dead bodies attacking me all the time that I fully realised how dangerous it was for us out there, how everything's balanced on a knife edge. It's better here, for sure, but this is nothing compared to what they've got at the Monument.'

'I get that—' Marianne started to say, but Vicky wasn't done.

'Now that I'm back here, my perspective has changed. I'll be honest, I have the mother of all downers on everything right now. I'm cynical, I'm angry, I'm downright frigging irritating to be around, but I'm able to put all that to one side because I realise we don't have a lot of choice here.'

'I'm not arguing with anything you've said,' Marianne continued. 'You're making assumptions. Yes, I think Dominic Grove is a complete fucker, the lowest of the low, and yes, it sickens me to the stomach to imagine having to speak to the bloke and breathe the same air as him, but I know this is all we've got, and I know we have to go. Doesn't mean I can't be a bitch about it. So, please, leave me alone, let me sulk, and let me know when it's time to leave.'

19

It was a bitterly cold night but being outside like this still felt like a novelty and it was worth it. Stan cradled a mug of bitter black coffee in his hands which took the edge off the chill. He'd found the steps they used and had come up onto the train tracks for a bit of air and to try and get his head around how much everything had changed in one day. He'd initially gone the wrong way, walking towards the black maw of Fenchurch Street station, and had spooked himself thinking about all those lifeless commuters trapped behind the ticket barriers, wandering the station concourse. The wreckage of the derailed train Dominic had also talked about formed a comforting barrier between Stan and the dead. The snarled-up carriages, on their side and twisted over, some blocking the tracks, others jutting up into the air, looked like an enormous abstract sculpture, like an impossibly oversized length of knotted rope.

Stan hadn't expected to see anyone out here, and he was surprised when he spotted another figure taking in the air. He was even more surprised when he saw who it was. He walked across and coughed politely to let Dominic know he was there. 'Evening'.

Dominic looked at Stan and nodded. 'Evening.' He was leaning over the railings, looking out over the area Piotr and his team had reclaimed earlier. Where before there had been corpses, densely packed for as far as anyone could see, now there was empty space. The waning moon was frequently hidden behind clouds and it was hard to make out any details. Below, a bonfire, a great pyre of body parts, had burned itself out to all but a dull glow, and the towering, tightly packed buildings made the dark corners darker still. Dominic stared ahead, perhaps hoping the other man would get the message and disappear, but he didn't. 'It's Stanley, isn't it?'

'Actually, it's Alec. Stanley's my surname. They call me Stan.'

'And what would you rather?'

'Don't mind, if I'm honest. I'm just happy I'm still around to be called anything.'

'Amen to that.'

They quickly ran out of things to say. Stan struggled with the silence. 'You had my vote last time, you know. Well, not you personally. Your lot.'

'Thanks, I guess.'

'From what I've seen, I think you've worked wonders here. People think politics is easy, but I know what a tough game it is. There's a lot of talk about the posh boys being bred for power and all that, but they still need to have the right people behind them to get anything done, don't you think?'

'I suppose. Didn't count for anything in the end though, did it?'

'You can't tell me someone somewhere didn't know all this was going to happen.'

'If they did, it wasn't anyone in government, that's for sure. I walked around the Houses of Parliament for hours after and I never saw another living soul.'

'Well, I'm glad you made it. I think this lot are lucky to have you. You need to have the right person at the helm, that's what I always say. I don't think they'd have got half as far as they have if you hadn't been here, coordinating things.'

'Appreciate that.'

'I know how it works, the government machine. I was civil service, you know.'

'I'd never have guessed.'

'My entire career, from when I left school to when I retired. It's a dirty business at times, I know that much, but I think it has to be. You're never going to be able to please everyone, are you? When you make a political decision, someone's going to benefit and someone will lose out. There's always winners and losers, don't you agree?'

'Absolutely. So, which are you, Stan?'

'Me? Oh, I've made a career of winning by not winning, if you know what I mean.'

'Haven't a clue.'

'I've always kept my head down, not made too much noise. I'm just saying the world needs folks like you up front, but it also needs backup from folks like me. You get me?'

'I think so. Not sure there's enough of the world left to need anything past what we've got right now, though.'

'But that's not always going to be the case, is it? We'll get back on our feet again. It's not like we're starting from scratch.'

'Do you not think? I don't know. It depends, I guess. I'd like to think that what we're doing here is giving the human race a fighting chance at survival, but then I also think we're just a few hundred people, doing our best not to die. Whether we succeed or not, it'll be many years before history judges us, and we'll be long gone. And that's assuming there's anyone left alive to record all this for the history books, of course.'

'They'll be writing about you if they do, Mr. Grove.'

'It's Dom,' he said. 'Mr. Grove died a long time ago.'

'Then they'll be writing about you, Dom. That must feel pretty special. Heck of a weight on your shoulders.'

'There's a lot to be done before we can talk about any of us going down in history, Stan.'

'Oh, I don't know. I think what you've achieved here so far looks pretty bloody spectacular from where I'm standing.'

'Thank you. I appreciate the support.'

'Anytime. And I mean that, Dom, I'm not just saying it.'

The conversation faltered again as Stan took a break from arse-licking to finish his coffee.

'I'll be heading back inside now, I think,' he said.

'Right.'

'You coming in? It's freezing out here.'

'Not just yet.'

'Surveying your empire?'

Dominic shook his head. 'Not much of an empire, is it? No, I'm waiting for Ash.'

'Ash?'

'One of our riders who went out this morning to draw the crowds away. The other lad we sent came home hours ago, but Ash isn't back yet. She's probably found herself somewhere better to stay for the night. A comic shop, knowing her. Wouldn't be the first time.'

'Think she's in trouble?'

'She can look after herself. She's a smart kid. Very spirited. Full of spunk.'

'I don't think you can say things like that anymore, Dom.'

'Really? I happen to think it's got to where we can say whatever we damn well like, Stan. The censors and the do-gooders and the political correctness police are all dead, in case you hadn't noticed.'

'And if you don't mind me saying,' Stan whispered, leaning closer, 'they won't be missed.'

'Here, here,' said Dominic.

It was daybreak when the music started playing.

The world was still drenched with a thousand shades of grey. Even the shadows had shadows. Almost all of the hundreds of survivors gathered in the Monument base were asleep, but most of them woke up instantly when the song began blaring out. They scrambled through the gloom to try and find out what was happening, heading for the various vantage points they'd found over the preceding weeks and months, nooks and crannies from where they'd peer over the barriers to keep an eye on the rest of the world. Some raced to the top of the Monument, others climbed the hollow staircases of empty buildings and hung out of windows. Many more swarmed up onto the railway, all of them asking why anyone would be playing that fucking song at that fucking volume at this fucking time in the morning in a place where even the slightest noise could have a devastating, disproportionate impact.

Phil Collins.

'You Can't Hurry Love.'

Track one, disc one.

'Now That's What I Call Music: Volume One.'

Ash's body lay next to her bike in the middle of the empty road which had been reclaimed only yesterday. Her face was ice white; her body drenched in blood from a single stab wound to her chest. On the tarmac alongside her, in letters as tall as Ash herself, someone had painted a message.

STAY AWAY

21

'For fuck's sake, all of you shut up!' Dominic yelled, and he slammed his fists on the table. The noise was loud enough to silence the rest of the room.

'This got anything to do with you?' Piotr asked, turning on Stan, who visibly recoiled.

'Absolutely nothing to do with my lot,' he said. 'You say she went north? We're from over to the west. We never went north. We hadn't been anywhere until we came here.'

'Hell of a coincidence.'

'And that's all it is, a coincidence. Bloody hell, what do you think we are, savages? None of our people would have hurt anyone like that. Not anyone who still had a pulse, anyway.'

'How do we know that for sure?'

'You don't, I guess. You'll just have to trust me.'

'Trust you?'

'Yes, trust him,' Liz Hunter said. 'Come on, Stan's no killer. Look at the state of him. He's too scared of getting killed himself to think about killing anyone else. And for what it's worth, I believe him. The people he came here with, they were wrecked. You could see it in their faces. I saw David almost lose his shit when we gave him a bowl of stew, for crying out loud. And that look he had on his face when Dom showed him around... you can't fake reactions like that, not to the extent I saw. None of us know who killed Ash or why, but the one thing I'm certain of is it wasn't any of Stan's lot.'

'Who then?' Piotr grunted. 'One of the dead?'

'What are you saying? That a corpse killed her, dragged her back here, painted a message for us on the road, then set the music blaring? Now that's dumb even by your impressive standards,

Piotr.'

He glared at Liz and she held his gaze, not intimidated in the slightest.

'Watch your mouth or I'll—'

'You'll what?'

'I'll—'

'You'll do nothing,' Dominic said, cutting across him. 'Liz knows what she's talking about.'

'How? She knows nothing. She's not taken a single step beyond the wall for weeks.'

'I'm a doctor. I understand people, that's how,' Liz said, still unfazed. 'What would anyone have to gain from killing Ash? What would it prove? What could it possibly achieve? We've opened our doors to Stan's group, and we've sent Orla back with them. There's nothing we have that we're not happy for them to be a part of, and as far as we know, there's nothing they have that we want. There's also no reason to think they won't share everything they have with us too. You saw them yesterday. You saw the state they're in. They didn't kill her.'

'Then who? And why display her body like that?'

Liz was about to speak again, but Mihai got there first. 'If it's not Stan's people, then clearly there's someone else out there.'

'Someone who wants what we've got,' Piotr said. 'It's obvious.'

'Why do you always have to go on the offensive?' Liz asked.

'Because some fucker killed Ash,' he yelled.

'Damn right,' Ruth said, sitting next to him.

Liz held her head in her hands. 'Jesus, I give up with you people. Let me put it a different way. Why do you automatically assume it's someone who wants what we've got here? Maybe it's the opposite? Maybe they're just trying to protect what's theirs?'

'But there probably is another group,' Dominic said.

'And is that really such a surprise? You've said yourself there's likely to be loads of other people out there. Scared people. No, not scared... people who are frigging terrified. People who are right on the edge, pretty much like we are.'

'Whoever it is, they are murderers,' Piotr said again.

'But they didn't kill any of the other kids who've been out there, did they? The fact Mark came back yesterday makes me more inclined to think that Ash stumbled on someone, instead of someone stumbling on her. I know this is hard to swallow and emotions are running high, but try not to overreact here. I liked Ash a heck of a lot, I think we all did. She was a lovely kid, always smiling. And weirdly, she actually enjoyed what we asked her to do.'

'What's your point?'

'I think whoever she came across might have seen her as a threat.'

'A threat?' Mihai laughed. 'Christ almighty, Ash wouldn't have hurt anyone.'

'Exactly, so killing her wouldn't have been a hard-fought victory, would it? I think they killed her to make a point, and if you think about it, that's pretty obvious. They brought her body back here, after all.'

'Yeah, like a fucking trophy.'

'No, not a trophy, a warning. "Stay away," they wrote, remember? Again, think it through. We tasked her with getting as many of the bodies away from this place as she could and dumping them somewhere else. I think she led them right to someone else's doorstep and they took exception. God, you'd be pissed off if someone turned up knocking on our door with a few thousand of those rotting bastards behind them.'

'We weren't best pleased,' Stan reminded them.

Piotr was running out of patience. 'None of this is relevant. We go out there, we follow the route Ash was supposed to take, and we find those fuckers and destroy them.'

His rallying cry was met with plenty of vociferous support. Dominic again gestured for restraint. 'Come on. Please...'

'I get that it's hard for you to keep your testosterone levels in check, Piotr,' Liz said, 'but is fighting really such a good idea? Abhorrent as it was, I stand by what I just said. What they did to

Ash was a warning.'

'They killed one of ours,' Ruth said, furious. 'What happens when another one of us just "stumbles" onto them and pays the price? We just let that go too?'

'But is this really how you're proposing we respond? By killing one of them? Or all of them? And if you don't get every last one and they come back to try and exact their revenge – their revenge for your revenge – then what happens next? It's a downward spiral that we might not survive. You take us down this route and we'll end up following a very predictable path that'll end up with most, if not all of us, dead. Don't any of you frigging Neanderthals understand? Did you never watch *The Walking Dead*, for crying out loud? It's a bit soon to be resorting to open warfare, don't you think?'

'So we're supposed to just sit back and let her death go unchallenged?'

'Yes,' Liz said.

'Bullshit.'

'Hard as that is to swallow, that's absolutely the right thing to do. Live and let live. Christ, we're all lucky to be living at all.'

'Ash isn't,' Piotr grunted.

'Thanks for that, Piotr. And let's face it, this isn't really about Ash, is it? For you this is just another dick-swinging contest.'

He was out of his chair and onto her. Ruth caught his arm and pulled him back. 'You fucking bitch,' he spat at Liz, 'I should—'

'You should what? Kill me as well? You do see what I'm saying here, don't you?'

Piotr shrugged Ruth off and stormed towards the door. Dominic got to his feet again and shouted after him. 'Wait. Come back, Piotr.'

Grudgingly, Piotr stopped. Dominic waited for him to retake his seat before speaking again.

'I'm devastated that Ash is dead, same as we all are, and I feel doubly guilty because it was me who asked her to go out there yesterday. It brings home the fact that the world we knew before all this, all the rules and logic we used to follow, it's all gone now. We need to think about life – and death – differently to how we used to. As hard as it is to accept, I think Liz is right. We can't afford for this to escalate out of control because right now we've got more at stake than we've ever had before. What happened to Ash was obscene and unwarranted but going out there with pitchforks to try and exact some ill-considered, half-assed revenge is a really, really bad idea. We've got the whole of the city, hell the whole bloody country to choose from, so we should do what the good doctor suggests and give those vile, brutish bastards as wide a berth as possible.'

'Who put you in charge?' Piotr demanded. 'I don't have to take orders from you.'

'No one put me in charge, Piotr, you know that, and you're right, you don't have to listen to me if you don't want to. But I'm thinking about the people here who aren't as strong as you, or who aren't as confident or certain. I'm trying to give a voice to everyone, no matter who they are or what they're capable of.'

'What, even Ash?' asked Mihai.

'Yes, even Ash. Do you really think she'd want us starting some kind of tribal warfare in her memory, when there are barely enough of us left to even form a bloody tribe anymore? If it was Ash sitting here and one of us had been killed, do you think she'd be demanding we go out and take an eye for an eye or whatever that bloody expression is? I don't think so. I do know a couple of things, though. First, I think that Liz is absolutely spot on with her reading of the situation and this was a warning, not a declaration of war. Second, I know that if she's wrong and we are attacked, then I'll be first in line to pick up a weapon and kill any fucker who tries to destroy what we've built here. I give you my word. I'll breathe my last breath defending this place.'

22

Late last night the group at the hotel had collectively agreed to leave. The decision was reached with little argument and even less fanfare. A substantial majority had immediately agreed that leaving the increasingly exposed hotel and travelling east to join the group at the Monument was their best option. Of the others, most had been reluctant to go simply because they were too afraid. For some, the prospect of setting even one foot outside the building was overwhelming. A stubborn few who didn't want to leave had to be reminded that if they stayed behind after everyone else had gone, their reprieve would only be temporary. There'd be no one left behind to bail them out anymore. When they got hungry, it would be down to them to go out and get food. There'd be no Sam, David, Gary or Charlie here to provide for them. David was honest with each of them, explaining that a risk-filled journey across London was their only viable option, but that what he'd seen of the Monument group left him in no doubt it would be a risk worth taking.

The view from the front of the hotel this morning had further validated their decision. First thing, Sam had looked down over Fleet Street from a third-floor window to gauge the immediate threat from the dead outside. They were still gathered around the front of the hotel in huge numbers, like a stain that had spread in all directions. It was hard to make out details from up high (fortunately), but he could see that those corpses nearest the building had been crushed over time, and more and more bodies were now climbing up on top. Death piled upon death. The flesh was drifting. Compacting.

'Where do you think you're going?' Sam asked Omar when he got back downstairs. The kid had his coat on, ready to leave.

'I'm coming with you.'

'You're not.'

'You need help.'

'I've got help. I've got Charlie and Sanjay coming with me.'

'You fancy Charlie.'

'Grow up, you jerk.'

'You do. I seen you looking at her. You're always looking at her.'

'You've got an overactive imagination, Omar.'

'Is Sanjay the bus man?'

'He's the man who used to drive a bus, yes.'

'Still think you need more help than just them two.'

'I don't. Thanks anyway.' Sam looked around the hotel landing and caught Selena's eye as she was passing. 'Hey, Selena, take care of this little shit, will you.'

'Why me?'

'Because he's doing my head in. Besides, he likes you.'

'I don't like her,' Omar protested.

'That's good, 'cos I don't like you,' Selena said. 'You're weird.'

'*I'm* weird? I'm not the one that thinks we're all gonna live happily after in some fairytale village.'

'It's not a fairytale, you asshole. My friend Kath—'

'Got a phone call from one of the fairies sayin' come and live with us and everything'll be happy ever after... yeah, yeah, yeah. You're so dumb.'

'You can't talk about Kath like that.'

'I can do what I want. Anyway, she's dead, ain't she? I seen plenty of dead people and they never did nothin' to me. I owned them all.'

'You think you're a big man, but you're just a puny kid.'

'I saved Sam, didn't I? And Sam had to save you and that Vicky I heard, so that means I'm better than all of you.'

'You're just a useless, immature little jerk. I'm not looking after you.'

'Good, 'cos I don't need looking after.'

They both looked around to voice their objections to Sam,

but he'd gone. He'd deliberately set them onto each other, then disappeared once the inevitable argument had started.

'I don't like him,' Omar said. 'He proper does my head in.'

'Yeah,' Selena agreed. 'Stupid damn crusty.'

Sam, Sanjay and Charlie retraced the convoluted hotel entrance/ exit route until they reached the church. Sanjay looked traumatised. 'How long's it been since you were last out here?' Charlie asked him.

'Can't remember,' he stammered. 'Weeks, I guess. Can't believe how many of them there are.'

'And it's the numbers you have to be careful about,' Sam explained. 'One slip, one fuck up, one tiny lapse in concentration and we could be screwed. All it takes is for a few of them to start taking an interest in us and we've had it.'

'Great. Thanks. I feel so much calmer now,' Sanjay smirked. 'Seriously, though, let me get my head around this again. We're going to go out there into the middle of those crowds, steal three buses, and drive them back to the hotel.'

'Yep.'

'Three bright red, really frigging noisy, really frigging huge London buses.'

'Exactly. But not to the hotel, remember?'

'We leave them across the Victoria Embankment, blocking the entrance to the Blackfriars Underpass.'

'Got it.'

'So the dead can't get past the buses, and when we're ready we can leave here straight through the underpass.'

'Pretty much. Good plan, isn't it?'

'You think it'll work?'

He shrugged. 'I think it might.'

'Christ, a little positively here, please,' Charlie said. 'Of course it's going to work. It has to.'

'And you're sure there are buses on the stands on Queen Victoria Street?' Sam asked, looking at Sanjay.

'Yeah. There were definitely a few when I last went past.'

'And when was that?'

'Couple of days after everything went shit-shaped.'

'You're absolutely certain?'

'One hundred per cent. Anyway, this is London. Bleeding buses are everywhere.'

'Right, so we find a bus each...'

'Turn them around if we need to, then drive north up New Bridge Street, turn left and use the side-roads to get across to Temple Street, then back down towards the river, onto the embankment, then straddle the mouth of the underpass.'

'Spot on. Simple.'

'You reckon?'

'Not really. Ready Charlie?'

'I'm ready.'

'Okay. Let's do it.'

As soon as they reached the Embankment, Sam split from the other two, intending to cause a distraction that would draw some of the dead away and reduce the pressure. With so many corpses still dragging themselves towards the hotel, there were fewer of them out here on the fringes. He adopted his tried and tested mimicking behaviour, matching the stilted, slothful movements of the vile populace, hoping they'd assume he was one of them. For the most part it appeared to work as it always had, but now and then he thought he sensed one or two of them watching, as unsure about him as he was about them.

He walked alongside a rotting woman for a time, step by wearisome step, and though he tried to match her pace and intent, out of the corner of his eye, he occasionally saw her lift her head and look at him. Sam forced himself to keep his own head down and fixed his gaze on the pavement just in front of his feet. She looked up again, then lunged over in his direction, and it was all he could do to keep walking and not react. He glanced back as she clattered into the side of a car and began pawing at her own reflection, distracted by a glint of sunlight on the dusty windscreen. The ugly noise drew others out of the shadows, taking the immediate pressure off Sam. In the brief respite, he smashed the windows of several other cars and set off their alarms.

The bus stops on Queen Victoria Street were only a few hundred metres away, but it felt like an endless trek to get there. Sam was relieved when he finally saw the first of the distinctive red, brick-like buses up ahead, though his head remained filled with a hundred questions he hadn't dared ask.

What if the engines don't start?
Will I remember what Sanjay told me about starting a bus?
What if the drivers are still in their cabs?
What if they're full of dead passengers?
What if the tyres are flat or there's not enough fuel...?

Sometimes he wished his mind was as empty as one of the vacant dead; he couldn't put the brakes on his pessimistic thoughts, and the closer they got to the buses, the bigger his doubts. *So, let's get this straight*, he said to himself, echoing Sanjay's earlier cynicism, *we're supposed to just stroll up here, nab three buses, then come back tomorrow and cart fifty people across dead London like nothing's happened? Yeah, right.*

Charlie had picked up a little speed. She'd adjusted the angle of her walk towards a specific bus. Sam watched her veer away from him and Sanjay. She was a copper. She could handle herself. He'd had plenty of run-ins with the police over the years and, politics apart, had quietly admired the self-confidence that many of them had demonstrated. Charlie was like that. She'd be absolutely fine. Ice cool. She had a better handle on all this than he did.

The rear door of the bus Charlie had chosen was wedged open just wide enough for her to slip inside. The vehicle was empty save for the driver in his cab, slumped forward. When she approached the corpse, it was as if he'd been plugged into the mains, because he immediately sat up and began to thrash around, trapped buckled up behind the wheel but doing everything he could to get to Charlie. His uniform was caked with corruption, hardened dribbles of decay and putrefaction, and he'd clearly been stuck in position too long because his body had swollen around his already wide waist like a partially deflated tyre. Charlie had been prepared for this. She took a long-shafted screwdriver from the back pocket of her jeans and plunged it into the dead man's temple. She bit her lip and fought against an almost overwhelming urge to vomit – this kind of attack was par for the course in the tacky zombie movies she used to love, but her undead reality was proving to be nothing like the movies. The momentary resistance of the dead man's parchment-like skin... feeling the tip of the screwdriver push through corrupted muscle, hitting the resistance of decalcifying skull bone then sinking into what was left of his jellied brain... And it wasn't instant, like in the films, either. The driver continued to fight for a couple of seconds longer before collapsing forward and faceplanting the steering wheel with a sickening thud and crack. Semi coagulated black blood dribbled from his broken nose as she sat him up and hefted him out of his seat. She dumped him in the road as Sanjay was shuffling past. 'You okay?' he mouthed. Charlie nodded then threw up in the gutter.

There were too many corpses milling around now for Sam's liking. He bent down and yanked a shopping bag free from the vice-like grip of an unmoving body, then mooched around inside for a tin of food or something similar he could put through a window as a distraction, but all he found was clothing and tat. Sanjay realised what he was trying to do. He prised an unopen can of Coke from another withered hand, then threw it hard as he could at a window across the street. The glass didn't smash but, in the vacuum-like silence, the noise of the can hitting the ground and spraying everywhere at least managed to draw a few cadavers towards it.

Sam gestured across the road to where two more buses were parked up close to each other. Sanjay took the front bus, which was empty. There was a handful of trapped passengers in the other. They watched Sam approach, increasingly agitated. He wrong-footed them by using a door midway along the length of the vehicle. They swung around as soon as he was onboard, scrambling down the aisle. The narrowness of the gap between the rows of seats made their movements easy to anticipate. He held his position and shoved each of them out of the door in turn, then shut it. He found the remains of the driver on the floor up front. As he shifted the man's remains, he heard a distinctive stutter and rumble outside. Sanjay had managed to get his bus going. It juddered forward, lethargic, and he turned around in the road and waited for Sam and Charlie.

Behind the wheel, Sam now cursed his luck. He'd picked a wreck, it seemed. He tried to get the engine to turn over, but it wasn't working. Then he remembered what Sanjay had told him and Charlie in the two-minute, hopelessly inadequate *"how to drive a bus"* conversation they'd had earlier. There was a switch. He flicked everything he could see, then pressed what was very obviously the ignition button, then relaxed when the massive vehicle rumbled into life. Sanjay stuck his thumbs up, equally relieved, and started to drive back towards the hotel. He passed Charlie's bus which was already pointing in the right direction. It was obvious from the bodies gravitating around the engine that she'd got hers started. She pulled out in Sanjay's wake, inadvertently cutting Sam up. He jumped hard on the brake and nearly tipped the thing on its nose. Almost immediately he could hear the *slam, slam, slam* of reanimated remains rear-ending the back of the massive vehicle.

The combined engine noise drew more of them from the shadows, but the buses were surprisingly effective at cutting through the crowds. They steamrollered the dead, their relatively slow speed belying their power. Sanjay accelerated, finally able to release some of the pent-up tension that had built during his incarceration at the hotel. He swung his bus around a corner and drove the wrong way into New Bridge Street, steering hard around the traffic islands and bollards designed to stop vehicles from travelling in this direction, and wiped out another pack of dead people in the process. It was foul, yet strangely cathartic.

Feeling the pressure, Sanjay struggled to remember the road layout. He knew the main routes and had driven them often, but navigating narrow side-streets in a vehicle like this was a different matter altogether. Take a wrong turn and they'd be knackered; drive down a dead-end and they'd be curtains. He missed the turn for Tudor Street and punched the steering wheel with frustration because that had been the road he'd intended to take them down. With Charlie and Sam so close behind it was impossible to turn around and try again so he kept going, knowing there were other turnings he could take up ahead. The next left – Bridewell Place – looked like too much of a risk. There was another left a hundred metres or so along, but though he might have been able to make the sharp turn, the others had less experience handling the buses and he doubted they would.

Bride Lane was next. He slowed down, but it looked so narrow he'd have struggled to get a regular car down there, let alone a bus. He was out of options and he cursed himself. The next left would take them onto Fleet Street - all was not lost. There were roads leading off Fleet Street that they could use to get back down to the Embankment and the Blackfriars Underpass. He checked in his mirrors to make sure the others were still following.

Sanjay hadn't realised they were so close to the hotel. *Hang on, maybe we're not?* It was hard to tell, because the crowd around the front of the building had swollen to such a size now that he couldn't be sure. It was like driving into the middle of a packed sports stadium, full of thousands, mid-pitch invasion. There appeared to be no end to the numbers of them up ahead. It was Bouverie Street on the left he wanted, but he couldn't take his eyes off the surging throng long enough to look. All details were lost in the chaos. Hundreds of corpses began to peel away from the central mass now, fighting with each other to get nearer to the three approaching buses. In numbers like this they appeared unstoppable.

There was a turning immediately on his left.

Whitefriars Street.

It was going to have to do. He wasn't going to get any closer.

At the last possible moment, Sanjay slowed down and turned the bus sharp left, then sped up again. Immediately behind, Charlie was too close and driving too fast. Not used to the size and handling of the bus, she overshot the junction. Sam was equally close but had a few extra seconds to react. As Charlie engaged reverse so she could shunt back and try again, Sam steered through the narrow gap between the back of her bus and the corner of Whitefriars Street then followed Sanjay down towards the Thames. He blasted on the horn for Sanjay to stop and gestured for him to angle the bus across the road and block it.

Huge numbers of corpses were already gravitating around Charlie's bus, making it all but impossible to see the junction clearly. She accelerated and swung the front of the bus around but collided with a road sign that had been obscured by a glut of lethargic figures. She tried to reverse out again, but this time there were too many of them. A double-width post-box and another road sign on the other side of the junction narrowed the gap still further. Charlie edged the bus forward, then shunted back, then edged forward again, but more and more bodies closed in around her, and she could manoeuvre no further.

By the time Sanjay and Sam were out of their vehicles and had made it back up to the junction with Fleet Street, Charlie was trapped. All her exits off the bus were facing into the crowd, no easy escape. The dead threw themselves at the exposed side of the vehicle, clattering against the metal bodywork, smearing greasy flesh stains over the windows and blocking all the doors. Inside, Charlie did what she could to ignore the noise and to focus. She'd been in worse situations than this before... she could deal with it. She tried once more to reverse out, but the size of the crowd made it impossible. She put the bus into drive and accelerated, but so many corpses had been dragged under the wheels and ground into slurry that she couldn't get any traction.

Sam screamed at her from the other side of the bus, protected within the confines of Whitefriars Street. 'Get out of there, Charlie! We'll use the other buses - just get out!'

Charlie remained behind the wheel, either ignoring him or unable to hear, stoically alternating between drive and reverse, and going absolutely nowhere.

'Charlie, GET OUT!'

The door Charlie had used at the back of the stuck bus was still wedged open slightly. When the first of the dead discovered it and shoved their sickly arms through the gap, it opened further and allowed more of them to pour inside. Flesh surged into the bus. The corpses struggled to climb steps and negotiate obstacles, but the collective force of the crowd behind made up for their individual inadequacies, pushing them forward and upward. Sam could see them piling into the vehicle in remarkable numbers with disproportionate speed.

Sanjay barged past him with a length of wood he'd found in the street and tried to smash one of the windows. It just bounced off the safety glass without even leaving a mark. The noise startled Charlie, though, and she looked up and finally saw what was happening. She got out of the driver's cab and tried to push back against the tide of decay, but there was no way through. She tried to wade through them and get to the steps up to the top floor, but there were already too many and her solitary attempt to move forward was no match for the collective force of the corpses coming the other way. She tried grabbing at them, tried ripping at their flesh, tried anything she could to find a way through, but it was all for nothing. Sanjay swung the wooden baton at the window again, but it had no effect. The dead didn't even react. They were only interested in one thing.

Sanjay swung at the window a third time, but it was already too late.

Charlie reached for the door at the front of the bus and pulled it open, but the entire section of Fleet Street she looked out onto was now swarming with decay. One huge, semi-coordinated show of force from the dead, and she was gone. They swept her off her feet and slammed her back against the protective screen separating the driver's cab from the rest of the bus with such force that both her skull and the screen cracked. It knocked her out cold. The loss of consciousness was the kindest thing.

Sam yelled out in anger and snatched the wooden baton from Sanjay. He smashed it again and again against the side of the bus, filling the enclosed side-street with noise. Inside the vehicle, the dead pressed their expressionless faces against the glass and pawed at it with greasy fingers, searching for another distraction now that Charlie was gone. Sam kept hitting out at them, and when Sanjay pulled him away and pleaded for him to come back to the hotel, he lashed out harder still. He turned on a couple of other corpses that had wearily dragged themselves up from the other end of Whitefriars Street. He swung at one and virtually decapitated it, then smacked the other across the knees and clubbed it again and again and again, reducing its head to an unrecognisable pulp.

Breathless, he finally stopped.

'We need to go,' Sanjay said, keeping his distance.

'Block the roads,' Sam said.

'What?'

'We need to block these roads and stop the dead getting any closer. Leave a clear route for people to get from the hotel to the buses.'

Sanjay ran down Whitefriars Street. There was a footpath on his right which, from memory, he thought would take them through to Bouverie Street, close to the hotel. There was a parked car with the driver still in its seat. He pulled the frantically animated cadaver out onto the street, then stamped on what was left of its face until it stopped moving. He released the handbrake and turned the wheel so the car blocked the road.

Sam took the cut-through to get to Bouverie Street, using the lump of wood to make short work of another half dozen bodies that greeted him when he burst out of the end of Magpie Alley. There was a sizeable crowd coming towards him from the direction of Fleet Street. South towards the river, the road had already been blocked by a crashed car. A builder's van had driven into the back of it. Sam dragged the remains of the driver out and started the engine then turned the van around so it was facing the right way and drove straight into the approaching crowd. He did a decent amount of damage with the first impact, but not enough. He reversed back then drove forward again, back then forward, again and again until, by the fifth impact, there was such a tangled mess of flesh and broken bones that the dead had virtually created an effective blockade themselves. He wedged the van diagonally across the top of Bouverie Street, preventing any more of them getting through.

The endless crowd in Fleet Street had been whipped into an uncontrollable frenzy. Thousands of them surged and thrashed against thousands more, reacting initially to the buses, then to each other. From the upstairs windows, Vicky watched wave after wave after wave of putrescence crash against the front of the hotel.

She could hear frightened voices elsewhere; David, Marianne and Sanjay arguing, their collective noise echoing along otherwise silent corridors. Sanjay was pleading with them to agree to evacuate now, whilst David and Marianne argued equally forcefully for them to stay. Every option felt like the wrong one. They couldn't leave because the group near the Monument wouldn't yet be ready for them, and the chaos outside meant that staying put was equally a risk.

Vicky studied the seething crowds below in abject horror. The chaos in Fleet Street was unstoppable and extreme. She searched for signs that the dead might be beginning to calm down the way they always eventually did when the survivors locked down and went back into hiding, but today they just kept on fighting.

She knew they were past the point of no return.

23

In the streets around the Monument, the reclaiming of the land from the undead continued at pace. The focus today was another stretch of the A1211. Once done, they'd turn north and clear Minories as far as Fenchurch Street. If all went to plan, tomorrow morning an army of volunteers would be used to clear Fenchurch Street at least as far as the junction with Lombard Street, hopefully further. David Shires had agreed to get his group to Bank station but, if they could clear a stretch of Lombard Street, it would make things immeasurably easier for them. In the process, the Monument group would also secure another swathe of buildings which could be stripped of supplies and anything useful. *Everyone's a winner*, Dominic had said when he'd heard the plan.

The backhoe loader was again being used to full effect, wiping out scores of bodies on the A1211. Buoyed up by yesterday's territorial gains, and incensed by what had happened to Ash, the bloodlust in certain sections of the group today was tangible. There was no shortage of volunteers to batter and destroy the hundreds of corpses caught out in the open once new roadblocks had been put in place.

The noise and the fumes and the chaos and the bloodletting were cathartic. Piotr was out on the blood-soaked streets himself today, barking out orders and releasing some of his own pent-up rage. He booted a random decapitated head as if it was a football that had been kicked over the garden fence by the neighbour's kids. 'We'll have this whole area cleared before afternoon,' he said to Ruth. 'Then I want some of those lazy fuckers who never do anything out here clearing up and stripping out buildings.'

'It's always the same faces, boss.'

'I know, and I'm sick of it. Day after day. I had Dominic and Lynette about it this morning. I said why is it always the same few people putting their necks on the line? Why is it always my people taking the risks?'

'What did Dom say to that?'

'He just came out with the usual bullshit. "There's no such thing as your people or my people, they're all *our* people," he said. Then Lynette starts giving me the same old spew about how some people still can't deal with what's happened... I told her I didn't give a shit. I told her things aren't going to get any better, and everybody needs to contribute. We need to stop wasting our time and resources on those who don't help. They're no better than the dead.'

'I can imagine how that went down. It's not the first time you've told them.'

'No, and it won't be the last.'

Dominic was watching progress from his usual vantage point up on the railway tracks.

'That fucker's not taken his eyes off you all the time we've been out here,' Ruth said.

'I don't care. I'm sick of his crap.'

'Once a politician, always a politician.'

'Once a cunt, always a cunt, I say.'

'I'll drink to that,' she said, laughing.

'He's the worst of the lot of them. He's all talk. We're out here every day, up to our necks in blood and guts, and he's up there giving out his fucking orders and drawing his fucking maps. I swear, Ruth, if he calls another fucking meeting today, I will break his fucking legs.'

'Touchy,' Ruth said, and she waved at Dominic who looked away, embarrassed. 'Just so you know, boss, we're all behind you.'

'I appreciate that.'

'Especially after what happened to Ash.'

'So you're good with what we discussed?'

'Absolutely.'

'You're sure? I don't want to lose you.'

'You won't. Anyway, it'll be too obvious if you go. Leave it to me. We can't afford to have a pack of brutal fuckers like that so close to this place. I swear, if they turned up here tooled-up and held a knife to his throat, Dominic fucking Grove would still try and negotiate.'

'Only one way you can deal with people like that.'

'I know. Don't worry, Piotr. I'll sort it.'

'What's your plan?'

'I'm taking a couple of the lads with me. We'll find out where they're based and scope things out. It's probably just a bunch of loonies going stir crazy holed-up somewhere. Or preppers who can't believe the frigging zombie apocalypse has finally happened.'

'That's what I'm thinking.'

'If it was anyone more organised than that, I think we'd have heard from them before now.'

'Who you taking?'

'Tayyab and Jonah.'

'Jonah's good, he's a smart boy. And Tayyab's good with his fists.'

'Exactly. That's why I picked them.'

'You be careful though, right.'

'We will. We'll be back before anyone even realises we've gone.'

'You're just sussing things out, yeah? Don't try anything stupid.'

'I won't.'

'Find out where they are, what they've got, and how many of them there are. That's all I want for today. Once we know that, we'll decide what we do next.'

24

Jonah took the lead. He'd spent time in the forces, and that experience was invaluable. Ruth was in charge though, no question. Tayyab brought up the rear. He was there to play more of a supporting role. He was almost as big as the other two put together. His size and strength would be an unquestionable advantage whatever – *whoever* – they found today.

They moved as quickly as they dared, not as fast as they'd have liked. The work that had been done around the base yesterday had been a success, but it meant that to get anywhere beyond the barricades today, the three of them had to navigate the larger, even more volatile crowds that had been displaced. Armed with bolt-cutters, crowbars, and other assorted DIY tools, they moved through buildings instead of going around them, only going back out onto the streets once they were far enough that the numbers of corpses had dropped sufficiently.

When they'd sent Ash out, they'd told her to focus on moving the dead into Commercial Street. She'd clearly had some success, because the area beyond the crossroads with Leman Street was still heavily congested. To avoid the swollen surges of rotting flesh, Ruth and the others instead used other roads which ran parallel, keeping moving in the same general direction while dodging the bulk of the insipid throngs. They stopped halfway along Old Castle Street where a cut-through between two angular-looking buildings would allow them to get a decent view of the rest of Commercial Street to the north. Tayyab gave Jonah a bunk-up alongside one of the buildings. He grabbed hold of the balcony railings outside a first floor flat and pulled himself up, then climbed up another two floors to get onto the roof. It was a trendy, modern development, and the roof had a covering of mossy sphagnum with occasional solar panels and a grey slab path which wound between them. Jonah smiled inwardly at the eco-friendliness of it all. He'd fully bought into all that climate-change stuff, but he guessed none of it mattered now. With only a handful of people left alive, the human race didn't seem capable of influencing its own destiny now, never mind the future of the planet.

Jonah ran along the roof then jumped down onto a lower section of the building and continued along until he was looking down over Commercial Street. To the untrained eye, it looked like any other road in undead London, but Jonah saw things differently. There were corpses milling around in surprising numbers, gravitating towards a couple of spots. And some sections of the street appeared bloodier than others. He'd seen enough to know the people they were looking for were close, and he ran back to the others. They spoke in hushed whispers in the shadows of the balcony he'd originally scaled.

'Do you know what's up there?' he asked.

'Spitalfields Market,' Ruth answered.

'Makes sense. Loads to loot. Looks like there are a lot of carved-up bodies down that way. Now I'm no forensics expert, but I'm willing to bet the blade that did all the damage up there was the same blade that finished off our pal Ash.'

'Okay. Anything else?'

'I didn't see anyone out there, but I have a hunch...'

'Go on.'

'It's just something about the way the bodies are moving. Some of them were going off in different directions.'

'So?' Tayyab said.

'You don't get out much, do you?'

'Keep up,' Ruth said. 'You've seen as much of the dead as we have. Unless something stops them or distracts them, they tend to keep moving in the same general direction.'

'Exactly,' said Jonah. 'So the fact I saw as many walking down the road as there were going up, makes me think there's either multiple things competing for their attention or—'

'Or there's something stopping them getting through,' Ruth suggested. 'Something like the kind of blockade we've spent the last month and a bit building to keep our place separate from everything else.'

'Exactly.'

'So, what do we do now?' Tayyab asked.

Jonah was quick to reply. 'Well, the one thing we absolutely don't do is march straight up to the front door. We need to be smart about this. Take our time.'

'They'll be expecting us to attack,' Ruth added. 'They provoked us, and they'll be ready for retaliation. There was a lot of bullshit being spouted last night about them dumping Ash's body as a warning, with bloody Dominic saying we should keep our cool and not react and all that shit.'

'Guy's a damn idiot,' Tayyab said, cutting across her.

'We all know it. I think it's more likely that whoever killed Ash is thinking along the same lines as us than Dom. They'll have been expecting us to turn up all guns blazing this morning.'

Jonah agreed. 'Totally. All the more reason for us to get in and out quick and without being seen. Any ideas?'

'I've been here a few times before. The market is pretty big, and they're likely to be protecting it, don't you think? Probably loads of supplies stored there.'

'Can we go around it?'

'Yep. If we cross Commercial Street here and keep going, we'll hit Brick Lane. We keep moving north, then cut back across when we're past the market and get a better look at what's going on up there.'

'Whatever we're doing, we need to do it now,' Tayyab said, and he drew their attention to an unsteady group of some twenty or so approaching corpses.

They split up but kept close enough to remain in sight of each other. Mimicking the dead, they dragged themselves across Commercial Street, then picked up speed and continued as agreed until they reached Brick Lane. The narrow road was far quieter, overlooked by many of the dead. They then continued towards Hanbury Street where they regrouped. Ruth broke into a coffee shop so they could speak more freely. 'Think we've gone far enough?' she asked Jonah.

'Probably.' He pressed his face up against the window. 'I'll go out and do a recce. I'll be quicker on my own. Less chance of being seen.'

Tayyab was already behind the counter, looking through packets of crisps and bottles of drink for things that were still in date. Jonah just looked at him.

'Christ, mate, how can you think about eating at a time like this?'

'I can eat anytime.'

Jonah shook his head then disappeared.

He crept along Hanbury Street to the junction with Commercial Street. It had been blocked off in a similar way to how they'd protected the base around the Monument. Vehicles had been parked across the road, with the gaps between them and underneath packed out with other stuff.

Wait.

There were four roadblocks here: the one he was crouched behind, one that spanned the mouth of Lamb Street on the opposite side of Commercial Street, one across the front, and another across the back of an odd-shaped yellow brick building, boxing it off. It had a red door on its protruding corner, and it looked curiously out of place, almost fortress-like, crammed in as if it had been built specifically to fit the available space. Its haphazard appearance was in stark contrast to the expansive metal and glass towers of Bishopsgate in the distance behind. From here, old London looked in risk of being overwhelmed and overtaken by the new. *Guess it's all old London now*, he thought.

The area immediately around the blocked-off building was reasonably well stocked. A couple of vehicles, crates of supplies, construction materials... even from a distance he could see that this was an established-looking operation. He shifted his position to get a better view of the front of the place and saw that the careful positioning of the barriers had turned this part of Commercial Street into a dead-end, and where the road abruptly terminated, the ground was carpeted with butchered human remains. There might have been hundreds of them; it was impossible to accurately gauge individual numbers as there were so many dismembered limbs lying around, far fewer complete corpses. The road was slick with blood. Those of the dead that were still mobile up here slipped and slid in the mire.

He noticed that not all of them were moving.

When Jonah looked closer, he saw that many corpses had been skewered on the ends of metal poles and railings which had been left sticking out of the roadblock in various places and at random angles. Was that a good sign, he wondered? Did it indicate that the preference of the people here was for defence over attack? But then he realised that most of the impaled cadavers were facing away from the barricade and several of them, he saw, weren't touching the ground. They hadn't done this to themselves by walking into the barrier; they'd been hung up as trophies. As *warnings*. This barrier was designed to keep people away, not just out. People like him, Ruth and Tayyab. People like Ash.

He worked his way back to the coffee shop.

'Well?' Ruth asked. 'What do you reckon?'

'They're fucking psychos, that's what I reckon. It's a bloodbath out there. What they did to Ash was one thing, but they've got corpses skewered on poles, all kinds of weird shit going on. Fucking crazy.'

'And exactly how many of them do you think there are?'

Jonah shook his head. 'Can't be sure. They're keeping their heads down, but I guess that's par for the course these days. They're boxed in, though, and judging by the amount of land they've got, I don't reckon there can be more than twenty or thirty of them, tops.'

'With those markets nearby I'm thinking they've got plenty of stash.'

'Yeah. Spitalfields could prove to be really useful for us. You know how hard it's been to get a decent supply route established. This place is literally just up the road. No reason why we can't deal with whoever it is we've got here, then block the sideroads off and come and go as we please.'

'We're going to need more information for Piotr. We'll go back out there and play dead. Mingle with the crowds. Try and get a better idea of their capabilities before we go back.'

They left the coffee shop and followed Jonah down to the end of Hanbury Street. They found a spot where the blockade was relatively low – easy enough for them to get over but impossible for the dead – then climbed across and merged into the milling crowd.

The three of them had done this previously, adopting the slothful gait and emotionless gaze of the dead, but it hadn't been for a while, and never in such an exposed location. And here they immediately found it was more difficult than it looked because the unexpected unpredictability of the dead made it hard for them not to stand out. The truncated road junction was a mass of random movement with corpses going this way and that and frequently colliding with their surroundings and with each other.

Jonah allowed himself to drift towards Lamb Street, Tayyab following at a distance. Ruth stuck close to the front of the building, confident she was well enough hidden by the main roadblock and the hideous, impaled corpses not to be seen. She noticed that some of the piked dead were still twitching... She shuddered and shuffled onwards, falling back into character.

The building itself wasn't heavily fortified. She thought the people hiding inside were relying on their gruesome barrier adornments to deter any would-be intruders, but she wasn't fazed. The way they'd dumped Ash's body and run made her think that these bastards were weak; overconfident and unbalanced.

She paused involuntarily when another corpse crossed her path. The temptation to react was strong, but she didn't. Instead, she kept going and collided with it, then caught hold of its arm and pushed its face onto one of the many metal spikes, all in a single subtle movement. Tayyab caught her eye and nodded his appreciation. She scowled at him and gestured for him to keep moving. He was a dumb bastard at times. If only he'd—

A glint of reflected light caught her eye. A window opened on the top floor of the building. She saw a flicker in the shadows, then someone hurled a petrol bomb over the barriers and into the street. She bit her lip to stop herself from yelling a warning to Jonah as the fuel-filled bottle flew over his head and landed several metres further down the road. The shattering of the bottle and the sudden whoosh of flame had an instant, inordinate effect on the nearby crowds. They surged towards the light from every conceivable direction.

Another bomb, this one thrown in the same general direction as the first. What the hell was going on?

There were many more bodies approaching now, a virtual stampede, and plenty of them were already on fire. They staggered about aimlessly, spreading the flames.

A third bomb, bigger this time, landed right in the centre of a pack, spewing out a huge, billowing burst of fire which engulfed several of them.

It's okay, Ruth thought, *they're not aiming for us.*

The petrol bombs had detonated so far from where she, Tayyab and Jonah were that they couldn't possibly have been intended for them. *Most likely*, she decided, *the people in the building are reacting to the movements of the dead, stopping them from getting any closer.*

But when she looked around at her chaotic surroundings, she realised she was completely wrong. The petrol bombs had never been intended to hurt them, they were designed to expose them, and it had worked perfectly. The fire had become the sole focus of all the nearest dead, whilst she, Tayyab and Jonah had all reacted in the opposite way by keeping their distance. She was okay for now, nestled up close to the roadblock, but the other two were both standing motionless, surrounded by oceans of space, transfixed by what was happening in front of them. As the dead continued their blindly foolish march towards the flames, she tried to attract Tayyab's attention without giving away her own position. She waved her arms wildly at him, but he was still just staring into the fire.

The single crack of a gunshot rang out.

It filled the air. It sounded directionless, echoing off every building and taking forever to fade away.

Jonah went down. She stepped to run towards him and help, but stopped because all that would do was put her next in the firing line. He was clutching his gut, rolling around in agony. He tried to stand up but barely managed to get onto his knees before collapsing again, howling in pain. As the flames began to fade, the dead began drifting towards his cries.

Ruth glanced back at the building behind her, but there were no signs of movement now, no one visible in any of the windows. She could see Tayyab looking for her and she pushed herself back against the impaled bodies, trying to disappear because she knew that dumb bastard would give away her location in a heartbeat. He started to run for cover, but had only made it a couple of metres when another shot rang out, hitting him in the back.

Ruth knew she was next.

She turned and ran, but the way back to Hanbury Street was blocked by the burning crowd. She sprinted straight down Commercial Street instead, desperate to put as much distance as possible between herself and the shooter. She scooped a cadaver off its feet, no weight to it at all, and held it in front of her like a battering ram as she charged into the masses, sending bodies flying in all directions. She knew she'd hear the next shot at any second, the shot that would inevitably take her out.

But it didn't.

The bullet brought down a body just ahead of her, so close that she had to leap over it as it dropped to the tarmac. Christ, if that was intentional it was a hell of a shot from such a distance. She was well away from the building now, level with the entrance to Spitalfields Market, deep in the rancid crowds. And then she looked over to her right and saw him: a single figure on the roof of the market with a rifle. Fuckers had been shooting at them from the other direction. Fuckers had been watching them all along. Fuckers had been toying with them.

She was still in the shooter's sights.

The fourth shot took down another randomly staggering cadaver just ahead and to her right.

Ruth threw down the corpse she'd been carrying and sped up, ploughing deep into another dense glut of undead creatures, knowing that their grabbing hands were less of a threat than the sniper on the roof of the market. Though they slowed her down, she was able to keep moving through them. She burst free then took a sharp left and raced away down Fournier Street.

She hid in a foul-smelling fast-food joint for hours, long enough to recover her composure and work out how she was going explain to Piotr what had happened. She knew exactly how he was going to react. He was going to bring an army of people up here and wipe the floor with these fuckers.

That was good. That was what she wanted too.

25

The dead were literally climbing the walls of the hotel now. Several hours since Sam and Sanjay had returned, and the furious reaction of the immense crowds in Fleet Street showed no sign of reducing. They'd continued to surge towards the building, and those cadavers nearest to the front continued to be trampled underfoot. More of them had been trodden down, and the semi-solid drift of flesh and bone had built up against the hotel frontage. Next to the main entrance steps, corpses had climbed the remains of their crushed brethren and were now hammering against large windows they'd previously been unable to reach, in full view of the survivors trapped inside. Dead faces were pressed hard against the glass; countless pairs of clouded eyes staring into the building.

After weeks of enforced inertia, the building was now a hive of frantic activity as the group prepared for evacuation. With little discussion, the group had split itself into two unequal parts: those who actively wanted to leave, and those who were simply too afraid to stay. The chaos inside the building served only to increase the fury out on Fleet Street.

Sam was in the shadows, watching the dead watching the living. 'We don't have time to stand around,' David said.

'It's my fault.'

'Just get a grip,' David said, losing his patience. 'How many times are we going to have this fucking conversation?'

'I should have waited for her. I took the turning before she did. I cut through, and I left her behind.'

'And if you hadn't, we'd have likely lost both of you. It wouldn't have made any difference. There was nothing you could have done.'

'And how the hell would you know? You weren't even there.'

'Because you've already told me, and we've been over it time and again since you got back. And Sanjay's been over it repeatedly as well. As fucking awful as it is and as hard as it is for any of us to accept, Charlie's gone. We have to move on. We don't have any choice.'

'You. Weren't. There.'

Vicky was walking past with another load for the buses. She overheard the conversation and stopped. 'We've all lost people. It hurts. Deal with it.'

'You can be an absolute bitch at times,' he said, glaring at her.

'You don't know the half of it. I have every bloody right to be.'

'You can't come here and start...'

Sam stopped yelling. There was no point. Frigging woman had turned her back on him and was walking away again. He went to catch up with her, to tell her exactly what he thought of her, but David stopped him. He grabbed Sam's shoulder and dragged him around the corner then pushed him up against the wall, blocking his way out. 'This isn't the time. What the hell's going on with you, mate?'

'What do you think? I can't stand that bloody woman...'

'I know you better than you think. I know she gets under your skin, but I don't think it's got anything to do with Vicky. I don't think it's all to do with what happened this morning, either.'

'I watched Charlie die. Is that not enough for you?'

He tried to get away again, but David pushed him back and held his gaze. 'There's more to it, isn't there? Is it something to do with Dominic Grove? You've made it clear what you think of him.'

'I have absolutely no desire to lock myself away with a mouthy, opinionated little gobshite like that, but...'

'But what? Come on, man, talk to me.'

Sam hesitated before speaking again, but it was clear that David wasn't going to let it go. 'It was different out there again today.'

'Different how?'

Resigned, Sam lowered his voice to explain. 'Do I have to spell it out? Look at what's happening with the bodies at the fucking windows, David.'

'They're wound up. All this noise and movement after nothing for so long has made them—'

Sam cut across him. 'I thought I was imagining it while we were out there, but now I know I wasn't. The way they swarmed the bus and got to Charlie... the speed those things were moving... the ferocity they were showing... They're getting far, far worse. Just look at them now. They're fucking rabid, mate. Wild.'

'It doesn't make any difference. Once we get to the Monument and get ourselves on the other side of the barricades, we'll be okay.'

'Yes, but we've got to get there first and that's what I'm worried about. Christ's sake, we've got people here who are scared of their own bloody shadows... how do you think they're going to cope when they get outside? I don't know if you've worked this out yet, but once we leave this place, it's every man, woman and child for themselves. If anyone gets into trouble, they're screwed. We won't be able to go back and help them.'

'Look, you've had the mother of all shit days. I know you liked Charlie and I know you—'

Sam pushed him away. 'I told you, it's nothing to do with Charlie.' He pointed at the front of the hotel. The windows were a mosaic of dead faces, decaying hands stretching ever upwards, pawing to get inside. 'They're climbing up the fucking building!' he yelled.

David pulled Sam closer until their faces were just millimetres apart. 'Listen, I get it, I really do, but you need to keep this kind of talk to yourself. Hysteria breeds hysteria.'

'You think I'm hysterical? Fuck's sake...'

'I think you're probably in shock. And I also think that if some of these folks get wind of you talking like this, they'll—'

'They need to know. Seriously, they need to know what we're up against. You said you understand, but I don't think you do, because if you really did then you'd be announcing it to the whole fucking group instead of standing here in the corner, whispering at me to keep it down.'

'Maybe later we'll have that conversation with them. The key thing for now, though, is getting ready to leave. We need to get this place packed up as quickly as we can and get everyone rested so we can leave at first light. Our biggest problem is going to be at the other end. If they haven't got the area cleared like they said they would, we could really be in trouble.'

'I can't think that far ahead. If that crowd out front gets any bigger, no one's going anywhere.'

26

It was well after dark when Ruth made it back. She was cold, exhausted, and nervous as hell, but she knew she had to find Piotr and tell him everything. She retraced the route through empty buildings that she'd taken earlier with Jonah and Tayyab then paused at the side of a bonfire in one of the cleared streets to compose herself. Flesh and bone and scraps of clothing burned intensely. She stared at a blackened skull, hypnotised by the flames licking at its vacant eye sockets. The air was filled with sickly sweet barbecue tones. Normally the smell made her hungry, but tonight she just felt sick.

She tried to get through at an access point in Coopers Row. There were people out here working late. One of them came at her with an axe. She held up her hands in submission, too tired to explain.

'Christ, Ruth, is that you? What happened? You look fucking awful.'

She looked down at herself. She was covered in all kinds of shit that had gushed and dribbled from corpses, making it hard to distinguish her from one of the undead.

'Bad day,' she said.

'It nearly got a lot worse - I almost cut your fucking head off. Where the hell have you been?'

She didn't answer. 'Where's Piotr?'

'I saw him in Tower Place with Grove a while back. Think he said he was going back to his apartment for a kip.'

'And where's Grove?'

'Still in the boardroom, I think.'

She nodded, then carried on walking.

*

Space in the apartment building was at a premium, but Piotr had bagged himself one of the penthouses early days, giving him more real estate than pretty much anyone else. No one had the guts or the inclination to suggest he share or maybe move to a smaller room if he wanted to maintain his privacy. Ruth had only been up here a handful of times before; she tried to avoid house calls if she could. The staircase seemed to go on forever. She almost stopped. All this effort just for him to go mental at her.

She knocked on Piotr's door and waited. It was dark all the way up here. She hadn't brought up a light, and she was relying on memory. She wasn't even completely sure she'd got the right apartment, but from what she could see this one looked about as ostentatious as she remembered. She was about to knock again when the door opened inwards.

If this had been the kind of clichéd post-apocalyptic life she'd seen the movies, the boss of the chain-gang would have been living it up on the top floor of this once-exclusive building, feasting on good food and quality booze, anything else he wanted on tap. The reality of Piotr's home life was about as far removed from old-world dystopian fiction as possible. He was half-dressed and alone. The cluttered apartment stank of him. He didn't even acknowledge her, just went back to what he was doing. He had piles of books around the end of his bed which he was sorting into order. 'I'll get through them all one day,' he said, barely looking up.

She shut the door behind her. The room was illuminated by several candles, some new, others burnt down to bulbous-looking nubs that dripped onto the expensive, but filthy, carpet. Piotr took a bottle of beer from a crate at the side of the bed (he had a few crates, she noticed), opened it, and passed it over. She drank as much as she could before the gas got the better of her. She wiped her mouth with the back of her hand, reluctant to speak.

'Well?' he said. 'I'm guessing it's not good news.'

'Tayyab and Jonah are dead,' she said, and Piotr just nodded, no other visible reaction. 'We found the place where Ash was killed. Commercial Street, like you thought, up past Spitalfields Market. They're smart bastards, Piotr. They were hiding, then they firebombed us when we got too close and shot at us from a completely different direction. Fuckers had a sniper on the roof of the market.'

'How many of them?'

'Nowhere near as many as we've got here. I swear, Piotr, I was lucky to get away.'

'You think? Luck had nothing to do with it. If they're as smart as you say, then they let you go. You said they had a sniper, and you were looking in the wrong direction. If they'd wanted you dead, they'd have killed you.'

'But that makes no sense. If they—'

'It makes total sense, you moron,' he yelled at her. 'Fuck me, Ruth, I sent you out because I thought you were better than this. They let you get away so you'd come running back and tell me how they beat you. And they beat you because you didn't think it through. You got caught.'

Ruth was angry, but she swallowed it down. Instead, she found herself apologising. 'I'm sorry, Piotr.'

'How many people?' he asked again.

'Jonah reckoned around thirty, but I can't be sure. Their building's relatively small and—'

'And you're making assumptions. Not a good idea. I did a job at Spitalfields last year. It's a big place. There could be hundreds of them, hidden away. The building you were focused on could just be a decoy. These people are smart, I think. Smarter than you've been. They're playing with us.'

'I'm not so sure. Why go to all the trouble of setting up a decoy like that? They might not have even known about us until Ash got too close, same as we didn't know anything about them.'

'They knew where to dump her body, didn't they? They've been watching, I know they have.'

'What do you want to do?'

'Beat them at their own game. Out-think them.'

'Is it worth talking to Dominic about—'

'You don't say a word of this to Grove or anyone else. I'll tell him when the time's right, got it?'

'Got it.'

'You didn't see anybody else out there?'

'Other than the guy with the rifle and whoever chucked the petrol bombs, no.'

'Sounds like there isn't many of them. They'd have made more of a show. They know they're outnumbered so they're trying to intimidate. They're trying to warn us off because they don't want a war. Way I see it, we either leave them to their own devices, or we attack.'

'We can't just forget about them; they've taken three of us now. We have to go on the offensive.'

'I agree.'

'When, Piotr? The other group will be arriving tomorrow.'

'I know.'

'Everyone's going to be focused on getting them in here safely. We'll leave ourselves prone if we're all looking in the other direction.'

'Correct. So maybe we don't have any choice after all. Maybe the decision has already been made.'

Later, Piotr found Dominic in the board room of Tower Place with Lynette. Idiot was planning and projecting again, working out how they were going to accommodate the new arrivals tomorrow. *He could be so childish*, Piotr thought. He reminded him of a nerdy kid building a world out of blocks in a stupid computer game. And just like the geeks and their games, for all the effort and energy they put into their virtual creations, in reality none of it made a fucking scrap of difference.

'Just the man,' he said as Piotr entered. 'I wanted to talk to you about something. When are we going to be ready to start clearing the houses in Wapping?'

'That's months away still. We agreed we'd open up the hotel

over by the docks for now, remember? Makes more sense.'

'Yeah, I know, but we need to be looking longer term. We've potentially got another fifty people arriving here tomorrow and there's not enough space in the apartments. The hotel will be okay as a stop-gap, but we need to get moving on the Wapping reclamation.'

'That's low priority. Right now, they go in the hotel. If they don't like it, tough shit.'

'What's with the attitude? We've talked about this. We need to start thinking about what happens in six months from now, a year... the planning is as important as the doing.'

Piotr just looked at him.

Lynette scooped up her stuff, sensing tension. 'Are we done, Dom? I need to get some food then make sure everything's ready for tomorrow.'

'Yeah, sure,' he said. 'I'll catch up with you later.'

Piotr waited for her to leave, then shut the door behind her.

'Problem?' Dominic asked.

'Big problem.'

He sighed. 'To do with Ash?'

'Yes.'

Dominic leant up against the window and massaged his temple. 'Go on. Tell me.'

'It's not just Ash. Tayyab and Jonah were killed today.'

'Fuck's sake. How?'

'Sniper.'

'Jesus Christ. Are you serious?'

'You think I'd joke about my men being killed?'

'Sorry, no, of course not. Where?'

'Commercial Street. Whenever we've pushed the dead back, I've sent people scouting around looking for anything useful. Turns out Jonah and Tayyab stumbled on the building where the people who killed Ash are holed-up. They're right on the edge of our territory. Closer than we thought.'

'How many?'

'No more than thirty, we think, but there's no way of knowing for sure. Look, Dominic, we need to do something about this. If they'd been further out of the way, then we could have left them, but it's too much of a risk, too many lives at stake. I'm concerned they'll try to hit us when the others come in tomorrow. We'll be prone. We'll be looking in the wrong direction.'

'Can we talk to them? Negotiate?'

'Three of our people are dead, one of them just a kid. Do you think they're interested in negotiations?'

'What's the alternative? Full-scale war?' Piotr's silence made Dominic uncomfortable. 'You're not serious? Bloody hell, Piotr, the absolute last thing we need to do is start a turf war. We've already got several million dead bodies to deal with, for crying out loud, we don't need any more.'

'You think I don't know that? I'm the one who's out there dealing with all this, remember?'

'So, what do you propose we do?'

'We just need to get through tomorrow. Get the others in here safely, then we can sit tight and keep ourselves to ourselves. But it's getting through tomorrow that I'm worried about. I'm going to send people out to watch their camp, make sure they don't attack. We know where they are now. We'll seal the roads around them, stop them getting too close.'

'So, this is just a precaution? You're not going out there looking for a fight?'

'None of us want a fight, Dominic. We'll keep our distance. They won't even know we're there. As you say, just a precaution.'

'But if they do try and start something?'

'Then we'll deal with them on their turf, keep the trouble away from here. The alternative is we put guards on the perimeter of this place, but all that's gonna do is freak people out.'

'I really don't like this.'

'I don't like any of it, but we don't have a choice. We can't risk not defending ourselves.'

'I understand the logic of what you're saying, but you're sure there's no other way? I could go out there and at least attempt a diplomatic solution. I'm happy to try if it means—'

'After what happened today, you'd have a bullet in your head before you got anywhere near.'

'Dammit,' Dominic said. 'Why does it always have to be like this? Why can't we just get on with each other?'

'It's human nature. This option is best for all of us. They won't even know we're there. We'll only react if we have to. I just want to keep the peace and make sure everyone gets home safe, same as you.'

'But who are you going to send out? Will they see things the same way?'

'I'll make sure they do.'

'I don't want any vigilantes.'

'I get it. Neither do I.'

'Then I guess that's the way we go. Keep this to yourself, though, and only involve the people you absolutely have to. I don't want everyone getting spooked. No more than they are already, anyway.'

'I understand.'

Dominic collapsed into his seat at the head of the boardroom table and swigged from a flask. 'Sometimes I feel so bloody naïve. I get carried away with the world building, you know? There's so much potential here... but the fact we're having to have a conversation like this is heartbreaking.'

'I know, I know, Dom. Like I said, it's human nature. Lock two people in a room with one bottle of water and they'll fight over it rather than share. It's the way we've evolved.'

'I was just hoping we might have evolved a little further after everything that's happened.'

'Maybe one day. Not yet.'

'Yeah, maybe. Thanks for telling me all this, Piotr. I'm so glad I've got you onside.'

27

DAY FORTY-FOUR

Shortly before four, hours before sunrise, one of the windows at the front of the hotel finally succumbed to the relentless pressure of the dead outside.

Sam was on his feet in seconds. He'd been sleeping alone on the ground floor, tucked away in an alcove set back from the front of the building, waiting for the inevitable. He crept forward and could see crawling movement in the shadows. When he switched on his torch and swept the light across the ground floor lounge, he saw corpses oozing in from outside like a viscous, semi-coagulated liquid. They seemed to flow then fall, losing control and dropping from the broken window, then picking themselves up again and beginning to advance deeper into the hotel. It was a horrific, terrifying sight, almost abstract in its unpleasantness. Bones were broken in the uncoordinated drop from a height. Many of the cadavers hit the ground and stayed there, incurably crumpled on impact, but others picked themselves up and moved forward as best they could. Some walked, some dragged, some crawled. The decay was about to spread through the building like a slow-motion slick.

The rest of the group had taken refuge in and around the bar, spending their final night at the hotel in less than comfortable surroundings, all the rooms and beds on the other floors now empty. Sam was about to run to alert them when the second window gave way and another torrent of bodies crashed through. The noises from the first incursion, along with the sudden release of densely compacted pressure as corpses had been forced through the opening, had resulted in another furious surge outside on Fleet Street. He flicked his torch upwards and saw that some of the glass had remained in the second frame, and those corpses that were pushed against its razor-sharp edges were being sliced as they fell. He watched lopsided figures that had been slashed to ribbons picking themselves up off the hotel carpet and staggering towards him as if nothing had happened.

Sam backed away from the hundreds of barely human creatures spilling into the building, wanting to run but feeling like his feet had been nailed to the floor. He scanned his torch around continually, trying to make sense of the oncoming wave of decay. In places, the remains were so deep that those bodies somehow still on their feet looked like they were swimming through the endless morass. Distinguishable body parts were frequently visible: an arm here, a pelvis and legs over there... He saw innards draped like paperchains, a face at an impossible angle with unblinking eyes that stared right through him...

He was so consumed by the horror in front of him, that he didn't give any thought to the endless madness out on Fleet Street until it was too late. The cumulative effect of the pressure changes and movements on the thousands of bodies that were still outside reached a crescendo. The door to the hotel finally gave way, and an unstoppable tsunami of rot swamped the ground floor.

Sam sprinted along the labyrinthine corridors of the hotel. He'd been here for weeks, but every scrap of familiarity had been stripped away by the dark and the fear and the presence of the encroaching dead. He ran one way then stopped and doubled-back on himself, realising he wasn't where he thought he was. Gary had just left the bar to see what the noise was. Sam came around the corner at speed and crashed into him. 'We need to get out.'

Gary held him at arm's length and tried to decode the look of terror in his face. 'Mate, if you need us to—'

'We need to get out NOW,' Sam screamed, pushing him away. He burst into the bar. 'Everybody out. The dead are inside.'

'What the hell?' David said, sleep-slurred, picking himself up off the carpet.

'They're in,' Sam said, starting to wake those nearest to him who were somehow still sleeping.

Marianne tried to stop him. 'But it's not time. They won't be ready for us. If we leave now, then—'

'Did you not hear me? They're inside the hotel. They just brought the door down.'

The panic in Sam's voice was contagious. Inside the bar, and wherever else other members of the group had chosen to try to rest and prepare themselves for morning, there was sudden, frantic movement. The dark space was filled with criss-crossing light from a rapidly increasing number of torches.

'Get to the buses,' Sam told them, marginally calmer now that he could see people beginning to move. 'Where's Sanjay?'

'I'm here,' Sanjay replied, scrambling to gather his things together and get his rucksack onto his back.

'Lead the way, mate,' David told him, and he handed him a torch and pushed him towards the exit. Once the stampede was over and the bulk of the group had passed, he shone his light around the empty bar. Marianne wanted him to move, but he refused and pushed her away. 'You follow the others. I want to make sure everyone's out.'

In the sudden silence, David did a final sweep of the area. He found no one, and he was sure they'd all gone, but he kept looking, anxious not to leave anyone, picturing a kid like Omar crawling under a table in terror and being forgotten. There were people here who'd been virtually catatonic since arriving at the hotel. He didn't think he'd be able to live with himself if any of them were overlooked.

The building should have been silent, but it wasn't. He could hear the dead dragging themselves tirelessly along the corridors and halls. Curiosity got the better of him and he walked a little way back into the building, perhaps not fully believing what had happened so quickly here. Everything had changed in a heartbeat. Surely the dead outside couldn't have had that much of an impact, could they? They were dumb, lethargic, emotionless lumps of reanimated flesh. How could they have wreaked such havoc?

David needed to understand. He needed some validation. He needed to be able to rationalise the sudden panic that was forcing them from this building and out into the night.

He'd barely made it halfway along the corridor connecting the bar to the rest of the hotel when he saw the first of them. At the outermost edge of the circle of illumination from his torch, he saw a shifting mass edging towards him. From here it really did look as if the hundreds of corpses that were now inside the building had become a single entity; an all-consuming, corpulent tide which rolled towards him at a speed he could easily outrun, but with a tireless intent. It was as if they were saying, *we're taking our time, but we'll catch you in the end...*

He felt something near his foot. A rat, perhaps? There'd been enough of them around the hotel recently. He shone his torch down as the outstretched hand of a cadaver brushed against the toe of his boot. It seemed to feel the shape of the toecap the way a blind person might run their hands over someone else's face.

We'll catch you in the end...

He stamped down on the hand, crunching bone.

There was another one of them to his right, and another lurched into the light from his torch. He turned and ran for all he was worth, bursting from the hotel into the hammering rain. He missed Magpie Alley and the cut-through for the bus. He was on the verge of panic, doing everything he could to calm down and not lose his grip completely, when someone appeared in front of him, carrying a burning torch.

'You took your time. Did you have trouble checking out?' Vicky asked.

David didn't answer. Shaking, he pushed past her and walked towards the buses.

Vicky returned to the hotel with Gary and Damien and torched the place. 'Should give them something to focus on that isn't us,' she said, and she walked back to the others, glad to be leaving.

*

They shifted the cars that had been blocking the road then waited in absolute silence inside the buses. They'd hoped they'd be able to sit it out until the sun rose to guide them to the Monument, but that was wishful thinking. The burning hotel building was a beacon to the dead.

The group settled in, expecting to wait there for hours, but less than thirty minutes had passed before David said: 'We need to get moving.'

Sam weighed up the odds. Whatever option he took felt like the wrong one. 'Fuck it,' he said. 'You're right. Go tell Sanjay. Let's get out of here.'

Gary ran down the street and boarded the other bus. Sanjay started his engine and followed Sam as he drove away.

Across Tudor Street, into Carmelite Street, then down onto the Victoria Embankment. Their original plan to use the Blackfriars Underpass to avoid a swathe of London streets had gone out the window – they were already well past the entrance, and there was nothing to be gained from trying to turn around. They could only keep driving and deal with whatever they came across.

28

There was no shortage of volunteers when Piotr put out the call. He had more than fifty people lined up ready to fight, all aware of what they were likely heading into. Piotr knew that a show of force was the only thing those fuckers at Spitalfields would ever understand and by Christ, the men and women who'd stepped up this morning were ready to give them exactly that. They were ready to avenge the deaths of their friends.

Fuck Dominic Grove.

What was he going to do about it? Was he going to stand in the middle of the bloody road to try and prevent them leaving? Was he about to grow a pair of bollocks and lead the charge north to sort the problem out? No fucking way. Piotr told his army they had to forget about the politician and all the thinkers and talkers he surrounded himself with. He told his crew that those people counted for nothing in this new world order. When all's said and done, he said, it's the workers and the fighters who'll make the difference. It'll be the doers, not the talkers.

It'll be *us*.

And these people were thirsty for battle... Piotr reckoned he could have found twice as many volunteers if he'd wanted. The anger and frustration that had built up inside each of them since the rest of the world had died was immense. These people had been stripped of their lives and their loved ones and their very reason for being. They needed justice, and building a barrier and wiping out a few thousand useless corpses every so often only went so far to appease them. The people up near Spitalfields might not have been directly responsible for their suffering, but they were the ones who were going to pay.

They'd gathered under the railway at the furthest point the group had secured to the east. Piotr had been storing basic survival gear, trucks and other vehicles up here for weeks as an insurance policy, primarily in case they needed to evacuate at speed. But they were just as useful for carrying people into war, and that was what this felt like. It was a show of force. They were going to make it clear to those fuckers there was no messing with the Army of the Monument. He liked the sound of that. He liked the idea of being commander-in-chief.

As a distraction, at the other end of the compound, the work to clear and secure Fenchurch Street began early. 'Don't need to worry about pissing off the neighbours these days,' Piotr had told Dominic last night. 'We'll start at dawn to make sure we're set for when the others arrive.' His idea had been met with little resistance, and he could already hear the backhoe loader eating through the frenzied undead over to the west. The chaotic noise there would camouflage anything Piotr's team did.

London had always one of the most diverse cities on the planet. Piotr himself had come here from Poland, lured by a girl, then kept here by his work. And even now, when the living population of the city had been reduced from millions to less than a thousand, the diversity of his army was remarkable. There were people here from every continent and from every walk of life, all of them united in their desire to stay alive and to do whatever was necessary to protect and defend what was theirs. And alongside those who'd come to London from elsewhere, there was also a sizeable number of locals who knew the area backwards. *A multinational taskforce*, Piotr told himself. *Closest thing left to the United Nations in the whole fucking world.*

There was no point trying anything other than a direct attack. The quiet of the dead city was such that to sneak up on anyone these days was all but impossible, and though they could have gone earlier on foot and used the darkness to their advantage, it would have been too much of a risk. Instead, they came at the building near Spitalfields from a number of different directions at once. If nothing else, the tumultuous noise confused the dead. They literally didn't know which way to turn.

Piotr had Ruth riding shotgun with him. 'That's it,' she told him, pointing out the building as they approached. She needn't have bothered; the roadblocks and impaled corpses were a giveaway. 'Fuckers firebombed us from that window on the top floor.'

He accelerated and ploughed his truck through the crowds at speed. In his rearview he saw other vehicles breaking away towards Spitalfields Market as he'd ordered, ready to deal with the sniper. They might lose a couple more people, Piotr had thought, but the shooter would only be able to kill one person at a time, and the moment they fired their first shot, they'd give away their location.

He sped up again and punched a hole through the blockade in front of the building, picking a weak spot between the impaled bodies. He brought the truck to a screeching halt directly outside the red door. Another three drivers followed Piotr through, the last one blocking the breach in the barricade with the back end of his car.

No signs of life. No counterattack. Yet.

They'd caught these people napping. Their multi-directional assault had come out of nowhere and, unlike yesterday with Ruth, Tayyab and Jonah, they hadn't given whoever was holed-up inside the building any time to react. Chapman – no one knew his first name – was an ex-copper who'd been on duty when the rest of the world had died. He'd taken the opportunity to purloin a few tools of the trade before leaving the station for the final time, and he came at the door of the building with a battering ram. With the speed and precision of a veteran of many dawn raids, he swung twice at the lock and the door flew open with ease. Piotr, Ruth, Chapman and several others crashed through.

Inside, the building was dark.

Cold.

Silent.

It felt empty. Full of shadows and echoes, nothing else.

They split up and went room to room on the ground floor but

found nothing and no one. Some clutter and detritus. A moderate stash of supplies. Little else.

'Fuckers have already cleared out,' Piotr said. 'They knew we'd be coming for them.'

'I don't like this,' Chapman said, and he raced up the stairs, Piotr close behind. The second floor was as empty as the first. Apart from a few more piles of provisions, everything appeared long untouched. There was no indication the place had been abandoned in a hurry. The rooms felt like they'd been empty for a long time, as desolate as almost every other room in every other building in London. This place wasn't anywhere near as big as it had appeared from outside. It felt very makeshift. Haphazard. 'Feels like no one's been here for weeks.'

'Well there was definitely someone here yesterday,' Ruth said. She peered out of the nearest window to try and gauge the size of the inevitable undead problem brewing outside. They were approaching from all sides, but for now their numbers were manageable. There were enough boots on the ground out there to deal with them.

'This feels like a set up,' Piotr said. 'Someone could have tipped them off.'

Ruth was unsure. 'You think?'

'Don't you?'

'Why go to the trouble of blockading a building and securing it like this if they weren't going to use it? Jesus, you saw the bodies on the spikes outside. It's a bit over the top for a trap, I reckon. I think they heard we were coming, realised what they were dealing with, and split.'

Chapman laughed. 'No offence, Ruth, but if you were coming for me, I'd fucking disappear too.'

'I'm serious,' she said. 'They know where we are and who we are, they know there's hundreds of us. Okay, so they tried to show us who's boss by killing Ash and picking off Tayyab and Jonah, but if these people have got any sense, they'd have worked out we're a real fucking threat and crawled back under their rock.'

'Why are we risking our necks out here then?' someone else asked. 'This is a waste of fucking time.'

'Shut up!' Piotr yelled, and his voice filled the entire place with noise, echoing off the walls.

'We should just take whatever useful stuff there is and get back,' Ruth said. Piotr stood his ground.

'Not yet. There's something we're not seeing here... something we're missing... I want you to—'

He stopped talking abruptly.

'What's up?' Chapman asked.

'Shh... listen.'

The group became quiet, and then they heard it. Movement on the floor above, almost directly above their heads. There was an immediate rush for the staircase, Piotr leading the charge.

The top floor of the building looked a lot more lived in than the other levels. There were more supplies up here, stuff piled high on either side of the landing that left barely enough space to get through in single file. All but one of the doors were unlocked. Piotr stepped back to let Chapman through with his battering ram and he smashed the remaining one open.

The room was empty save for a mound of bedding at one end beneath a window. There was a woman lying on it, thrashing around and doing what she could to crawl further into the corner and disappear. She tried to make herself as small as possible but struggled. She couldn't get up. Piotr saw that her left leg was strapped up and splinted. Someone had tried to deal with her horrific looking injury but without the equipment and knowledge to do it properly. It was festering. He could smell her from across the room. She tried to move again but couldn't. Her face was scarred on one side, horribly burnt.

'What the fuck is this?' Chapman asked, confused.

The crowd in the room was agitating the already terrified looking woman. Piotr gestured for them to hold back.

'Sweet Jesus,' Ruth whispered. 'They must have left her behind. Fuck, that's awful. Look at the state of her.'

'Maybe we did scare them enough to make them disappear after all,' Chapman said. 'No sense carrying a cripple, she'd have only slowed them down. And judging by the stink in here, that's the kind of wound that's not going to get any better.'

'It's fucking barbaric,' Ruth said, her voice filled with disgust.

Piotr still wasn't convinced. 'I don't buy it. Keep an eye on the exits. She could just be bait.'

He took a few hesitant steps forward. The woman watched his every move with wild, unblinking eyes. She started to sob and tried to swallow the fear back down, almost choking on it.

'Where are the others?' he asked.

'No others,' she said, barely audible.

'Where did they go?'

'No others,' she said again, a little louder. She had a northern accent.

Piotr took another step closer to her, then put his boot on her broken leg and pressed down. She screamed in agony.

'Do you think I'm stupid? You're crippled, but you've got food and drink. I don't smell shit in here. Someone's been letting you out to shit and piss and keeping you clean. Who is it that's looking after you?'

'Just... Taylor.'

'Who?'

'Taylor.'

'Where?'

'He's not... here.'

'Then where is he?'

His boot was poised just millimetres above her leg. The woman's eyes flashed from his foot to his face and back again. 'Not here,' she repeated.

He stamped on her ankle. Her agony filled the building.

'Piotr, come on,' Ruth said. Piotr turned around and glared at her, then turned back to the woman.

'Tell me where he is or so help me, I'll break your other fucking leg too.'

'I'm sorry,' the woman said.

'Sorry for what?'

'Was she your friend, the girl on the bike?'

'She was more than just a friend. She risked her life for us.'

'I'm sorry...' she said again, wiping tears from her eyes.

'Was it you? Did you kill her?'

She shook her head.

'Taylor?'

She shook her head again. 'Not him.'

'Tell me.'

'It was an accident.'

'Bullshit.'

'I swear. It was her fault. Too much noise. They got her.'

'They? Who is *they*? Talk, damn you.'

'The dead people.'

Piotr put his full weight on her ankle again, and the woman screamed herself hoarse. 'Please...' she begged. 'Please stop...'

Her face had blanched. The room smelled as if she'd soiled herself. Piotr lifted his boot and she writhed in agony among the dirty bedding.

Ruth crouched down next to her, then helped her sit up, back to the wall. She found a half-drunk bottle of water amidst the detritus and held it up to the woman's dry lips. 'Here. Drink this.'

Piotr was not impressed. He walked over to the window and looked down at the growing crowds in the street. 'We don't have time for this bullshit.'

'What's your name?' Ruth asked.

The woman hesitated, as if it was a struggle to remember. 'Helen.' She began to appear marginally more composed. She looked at Ruth, who nodded, encouraging her to talk. 'Your friend... the dead people came at her and she couldn't get out of the way because of all the stuff Taylor left in the road.'

'She was stabbed,' Chapman said. 'I've seen thousands of those dead bastards, but I never saw one carrying a weapon.'

Helen shook her head. 'She tried to climb over and get away...

slipped... she fell onto the spikes. It was an accident...'

'You seriously expect us to believe that?'

'Taylor tried to help her, but she was already dead. He had to cut up dead people to get through to her. He told me he knew where she'd come from. He said he'd take her back because you'd be worried if she didn't come home...'

'Take her back? He dumped her fucking body in the street,' Piotr said. 'He told us to stay away.'

'Dangerous up here.' She turned her attention back to Ruth. 'I've seen you... you came here before. I tried to help you too...'

'Hardly. You threw firebombs at us.'

'Not at you, at *them*.'

'And then your friend Taylor killed two of our people.'

She nodded again and swallowed hard, almost overcome with nerves. 'I know. I told him that was wrong, but he said what else could he do? He said you'd keep coming if he didn't warn you off. He was just trying to look after me, that's all. He says he can't fix my leg, but he's doing what he can. He's a good man. We're both good people. We don't want any trouble...'

'Fucking crazy people,' Chapman said.

'What's happened wasn't his fault. He wanted to help...'

Chapman was losing patience. 'A sniper with a conscience, Fuck me, I've heard it all now.'

'I just wanted to help the dead ones. Stop them suffering. I got hurt and Taylor found me.'

'Help them? How?' Ruth asked.

'Killing them again. Putting them to rest.'

'Why should I listen to any of this?' Piotr said. 'Three of my people are dead.'

'Taylor says why can't you stay away and leave us alone? He says London's big enough and you've got all that space... why keep coming up here?'

'Wait. Exactly how much does he think he knows about us?'

'He knows everything. He's seen it all. He's been watching you from the start. He tells me he doesn't want any trouble. He says the dead people are the problem, really.'

'He kills my people and says he doesn't want any trouble? That's a bit fucked up if you ask me.'

'He said he had to do it.'

'This is a fucking joke,' Chapman said. 'We've wasted our time on a deluded cripple and a lone wolf vigilante. Fucking ridiculous.'

Piotr pointed at Ruth. 'You told me there was thirty of them here.'

'We thought there were more. It's not my fault we—'

'Save it. I've heard enough bullshit for one day.' He turned to face Helen again. 'I'll ask you once more, where is he, this Taylor?'

'I already told you, I don't know. He never tells me where he goes.'

'Probably on his way back to the Monument,' Chapman said.

Piotr agreed. 'Yeah, that's what I'm thinking. There's nothing more for us here. Strip everything useful from this place and let's head back home.'

'Don't,' the woman said, and she shot out a hand and caught hold of Piotr's leg. 'Please. Don't take Taylor's stuff. Don't make him angry. He's a good man, but he's dangerous. He'll—'

Tired of listening, Piotr shook himself free of her grip then stamped hard on her ankle. Bone cracked. Helen screamed even louder than before, so loud it caused the dead to surge in the streets outside. Ruth barged past him and left the room. Piotr watched her leave, disappointed.

'They're getting fruity out there, boss,' one of the crew warned.

'You heard what I said. Clear the place out, then leave. And watch out for Taylor, the big man. One joker with a rifle against all of us! Fucker doesn't have a hope in hell.'

'What about her?' Chapman asked, nodding dismissively at the wreck of a woman on the ground.

'Please...' she begged.

Piotr gestured for him to hand over his battering ram, then swung it into her face. 'If you see Taylor, give him a message from me,' he told her corpse.

They'd been loading the vehicles for several minutes before anyone realised what had happened. It was Ruth who saw it first. She hammered on the side of the van she was loading. 'We need to leave. Right now!'

There was a new flood of dead flesh approaching. Hundreds of corpses were clogging Commercial Street, moving north from Spitalfields.

'Where the hell did that lot come from?' Chapman asked.

'Taylor,' Ruth replied.

When the others saw what was coming, they immediately stopped what they were doing and returned to their vehicles. Piotr revved his engine angrily, no longer concerned about the impact of any noise. The car blocking the hole in the barrier reversed backwards, its progress slowed to a crawl by the huge wave of corpses now coming the other way. The sheer density of the mass of advancing dead flesh stopped it moving altogether. The creatures swarmed all over the vehicle, the driver and his passenger trapped inside, unable to escape, and then began to pour through the compromised roadblock.

Piotr didn't care. Those idiots who'd got caught... well, that was just tough. They were on their own. If they couldn't deal with a few corpses by now, they weren't worth his time. Except they weren't dealing with a few corpses anymore, he saw, they were dealing with hundreds upon hundreds of the fucking things. In his rearview he saw that the gates at the front of Spitalfields Market had been opened, setting free a seemingly endless procession of the dead.

Piotr accelerated and drove forward through the blockade on the other side of the building, knowing there would be far fewer bodies on that side. Those drivers who were able to get to their vehicles followed his lead.

Piotr knew that Taylor was responsible for what had just happened, and he was going to make him pay for it.

Whoever he was.

Wherever he was.

29

The buses rumbled east, making slow progress along streets overfull with corpses. The sun had dragged itself up from below the horizon at last, as if reluctant to illuminate what was left of the world this morning. Better, perhaps, that this endless parade of foul sights should remain shrouded in darkness. Light or dark, it didn't matter; up front it was hard for Sam to see where he was supposed to be going. With so many rotting creatures swarming all around them, it was all but impossible to make out the curves and turns of the road. He took his lead from the buildings on either side, doing what he could to keep the bus equidistant. He should have let Sanjay take the lead, but he had no way of getting a message to him now and, even if he could, there was nowhere on the overcrowded streets to overtake. The corpses covered everything with a bottomless wash of deteriorating human remains. Occasionally he saw built-up drifts of flesh around other buildings like the devastating one that had formed against the front of the hotel. He wondered if there were other survivors trapped inside those places. Even if there were, there was nothing they could do to help them. For now, their focus could only be on themselves.

It was getting even harder to see clearly. As Sam drove through the crowds, crushing, smashing, obliterating anything that got in the way of the bus, the vehicle became increasingly coated in a sheen of gore. The wipers clattered from side to side, but rather than clearing the glass, they just worsened the smears and stains. And the cadavers obscured obstructions, sometimes forcing him to change direction at the last second when he found he could no longer keep moving forward. It was a constant reminder that out here the line between safety and catastrophe was impossibly slender. He thought non-stop about what had happened to Charlie. She'd overshot a junction, nothing more than that, and had paid for it with her life. She'd died just metres away from him, yet hopelessly out of reach. A horrific final image of her was seared into his mind from when they'd loaded up the other buses, hours later. An image of parts of her, anyway. He'd seen the back of her head, and one of her arms stretched outwards and upwards like she was drowning, still signalling for help. Everything else had been obscured from view, buried deep in the toxic slurry of human remains that had filled the bus.

And all she did was overshoot a junction...

It scared Sam to think that one minor lapse in judgement and it could all be over. It scared him even more to think he had responsibility for everyone else too. The lives of all the people in this bus and potentially all those following behind, were in his hands.

'Jeez, watch out,' Omar screamed. He was standing next to the cab, gripping onto the front rail like an impatient commuter waiting for the next stop. Sam had told him repeatedly to go sit down, but he'd refused to move. He pointed into the chaos ahead. 'Watch the road!'

'I can't even see the bloody road,' Sam yelled at him, and they both winced and looked away at the same time when a random corpse pushed its way into a small bubble of space before being ploughed down. Its head smacked against the windscreen, popping like a balloon filled with sticky black blood.

'Gross,' Omar said. He was staring gleefully into the gory mire, the expression on his face equal parts fear, disgust, and wonder. He was really starting to piss Sam off. As if he didn't already have enough distractions.

'Go and sit down,' he shouted again.

'Why?'

'Because you're an annoying little shit and you're putting me off. I thought I told you to travel in the other bus.'

'With him?'

'With who?'

'Gary, the psycho social worker. No thanks.'

'Grow up, you little idiot.'

Omar was about to argue back when the bus clipped the kerb. The entire vehicle jumped up then crashed down hard again. The unexpected jolt threw Omar sideways and he smacked his head. It was the last thing Sam's passengers needed. They'd been unnaturally quiet for much of the journey so far, but were now deafeningly loud in their protests, making so much noise Sam wondered if the dead had somehow managed to get on board.

'Fuck!' Omar said.

'For the last time, will you bugger off and let me concentrate.'

'No, look... that's not good.'

Omar was pointing into the kerb-side wing mirror. Sam squinted through the chaotic movement and immediately saw what was wrong. 'Shit... you're right, that's not good at all.'

The other bus – a bright red block of colour which stood in sharp contrast against the greys and muddy browns of everything else – had stopped. David ran the length of the bus. He'd seen it too.

'I know,' Sam said, before he had chance to speak.

'We need to stop.'

'We can't.'

'But they might—'

'We can't risk it. It's too dangerous. We have to keep going. I don't know what's happened back there, but we have to hope they get it sorted. Sanjay can follow the trail I leave behind. I'll slow down as much as I can, but there's no way we can risk stopping.'

'They're carrying on without us,' Marianne said from her seat just behind Sanjay. Sanjay hadn't noticed. Wasn't interested. He'd got bigger problems to deal with. 'Did you not hear me, Sanjay? They're leaving us behind! They're not stopping!'

'I hear you,' he said under his breath, but his focus was on trying to get his bus moving again. When Sam had oversteered just now,

Sanjay had overcompensated so as not to make the same mistake, and as a result he'd driven through a dip in the road which had been camouflaged by corpses. The dip itself had already been full to the brim with a putrid, semi-solid slurry of body parts and decay. One of the back wheels had sunk into it, and trying to get it free was proving impossible. No grip. Going nowhere. Sanjay accelerated, but they only sank deeper. 'Shit!' he yelled, and he banged his fist against the window in frustration.

The nervous noise building inside the bus was being drowned out by the godawful din coming from outside. Hundreds of corpses clamoured to get closer to the living, spurred on by the relentless whine of the engine. Many of the terrified passengers hadn't been this close to the undead in weeks, and now they were trapped, forced to stare at thousands of them in close proximity. The deterioration in their ghastly appearance proved too much for some, who became hysterical. The last time they'd been up-close, the dead had, by and large, still been recognisably human. Now they were little more than foul caricatures of the people they used to be, hopelessly deformed monsters. Some of the faces that peered into the bus looked like they'd melted, others like they'd been left out in the sun too long and baked. Their colouration was all wrong, and their features were distorted; bulbous eyes, missing eyes. Drooping mouths with swollen tongues and loose, blackened teeth. Noses eaten away by rot... Anyone who'd spent any time in London had been used to a vibrant, multicultural community with people from all walks of life and all corners of the world. Today, all that individuality had been erased. It was as if all the corpses belonged to a single grotesque undead race.

Gary had his face pressed against the window nearest to the stuck wheel, trying to look down. It was so busy out there he could hardly see anything. He pushed through the crowded lower deck to get to the front and speak to Sanjay. 'I'm going out there.'

'And do what?' Sanjay asked. 'Politely ask them to move out of your way? They'll tear you apart, mate.'

'We need to get back there and shove something under the

wheel, see if the tyre can get a grip.'

'Are you serious?'

'Yes. We're desperate.'

'I'll help,' Vicky said. 'If we don't get moving soon, we're dead already. Give us a second then open the back door, Sanj.'

Vicky and Gary grabbed stuff as they made their way back along the bus: coats, bags... whatever they could lay their hands on. When the mechanism hissed as Sanjay opened the back door, those passengers nearest to it scrambled out of the way, fearing the dead would come surging inside at them. Vicky dumped the stuff she'd collected, then took out her crowbar. 'You sort the wheel out. I'll try and hold them off,' she told Gary.

'Got it,' he said, sounding less than confident, and he stepped down into a pool of semi-liquid flesh, sinking almost to his knees. The dead began to snatch and grab at him as he dropped down. On his belly now in the unspeakable filth, feeling bones and body parts shifting under his weight, he started to cram whatever he could get hold of into the space in front of the wheel. Vicky stood guard, swinging her crowbar at any creature that stumbled into range. She was impossibly outnumbered, but her strength and coordination gave her a slender advantage. Several other passengers followed her lead and joined the fray.

'Fuck me,' she said to the footballer Damien who started fighting next to her. 'Things must be bad for you to get off your arse and start fighting.'

Between six of them, they were just about managing to hold the swarming dead at bay and give Gary space to work. He slapped his hand repeatedly against the side of the bus and Sanjay revved the engine and tried to move. The wheel rocked and almost gripped, only to start spinning wildly again, spraying gore behind but still going nowhere. Gary looked up at Selena, who was waiting on the step at the back of the bus. 'Tell Sanj to give me another thirty seconds, then try again,' he said, and she ran down to pass the message to the driver.

All around him now was a protective bubble of his fellow

survivors. More jumped down from the bus and joined the fight, their fear of the dead overcome by their fear of dying out here on this flesh-filled road. They fought with shovels, umbrellas, bags filled with junk, random tools, kitchen pots and pans... it didn't matter as long as whatever they used was hard or heavy or sharp enough to either incapacitate or obliterate. Despite everything, it sickened Vicky to have to do this. It was stupid and illogical, but it bothered her more and more with every single one of them she hacked down. *These were people once. These were people like me. They don't deserve this...*

She was too tired and broken to care about her own safety anymore, but she felt a huge responsibility when Selena reappeared and joined the fight. It made her think about Kath and the promise she'd made to her, then how Kath had sacrificed herself so that she and Selena would have a chance of staying alive. Much as she'd loved Kath, her legacy was a pain in the ass. It was her fault Vicky couldn't just roll over and give up. It was her fault she had to keep fighting.

Gary reached further under the bus and yanked out a troublesome bit of bone – a tibia or fibula... something leg-like – then screwed his face up in disgust and scooped out several more armfuls of the putrid offal. Until now nothing he'd done seemed to make the slightest difference, but at last he felt his hands scraping the tarmac. He wedged more and more dry stuff in front of the tyre then stood up. 'If this doesn't do it, I don't know what will.' He was knackered and soaked with decay. With real effort, he hammered on the side of the bus.

Sanjay accelerated, and with infuriating ease, the vehicle began to move. For a second Gary and the others watched it drive away, exhausted and relieved. Then, remembering it was their sole remaining lifeline, they ran after it, tripping and slipping through the bloody slush.

Vicky was the last to alight. 'All on,' she shouted, and Sanjay put his foot down, making the most of what was left of the tracks the other bus had left behind. The lines Sam's vehicle had carved in the muck had almost disappeared.

30

Piotr and the remains of his army thundered back towards the Monument base, heading for their hidden access point over towards Wapping. He'd counted them all out, and he counted far fewer back in. 'We're missing about ten,' Ruth said. Piotr shook his head, dismissive.

'Some of them will make it back, some of them won't. What about the vehicles?'

'Three down, I reckon,' someone answered.

'Fuck,' he cursed.

Chapman had ridden shotgun on the back of a pick-up truck. 'Did you see it, boss?' he asked. 'Fucker had hundreds of corpses locked in the market. Bastard.'

'Doesn't matter,' Piotr said. 'We got rid of the woman, we destroyed the roadblocks, we took his supplies, and we gave his building to the dead... letting the bodies out of the market was Taylor's final throw of the dice.'

'Yeah, but where is he now?' Ruth asked.

'Who cares? There's only one of him, remember. There are hundreds of us. And there will be even more when those others get here. I want everyone over in Fenchurch Street now, help with the clean-up.'

He marched back towards the centre of the compound. Ruth ran after him. 'Wait, Piotr,' she said.

'What?'

'Can I talk to you?'

'Is it worth me listening? I'm disappointed in you.'

'Me? Why?'

'You even have to ask? The way you handled that woman back there... no, the way you *didn't* handle her. Too soft. And don't forget, we got into this fucking mess because you fucked up with Jonah and Tayyab. I expected more of you.'

'Look, Piotr, I'm trying my best here. That stuff with the woman back there... I used to collect debts door-to-door. It doesn't always work if you go in and start throwing your weight around. If you'd only—'

'So now you're telling me I got it wrong?'

'I didn't say that. It's just sometimes you have to adapt the way you deal with people to suit how they—'

'You *are* telling me I was wrong! I'm supposed to take advice from someone who was beaten by a cripple?'

'You heard what she said. She said she was trying to help us.'

'By firebombing you? By killing Ash?'

'But if she's telling the truth and it was an accident then—'

'Jesus Christ, Ruth.' He walked away again.

'Wait,' she said. 'Piotr, hold on.'

'What?'

'This Taylor guy...'

'Yes.'

'He's still out there.'

'I'm well aware of that.'

'The woman said he'd been here, that he knows where we are and what we've got.'

'So?'

'He's a frigging sniper. He could take us out one by one.'

'He's no sniper, he's just a guy with a rifle who thinks he's something.'

'Sounds like a sniper to me.'

Piotr turned on her. 'You're really starting to piss me off, Ruth. Do you have a point to make?'

'We're surrounded by empty buildings with hundreds of windows. He could be anywhere. He could be watching us right now, about to pull the trigger.'

'You think I haven't thought of that already? We've forced his hand. For what it's worth, I think you're right. He'll come here and we'll lose a few more people, but when he starts shooting, we'll track him down and string him up. One of him, hundreds of us. Now go and do some work and leave the thinking to me. Everything is under control.'

31

Sam had been driving as slowly as he'd dared since they'd lost sight of the other bus, making sure they maintained enough speed to keep moving forward through the sea of death and not be overwhelmed whilst holding back in the hope the others would eventually catch up. Keeping the bus moving took all his concentration, but the distractions were greater than ever. If it wasn't the grotesqueness of the individual cadavers, it was the horror of seeing tens of thousands of them. If it wasn't catching sight of some iconic London building unexpectedly, it was seeing the next famous landmark reduced to a shell. And if it wasn't any of that, it was ever-present thoughts of Charlie and the loss of the other bus that plagued him. Out here, on their own and cast adrift from all safety, the journey felt like a fool's errand. A stupid, dangerous risk too far. He thought it would only be a matter of time before he inevitably let down the remaining people who had trusted him to get them to safety, provided they lived long enough to be let down. Everything else had gone wrong so far, hadn't it?

'Anybody know London well?' he shouted back to the others.

'Parts of it,' Orla replied, getting out of her seat and moving forward.

'What about this part?'

'What do you want to know?'

'Start with the basics. Just tell me where we are and how far we still have to go.'

'We're getting close now. You see those buildings right at the end of this road? Greek or Roman looking? All the columns on the front?'

'I see them.'

'The Bank of England's up there somewhere. A little way beyond that is Bank Station. That's us. Almost there.'

'Thank Christ.'

The bus stopped dead when Sam drove into something hidden by corpses. It was a waist-height 'Keep Right' road sign; an upturned metal U-shape on a raised island. Sam kept the engine running but struggled to work out how to get the bus into reverse so he could shunt back then steer around it.

'Par for the course,' David said under his breath. 'If things can go wrong today, you can bet they will do.'

They'd only been stationary for a few seconds, but that was already time enough for the dead to make their presence known. The bus was surrounded, the engine struggling. Sam found the right gear and was able to roll back, but when he engaged drive and tried to move forward again, nothing happened. They'd lost all momentum. The tyres were just spinning, their treads filled with rot.

'Reckon we could risk getting out and pushing?' David asked, running out of options.

'Push a bus?' Sam said. 'You serious?'

'Too far to make a run for it?' Orla suggested.

'Equally stupid suggestion.'

'You've walked through crowds bigger than this,' David reminded him.

'Yeah, on my own. There's, what, around thirty of us in here? Think they're gonna let that many people walk through without a load of grief? Half of this lot probably don't even know where they're supposed to be going. See, this is what happens when you have a load of folk who—'

'Hold on!' someone shouted from the far end of the bus. Sam looked up and then braced for impact as Sanjay drove the second bus into the back of the first, shunting them forward. He steered around the road sign then pressed down on the accelerator, desperate to keep the momentum, relieved when the heavy vehicle kept moving and the one behind kept following.

'Well, that was a stroke of luck,' he said. 'Thank fuck for that.'

The celebrations inside the bus were deafening, but short-lived. Up ahead, around the general vicinity of the Monument, there was a huge explosion.

32

'What the fuck was that?' Dominic cursed as the explosion rocked the compound. He looked out of the window of the Tower Place boardroom but couldn't immediately see anything other than the frantic reactions of the crowds of people outside.

'I don't know...' Lynette said, equally confused. 'Wait, look over there.'

There was a great pall of dirty black smoke rising up from somewhere beyond the train track. 'Christ, is that—' Dominic started to say before a second explosion silenced him. More smoke billowing now, further west than the first blast. He ran downstairs and collided with Mihai coming the other way.

'What the hell's going on, Dom? Have you seen Piotr? Is this something to do with the work his lot were doing by the—'

Third blast in quick succession. This one was out in the deadlands far beyond the barricades, out towards Bank tube station.

'Ring the breach bell,' Dominic ordered. 'Get people into the Tower.'

'But don't you think we—'

'Now, Mihai. For Christ's sake, we're under attack.'

Dominic sprinted towards the Monument and climbed the three hundred steps to the top. Despite the height, the view was frustratingly limited. He could see the plumes of drifting smoke, but the blast areas were hidden from view by other buildings. Crowds of people were running south from the direction of the clearance work on Fenchurch Street. He saw Piotr down there and yelled at him. 'What did you do!?'

Piotr looked around and then up. He climbed the Monument steps to Dominic and burst out onto the viewing platform, breathless. 'Take it easy. It's just one man. I can handle it.'

'Take it easy? Are you out of your fucking mind? What the hell's going on, Piotr? What did you do?'

'I did what I said I was going to do. It's not like we thought. There was only two people up near Spitalfields, and we killed one of them.'

'Jesus Christ...'

'She was half-dead anyway.'

'But you told me there was about thirty. You told me you were going to keep your distance and stop them if they tried to attack. You said you weren't going to provoke them.'

'Ruth got it wrong. Turns out this is just one fucked-up vigilante who thinks he's some kind of assassin.'

'Who is he? *Where* is he?'

'His name's Taylor, and I don't know where he is. He had a whole crowd of corpses corralled up in the market and he let them loose on us... like I said, it's just one man, Dominic, nothing to worry about.'

'You're telling me those explosions are nothing to worry about? You fucking idiot. I told you something like this would happen. I told you not to pick a fight, you moron.'

'For the last time, it's just one man.'

'Yeah, just one man who's managed to murder three of our people and compromise the safety of everything we've worked hard to build up here. He's undoing everything we've done.'

'It's under control.'

'Under control, how?'

Piotr shook his head. 'We're still safe. He's hit the outer barrier. Nothing's changed. We just need to push the bodies back again.

'We might still be safe, but what about the group that's out on the road? They're never going to get in here now.'

Dominic shoved Piotr out of the way and ran back down the stairs to street level. He pushed through the anxious residents heading towards the Tower of London, ignoring those who tried to stop him to ask for explanations or reassurance, because right now, he couldn't give them either. He climbed up onto the railway bridge to the viewpoint from which he'd watched much of the work being carried out over the last few days. It was just as he'd feared. Gaping holes had been blown in the second-level barricades they'd erected to keep the dead back at a distance from the perimeter of the compound. Now thousands of corpses were pouring through unchallenged.

Days of effort undone in seconds.

Dominic tried to look for answers, for solutions, for explanations... but he was lost. Piotr appeared next to him. 'I know this looks bad, Dom, but it could have been worse. Like I said, we're still safe, and that's all that matters. I'm sorry about the others, but people we already have here come first.'

Dominic didn't react. Instead, he continued looking out over the expanse of open land below him which had been hard fought for and which was now rapidly being lost again. Massive crowds of decaying figures were dragging themselves closer to the railway line, moving with remarkable speed. He knew that this was just what they did, that their behaviours were nothing more than instinctive reactions triggered by sudden changes to their immediate physical surroundings, but Christ, the damn things looked arrogant as hell. He'd seen utter terror in the faces of the survivors he'd passed just now, barely contained hysteria. Among the dead, though, there was nothing. No fear. No emotion. Totally unfazed. They almost had a swagger about them now; loping and striding and slipping and crawling and dragging and stumbling ever closer without a fucking care in the world. It was as if they were saying, 'This is all ours now'.

There was another almighty explosion. Number four. This time it came from the opposite end of the compound. Dominic saw the next pall of smoke rising over the Thames and immediately deduced what had happened. 'London Bridge,' he said, punch-drunk. 'Oh my god, he's blown the blockade on the bridge.'

The implications were devastating.

Hundreds of thousands of corpses on the south bank were now able to flood north across the river unhindered, straight into the heart of the compound. There was no longer anything separating the living from the dead.

33

They kept the buses moving forward because there wasn't anything else they could do. To slow down here or to attempt to change direction would be catastrophic; to turn back, unthinkable. 'What the hell's happening, Orla?' Sam demanded.

'How am I supposed to know? I'm on the bus with you, remember.'

'But those explosions...'

'Do I have to spell it out? I'm here, they're there. I have no idea what happened.'

'Could it have been an accident? Did you keep anything flammable in storage?'

'Nothing that could have gone up like that, I don't think.'

'And not in so many places at once, I guess,' David added, watching the various plumes of oily smoke continuing to billow up into the grey morning sky.

'Some kind of attack?' said Sam.

'Has to be. But from who?'

'The dead?'

'Are you serious?'

'Do you lot even have any weapons that could do that kind of damage?'

'Weapons? We're like you, remember, limited to sticks and stones.'

'Stop clutching at straws. We'll find out soon enough,' David said, frustrated by the pointless conjecture.

From here they should have had a relatively clear run to Bank underground station, but from what they could see over the heads of hundreds of swarming corpses, the entrance to the station had been destroyed, the underground route into the Monument compound now permanently blocked. Thousands of cadavers were converging on the site of the explosion, drawn there first by the noise and then by the reactions of countless others.

'We need to make a decision,' Sam said. 'We're rapidly running out of road.'

The bus was brought to almost a complete stop by the impassable crowds. Behind the wheel of the second bus, Sanjay was sailing blind and only just managed to avoid driving into the rear of the first.

'Is there another way in, Orla?' David asked. Orla was looking around, as if searching for inspiration, but all she could see was rotting flesh. 'Can we get closer to the railway?'

'That's Lombard Street up ahead,' she said. 'That would do it, but there's no way through.'

'We need to do something...' Sam said, still nudging the bus forward, inch by inch.

'King William Street,' she said. 'Take a right here. Keep going and it's right again at the fork in the road.'

Orla pointed the way. At first all Sam could see was another endless confusion of undead movement, but the building frontages again gave him an approximation of the route she was suggesting. 'Where's this going to take us?'

'Keep going down King William Street and we should be right on top of the blockade across Cannon Street. We might be able to get through there, maybe climb over?'

'It's worth a shot,' Sam said.

'It's the only suggestion I've got.'

'Some of us might manage it,' David said, 'but not everyone.'

'If you've got a better idea, I'm all ears.'

King William Street had a gentle downward slope. Sam steered right and accelerated again, finally managing to pick up speed. But even larger crowds were waiting for them down at the junction with Cannon Street.

'I'm starting to think your base might not even exist anymore,' he said.

Orla shook her head. 'I think you might be right. God only knows what's going on here.'

By the time the barrier across the river had been blown, most people had made it to safety inside the Tower of London. Piotr dragged many of them back out again, strong-arming them to help plug the gap and stem the tide of corrupted flesh now streaming into the compound through their brutally ruptured defences on London Bridge. He ordered them to take vehicles from the car lot in the square next to the Tower. Drivers raced through the streets until they were in sight of the furthest advanced corpses, then stopped. They blocked Lower Thames Street and Great Tower Street, ramming cars into each other to seal off the roads and prevent the dead from getting any closer to the Tower. After, more people were press-ganged to fortify the makeshift barriers. They worked with a feverish urgency, realising their personal safety was on the line. It was unlikely any of the corpses would get over the first row of cars, but they kept on building, not taking any risks. The unemotional tenacity of the undead was sobering. Pile things up ten feet tall to try and stop them, and you could still imagine those horrific, diseased fuckers crawling up and over the top.

Dominic and Lynette were standing on the roof of an otherwise empty office block, all marble and glass and odd-shapes and angles. Until today it had been deep in the heart of the compound, earmarked for future expansions, but everything had changed in the last hour. Its position was now on the very edge of their remaining territory, its outer walls forming part of the compound's weakened defences. A great swathe of land had been lost, taken from them with ease by the dead. The number of corpses they could see from up here was incalculable. 'I've never seen so many of them before,' Dominic said.

'Whoever did this knew exactly how to hurt us. They've boxed us in, cut off our escape routes. All the bodies we drove away from here, they've brought back. They're coming at us from all directions at once.'

Lynette was absolutely right.

To the north, tens of thousands that had been held at bay by the second-level barriers had suddenly been released. But their numbers had the potential to be dwarfed by those coming from the other side of the river. The dead on the south bank had been largely ignored for so long because blocking the bridges had been enough to prevent them getting anywhere near the compound. That had been one reason why they'd chosen this place. Having the river along their southern border had given them one less direction to have to defend, but the bridges had always been potential pressure points.

From here they could see that the final blast had blown a gaping hole in the roadblock across London Bridge, the force of the explosion so powerful that many of the vehicles they'd used to block the way had ended up a fair distance away, leaving the way clear for tens of thousands more corpses to march straight into the base. The bridge was an endless procession of rotting flesh along its entire length, no visible end.

'It was the people who killed Ash, wasn't it?' Lynette said.

'Yes.'

'So why did they stop?'

'Who says they have?'

She shook her head. 'They'd have finished us off by now if they wanted to. This could have been so much worse.'

Dominic turned on her, furious. 'How? How could it have been worse? Christ, Lynette, sometimes I think you must be as dumb as those diseased fuckers out there. We're trapped, don't you get it? We can't get out. We can't get food, we can't get supplies... we can't do anything. We're absolutely helpless.'

Lynette was unfazed by his anger. She'd seen it all before. 'Good lord, Dominic! Will you just listen to yourself? It's not all about your precious bloody walls and Piotr's bloody civil engineering projects.'

'What are you on about?'

'None of our people died, as far as we're aware. They didn't bomb the Tower or the offices or the apartment block, did they? Like I said, it could have been a lot worse.'

And she turned her back on him and left him alone on the roof.

34

The further the buses progressed down King William Street, the more their chances of getting into the compound seemed to reduce. The movements of the dead up ahead were more volatile than ever, increasingly unpredictable as the space around them was restricted. 'This is it,' Orla said. 'This is the perimeter of the compound.'

'I see it,' Sam said.

Though most of it was obscured, the top of the barrier the Monument group had erected was visible over the heads of the crowd. It was only a couple of metres tall and looked surprisingly haphazard in its construction, thrown together.

'That's it?' David said. 'That was enough to keep them out?'

'It had been until today,' Orla said.

'But you saw what they did at the hotel.'

'Yeah, but that was when you'd only a couple of rows of bricks keeping you and them apart. Don't forget, we had the advantage of space here. That's why we focused most activity in and around the buildings closest to the Tower, well away from the outskirts. The sound gets harder to locate. They forget we're there. That's also why Piotr's been putting in those second-level defences. We were trying to isolate ourselves.'

'Can we get through?' Sam asked.

'We can try and get over the top, I guess. But like David said, some of these folks will struggle to climb and—'

'No, can I drive through? Do you reckon the bus will do enough damage to make a hole and get us inside?'

'I don't know.'

'It's a heck of a risk,' David said.

'Getting out of bed in the morning is a heck of a risk these days.

249

I'm running out of options here. I need a decision.'

'But if we don't make it?'

'Then we revert to climbing. Those of us who can, anyway. At the very least I'm going to make a fucking mess of things. Even if we don't get all the way through, we'll likely do enough damage to make it easier to get over the threshold.'

'And if we do make it,' Orla said, 'we're home and dry. We'll be safer on the other side of the blockade, and it's not like you're planning to use these buses again, is it? Use them to block up the frigging gap.'

Sam's decision was made. 'Brace!' he shouted, and David turned around to try and make as many people aware as he could before the bus smashed into the perimeter of the base.

He only had a few seconds.

A wedge of bodies bore the brunt of the impact and cushioned the front of the clumsy vehicle as it collided with the barrier. Unsighted, Sam had driven straight and hard. It was good fortune that he'd made contact with a couple of relatively small cars and smashed them backwards, almost managing to punch a hole through.

Almost.

They were wedged half-in and half-outside the base. Stuck.

'What do I do?' Sanjay asked.

Vicky's answer was obvious.

'Ram it. Drive straight into the back of it. Hard as you can.'

The fact the second bus was following, not leading, meant that the short stretch of road between them was relatively free of corpses. Sanjay took full advantage of the space and floored it.

The impact hurled everyone forward. Sanjay snatched his hands away from the wheel, afraid of injuring his arms, and held onto the sides of the cab. The force was horrific, sending passengers flying and screaming in all directions, but it wasn't enough. The first bus moved forward a little, but it was still trapped.

Reverse.

Second attempt.

It was worse the second time around, the awful anticipation adding to the pressure. And although it hurt and although it was frightening, a little whiplash and a few minor abrasions were a small price to pay if they made it through to the other side of the Monument boundary.

'Hold on,' Sanjay yelled, and he put the bus into drive again and motored forward.

Both vehicles burst through, and the contrast on this side of the wall with the chaos they'd been travelling through all morning now was stark. It was pretty much clear, just a handful of bodies which followed them through the gaping hole they'd left in the Monument group's defences.

Up ahead, the other bus stopped. David and several others were already out, gesturing for more people to help them block the breach. They charged at the dead coming the other way and obliterated them with whatever weapons they could find. As they continued to fight, other people began plugging the gap with anything they could lay their hands on. Damien ran over to a car that looked to have only recently been used. The keys were still in the ignition. He drove it over and parked it across the hole. Gary did the same with another vehicle. He got out again and looked around the immediate area. There were signs of clearance work – piles of bodies that had been crushed or hacked to pieces, a digger, hastily improvised cordons across side-streets – but everything appeared abandoned and unfinished. 'I reckon the explosions happened while they were in the middle of doing this,' he said to Damien.

David saw that Orla was walking away from Sam's bus. She was standing in open space, looking down towards the river. 'What is it?' he asked.

'Look.'

Though the land on this side of the barrier had initially seemed to be clear, there were hundreds and hundreds of corpses approaching from the south, all coming this way. Their faces were expressionless, and their movements demonstrated little individual control, but *en masse* like this, they had the appearance of an aggressive marching army.

'Jesus Christ, one of those explosions must have blown the roadblock on London Bridge,' Orla said, sounding terrified. 'There are literally millions of them on the other side of the Thames, and now there's nothing to stop them getting through.'

David looked as far into the distance as he could. Orla's fears were completely justified. He could see all the way down to London Bridge and beyond. There was an apparently endless number of corpses coming towards them.

'At least we're inside the base. Which way now?' he asked.

Orla shook her head. 'We can't assume it's a straight run. They'll already know the bridge is lost and they'll have put temporary barriers in to stop the dead getting to the Tower. I still think the railway line is our only option. Fenchurch Street Station. They were supposed to be clearing the road for us.' She gestured further up the road to the north. 'We go up here, then right at that box junction up ahead.'

'Let's get everybody back on the buses and move,' David said. He could hear Sam revving his engine in anticipation.

'I've already seen it,' Sam said when he got back on the bus. 'That's not good.'

'Orla reckons Fenchurch Street Station is our best bet. I'll tell Sanjay and—'

'Wait,' Sam interrupted. 'There's another problem.' He accelerated again, but the bus didn't move. 'I think I fucked it driving through the barrier. We need to get everybody onto the other bus before that crowd reaches us. We need to get everyone onto Sanjay's bus and keep moving.'

'I can have a look at the engine. It's probably something just—'

'There's no time and no need. We can do it in one bus no trouble. There's more than enough space.'

David weighed up their options, realised they had none, then leant out and beckoned Sanjay over. Sanjay squeezed the front of his bus through the narrow gap between Sam's wreck and the pavement railings, then stopped when the two cabs were level. 'We're down to one bus,' David told him. 'Do you know how to get to Fenchurch Street Station?'

'Course I do. I was a bloody bus driver.'

'Good. Drive forward and open your doors so we can get everyone onboard.'

Sanjay nodded and did as he was instructed.

'We need everyone to load onto the other bus,' David shouted to Sam's passengers. 'Move quickly. Grab whatever you can get hold of and shift. We don't have a lot of time.'

Sam continued revving the engine aggressively, doing what he could to distract the nearest of the dead. Their pace was glacial, but there were thousands of them. He watched for signs of them taking the bait and was relieved when a number of the furthest forward began to drift towards his bus, ignoring everything else.

It was like a wall of death advancing towards them. The figures were far removed from everything that was human. Their movements were awkward and forced, their spatial awareness limited. Individually they were nothing, but together they were all consuming. A dead man at the front of the crowd started to slow down, but those around showed no mercy or concern when he tripped and fell and was trampled underfoot. Different creatures automatically assumed his position at the head of the pack without a single thought or any communication. Elsewhere, the dishevelled monsters fought amongst themselves, those that were more intact ripping at the putrefying flesh of weaker creatures to cement their advantage and be among the first to reach the living. The driven intensity they were displaying now was terrifying, their own physical condition of secondary importance to their desire to attack.

Sam stared deep into the oncoming masses. What hope did he and the others have against an enemy so dispassionate and completely driven to destroy?

The cross-over was completed quickly. With the first few bodies now uncomfortably close, the group had been forced to leave plenty of supplies and provisions behind. 'Doesn't matter,' Vicky said to David. 'We can replace all of it. It's only the people we need to be bothered about.'

Omar held back, waiting for Sam. He rapped his knuckles on the Perspex of the driver's cab, nervous. 'Come on, Sam. Time to go.'

'Get yourself on that bus, mate. I'm right behind you.'

Just the two of them left now. Sam got out of his cab and gestured for Omar to go across to where Vicky was waiting for him at the back of Sanjay's bus. 'This is messed up,' Omar said, craning his neck to look back at the oncoming hordes, so close they could make out what was left of their disfigured faces.

'Tell me about it,' Sam replied. Then he stopped. 'Shit. Sorry, I left something back in the cab. Go with Vicky, mate. I'll catch up.'

'Okay, Sam.'

It happened so quickly that no one realised what he was doing until it was done. Sam jumped back into the cab of the first bus, operated the control to shut the door behind him, then leant on the horn and drove away. He turned the bus towards the oncoming mass of bodies, then accelerated.

Omar tried to run, but Vicky caught his arm and pulled him onto the other bus. 'He told me the bus was broke.'

'I know, Omar.'

'He lied to me,' he screamed, hammering at the door with anger. 'He's a fucking liar!'

'What the hell is he doing?' David asked.

'Whatever he wants to do, same as always,' Vicky said.

Omar was sobbing. 'But he told me—'

'I know what he told you,' Vicky said, cutting across him. 'Sanjay, drive! Just go!'

The two buses were now moving in opposite directions, the distance between them increasing rapidly. The endless swarms of dead bodies were only interested in Sam's bus and he sounded the horn again and again and again to make sure that interest didn't wane. Sanjay's bus was all but ignored as he drove away from the river and the advancing dead army, taking advantage of the clearest roads they'd driven along all morning. Omar stayed at the back of the vehicle, his face pressed against the glass, watching Sam's bus as it picked up speed and hurtled towards the dead.

Sam gripped the wheel tight and tried to focus on London Bridge ahead of him, not on the corpses he was crushing and smashing and grinding into the road as he accelerated into the crowd.

Of all the places to end up, why did it have to be bloody London? He'd always hated the city and everything it represented. To be doing what he was doing in the shadow of the Shard and other modern corporate landmarks, symbols of the greedy capitalism he so despised, felt like a cruel irony. *But then again*, he thought, *maybe it is the perfect place to make my last stand*.

His intention, first and foremost, had been to distract the dead and give the others a fighting chance of getting to Fenchurch Street station, but he had an opportunity to do more than that. He was going to try and stem the endless flow of death that threatened to overwhelm everything, but he hadn't bargained on how difficult the road was going to be to seal off. There were two lanes in either direction, with a central reservation made impassable by regularly spaced streetlamps. Anti-terrorist barriers on the wide pavements on either side further narrowed his options. Fortunately, the progress of the dead was impeded by virtue of their massive numbers. Hundreds of them were being funnelled through a relatively narrow space that looked, from this speed and this distance at least, small enough that he'd be able to block it with the bus.

He was committed now, surrounded by death on all sides. There was no alternative. No going back. If he didn't do this, they'd keep coming and the Monument base would eventually be lost. He thought back to the hotel and what had happened there. *Maybe the base is lost anyway?* He hoped he'd give the others a fighting chance, but maybe he was just delaying the inevitable.

It was something of a relief not to have to fight anymore, actually. He'd never much fancied the idea of being sealed away with that arrogant arsehole Dominic Grove, truth be told. It had always felt like a bad idea. Sam didn't like locking himself away, full stop.

His elevated driving position gave him a clear view all the way across the bridge, and all he could see was death. More corpses than ever. Endless in number and with only one goal, they were a corrupted, unregulated, and utterly horrific occupying force.

He accelerated again.

Corpses flew in all directions as he ploughed into them. He could feel the vehicle threatening to run away with itself, the tyres struggling to grip the road as more and more emaciated figures were dragged under its wheels. Sunlight glinted off the top of the towering Shard, distracting him temporarily. He bumped up the central reservation and took out a lamppost, then steered back the other way and crashed down heavily onto the carriageway.

Not far now. All he could hear was a constant *thud, thud, thud*, as the dead smacked against the front of the bus like flies. He locked his arms and aimed for the hole in the roadblock.

There was a shallow blast crater in the road. Sam remembered thinking that whoever had planted the bomb must have been a pro, because they'd destroyed the barricade but left the bridge and the road intact. It was a pointless, fleeting thought. He steered hard to the left, hoping somehow to slide in the fleshy mire and plug the gap sideways, but then the bus began to lean. He instinctively leant back the opposite way to counterbalance, but it was already past the point of no return. It crashed over onto its side, crushing many more bodies. The hole in the blockade hadn't been completely filled, but such a small gap remained that the dead blocked the rest of it themselves. Incensed by the increased noise of the bus, so many of them surged forwards at once that they became wedged and couldn't get through, a densely packed scab.

Sam wasn't aware of any of this.

Sam was gone.

35

There were bodies up near Fenchurch Street too, but in nothing like the numbers they'd had to deal with previously. Sanjay was feeling the pressure, which had increased disproportionately once Sam had disappeared. Now there was no question; it was all on him.

He was disorientated, on the cusp of convincing himself he might miss the station turning. The noise in the bus wasn't helping. He could barely hear himself think and needed reassurance. 'We got any ex-commuters on here?' he shouted over the din. 'I could do with some help up here.'

Marianne pushed through the overcrowded chaos to get up front. She'd spent much of the horrific journey so far doing what she could to avoid looking outside, but there was no escaping it now. She looked out through the huge windscreen, wipers still flicking from side to side to clear away the gore. When they'd been driving through crowds of thousands, it had been easier to convince herself that the featureless masses in the streets were anything but human. Now that their numbers were massively reduced, though, their individual shapes were easier to discern. Up here front and centre, there was no escaping the fact they had once been people. Stick like figures, moving on their own and in small groups, dripping with decay, continued to throw themselves at the bus. Surely, she thought, hypnotised by the horror of it all, if they had retained any ability for comprehension (and they must have, because they were walking and reacting, weren't they?) then they would have known they were staggering towards oblivion... what was it they craved? Vengeance?

'This is right, isn't it?' Sanjay asked. 'Hard to tell with so much going on around here.'

'Give me a second...'

She could understand why he needed validation. Nothing looked like it used to. All the detail of the world had been blurred with an oily filter of grime. There were weeds in the gutters, packs of rats feasting on corpses without a care, rusting vehicle wrecks... It had been less than two months, but already it looked like nature was greedily reclaiming the city.

Sanjay was getting frustrated. 'You do know where Fenchurch Street Station is, don't you? I can't risk missing another wrong turning. The last one cost Charlie her life.'

'I used to use Fenchurch Street all the time. There's a tribunal just around the corner and—'

'I don't need your life story, Marianne, just a little validation.'

She continued to scan their crumbling surroundings, trying to make sense of the madness. And then she saw a set of traffic lights. She'd overlooked them at first because she'd expected them to be lit, and though they were dull and dark, she used them as a marker. They were close to the junction with Fenchurch Street.

'Turn right,' she said.

'When?'

'Now!'

Sanjay swung the front of the bus around, and when he glanced out of his side window, he saw that even though Sam had done what he could to block the road further down, there was still a multitude of corpses coming their way. It was a relief when the bus pulled into Fenchurch Street and the buildings blocked his view.

'This is definitely right,' Marianne told him. 'It's maybe a quarter of a mile down here...'

She was beginning to find focus in the shapes of the buildings and the lines of the road. On their right, a hundred metres or so ahead, rose the enormous, curved block of 20 Fenchurch Street, a building known locally as the Walkie Talkie. She looked up and was reassured by the familiarity of its unusual shape, the way its highest floors seemed to hang out over the road. Just for a moment it was as if she'd been allowed to peek back into the world she remembered, the world they'd all lost.

Sanjay literally brought her crashing back into reality.

There was a car on its side straddling the road up ahead. No time to stop or go around, he accelerated into the rear of the wreck and sent it pivoting around, taking out a handful of staggering bodies in the process.

'This is it,' Marianne shouted, her voice amplified by adrenalin and nerves. 'Right again.'

Up ahead now, partially obscured by detritus and decay, Sanjay saw the mid-nineteenth century station façade. There were newly formed piles of rubble here and abandoned vehicles which had been moved to the sides of the road; telltale signs of the other group's clean-up operations. But there were more of the dead too, scores of them trapped in the area immediately around the building.

'Can you ram the entrance?' David shouted from a little way back. 'See if you can get the front of the bus inside?'

'If I can get up enough speed I can try,' Sanjay said.

'Don't!' Marianne told him. 'You won't get through.' She pointed out a line of equally spaced, black-painted traffic bollards, installed specifically to stop idiots from driving vehicles into the front of major stations. 'Christ, the whole damn world is against us. Even the bloody safety barriers are stopping us getting safe.'

'We're not going to get much closer,' Sanjay shouted, loud enough so everyone could hear. He stopped abruptly. The brakes hissed, and the dead immediately began to converge on the bus. They were emerging from a multitude of hiding places, drawn out into the open by the engine noise like they'd been woken from hibernation.

'Sweet Jesus,' Marianne said. 'They're everywhere.'

They were dragging themselves out from the shadow-filled mouths of every side-street and alleyway. It felt as if every dead body left in the whole of the capital was converging on this particular spot at this exact moment.

Sanjay tried to shunt the bus as far forward as he could, pushing its snub nose deeper into the carnage around the station, but he could only manage centimetres when they were still several metres short, and every slight acceleration continued to rile up the rancid crowds.

David yelled for quiet, then barked out instructions. 'Just get into the station. Help each other. Make sure you pick up a weapon and if you have to fight, fight.'

The doors hissed open, and he led the charge with a baseball bat, flying towards the nearest corpses and swinging at them wildly. Others followed, and an uneven protective bubble was formed between the side of the bus and the front of the station. David dealt with several bodies with ease, clubbing at their skulls and taking each of them out with a single swipe, but at the back of his mind he knew no matter how many he hacked down, there were thousands more ready to take their place. It would take an army of fighters like him to maintain holding them back, and there were fewer than fifty people on the bus. He didn't know how long he'd be able to keep up this pace. Thirty seconds in and only half that number of kills, and he was already gasping for air. His clubbing arm was heavy as lead.

Marianne scrambled through the decay to reach the nearest station door. She'd used this place an incalculable number of times over the last few years, but today it felt alien and unfamiliar. She pushed the door, expecting it to open easily like it always did, but it was stuck, wedged shut by more dead flesh on the other side. She knew from the scuffling, shuffling sounds coming from inside that the station wasn't going to be the safe haven she'd hoped, but there was no alternative. She dropped her shoulder and shoved hard. Other people began pushing with her, and others pushed the pushers.

Marianne and the man standing next to her shoved the door at the same time and it opened inward, the gap just wide enough for them both to squeeze through. They ran straight into a crowd of restless corpses that had been trapped inside the building for almost two months. They seemed stronger than those outside, somehow less decayed. It was impossible to gauge their numbers. They just fought and kept fighting.

Back out front, at the rear of the abandoned bus, Gary saw that Damien was being overwhelmed by a sudden swell of undead movement. He went to fight alongside him, striking out with a carving knife he'd grabbed when he'd got off the bus. He slashed wildly at them, crisscrossing their putrid flesh, but the blade's impact was negligible. The corpses didn't react, barely even noticed. They just kept coming at him. He turned around to see why Damien had stopped fighting, but the footballer had given up and fled for the station, leaving Gary exposed. In the few seconds he'd been distracted, the nearest cadavers rushed forward again, and he lost his footing. He was on his back looking up, and he curled into a ball as the dead filled the space where he'd been. He covered his head and face to protect himself from the feet that trampled around him and from the putrefaction which dribbled from their emaciated frames. He rolled over onto his front, but all he could see in every direction was more of them. He started to crawl away, then realised he was moving towards the back of the bus, not the front. He managed to turn around, but they were so tightly packed it took an age and he struggled not to panic, doing everything he could to silence the voice in his head, screaming at him that if he didn't get to the station fast, it would be too late. *The others will barricade the door as soon as they are inside*, he thought. That was what he'd have done.

The dead were falling apart around him, eviscerating each other as they advanced towards the ruckus around the station entrance. Liquid gore rained down, drenching him again. He finally reached one of the black concrete crash barriers and tried to pick himself up, only for more of them to force him back down. On his knees now, they were all he could see. Wave after wave after foetid, rancid wave.

He could hear voices though. Sanjay was near, fighting to get the last few of the group through the door. Gary finally dragged himself back to his feet and lurched towards the front of the station, but he was out of position, way over to one side. He felt his way along the wall until he reached the edge of the group. He tried to get Sanjay's attention, but he was lost in the madness of everything else. All Sanjay saw was more of the dead and he lashed out at the crowd. In the next surge, Gary hit the ground again. Desperate now, well aware the effect any noise would have on the dead hordes, he screamed for help.

Vicky was dragging Omar through the door by the scruff of his neck when he heard someone still outside and stopped. Vicky was distracted, and he squirmed free and went back the other way. A blood-soaked figure came at him at waist height, scrambling through the disintegrating remains of others with unparalleled ferocity, and Omar lifted the wrench he'd been carrying as a weapon, ready to smash it into the foul thing's face.

'Don't, Omar. It's me.'

Without hesitation Omar dropped the wrench and grabbed Gary's gore-covered shoulders, trying to pull him free from the mass of cadavers he'd become a part of. With everyone else now inside the building, the entire repugnant crowd turned on Gary and Omar. Omar was losing his grip. He let the station door swing shut behind him then wrapped his other arm around one of the security bollards, refusing to let Gary go.

Just inside the station, Vicky looked around for Omar. 'Where'd that little bugger go?'

She could hear him kicking against the other side of the door. She forced it open again, saw him clinging desperately onto the bollard. She lunged forward, assuming that Omar was the one being dragged back into the crowd, then saw Gary's terrified face and realised what was happening. She called for help. Damien put his arms around her waist, and between the two of them they hauled Gary and Omar to safety.

Relative safety.

Vicky slammed the station door shut, blocking the hordes from view. The creatures outside were so tightly packed together now that they appeared as a single unending mass of decaying flesh, something snatched from a Lovecraftian nightmare. A wave of death broke against the front of the station. No longer being held back, they flooded forward, smothering the building with decay and blocking the light inside. It reminded Vicky of how they'd overrun the hotel earlier, and it chilled her to the bone because they never gave up. No matter what happened, no matter how badly broken or decayed they were, they remained resolute. Stoic. Unstoppable. They displayed no emotion, and yet when she looked into their horrifically disfigured faces, she felt nothing but pure hate.

Gary was gasping for breath. He peeled off his sodden jacket and used the inner lining to wipe his face and hands. Damien handed him a bottle of water and, shaking and nearly choking on it, he drank half then poured the rest over his head to wash off some of the gore. 'You hurt?' Damien asked him.

'Don't think so. No thanks to you, you prick.'

'What's that supposed to mean?'

'I went to help you, and you just fucked off and left me to it.'

'It was crazy, mate. I couldn't see what was happening.'

'Really? I don't think you give a shit about anybody else who—'

'Not now,' David said.

'There was too bloody many of them,' Damien explained. 'I couldn't see shit past my own hands.'

'Not now,' David said again. 'Seriously, just shut up. Keep the bloody noise down.'

He looked around, finally starting to make sense of the shadows. He'd naively expected the street entrance to take them straight into the station proper, but it didn't. It was a relatively small, enclosed space, with a single staircase alongside two long-since motionless escalators straight ahead which, he presumed, would get them to the platforms. The remains of freshly battered corpses littered the ground, and at the foot of the escalators was an enormous mound of trapped flesh that had accumulated over time as many of the cadavers wandering the station space upstairs had dropped down.

'Have we got everyone?' Gary asked.

'Don't know,' Vicky replied. 'Hard to tell.'

The conversation was interrupted by another random corpse making an undignified descent down the escalator. It tried to climb over the heap of flesh to get closer to the living. David quickly dealt with it with a swing of his baseball bat. He looked up as two more of them tumbled down from the upper level. There were even more behind. Faint light upstairs revealed more constantly crisscrossing shadows.

'What now?' Vicky asked, lowering her voice to a whisper.

'This is quite a small station,' Marianne explained. 'Only four platforms.'

'Small is good.'

'Busy, though. It would have been heaving when everyone died. Peak rush hour.'

'Great.'

'Can we get moving?' Gary asked. 'I'm frigging freezing.'

'We go that way, I guess,' David said, pointing to the top of the escalators.

'Yep. Then just head for the platforms. Any of them will do,' Marianne confirmed.

'From what we saw when we were here before, we just need to get down onto the railway lines. Once we're on the tracks we should be able to get into the compound.'

'If there's anything left of it,' Orla added unhelpfully.

They began to carve a way through the mound of corpses at the bottom of the staircase. Sanjay started to dig through the revolting mass of flesh with a shovel he'd taken from the bus. Near the bottom of the pile, the pressure had crushed the lowest corpses. The blade of the shovel cut through compacted, mud-like, once-human remains. Other people picked up individual corpses and dragged them out away, dumping them like sacks of rubbish, no thought for dignity or respect. There was teeming movement throughout the muck. Masses of insects, worms, and maggots were revealed. A rats' nest in a hollow was disturbed. Some of the dead bodies, even those buried deep, still juddered and twitched.

Once a path through the mound had been cleared, the group began to climb the stairs. Some were quicker than others. Some couldn't wait to get to the end of their journey, while others were traumatised, too afraid to take another step forward without being pushed. David urged the most reluctant of them to move. 'Come on,' he said, 'we're almost there. The hard part's done.'

Vicky dragged another corpse out of the way and reversed into Selena. 'Sorry, love. You okay?'

Selena nodded, uncharacteristically enthusiastic. 'Sooner we get this done, the sooner we can start planning to get to Ledsey Cross like Kath said.'

Vicky could only nod and smile. She couldn't bring herself to burst Selena's bubble and tell her that she was fairly certain they would never leave London. If she was honest with herself, leaving the city had felt like a pipe dream all along, and after the hell they'd been through today to travel barely a couple of miles, getting to Yorkshire sounded like a trip to the moon. Vicky wished she could be as trusting as the kid, free and unbound. She watched Selena race up the stairs, overtaking everyone else. *All she's been through, and she still keeps going...*

But then she stopped.

She was almost at the top of the staircase, just at the point where her head was level with the first floor. She froze, turned around and tried to go back the other way, but there were too many people close behind and she was stuck. Vicky forced her way up through the crowd to get to her. 'What's wrong?'

'Don't go up there, Vic,' Selena warned, but Vicky knew she had to.

There was another wedged mass of tangled corpses stretched right across the top of the escalators and stairs, a fleshy dam. Beyond this obstruction, the rest of the station was packed with decay. All of their potential escape routes had been sealed.

The bodies at the top of the steps had prevented more of them dropping down to the street level entrance, and the ticket barriers had stopped them getting onto the platforms and the tracks beyond. It was impossible to accurately gauge numbers, but Vicky guessed there were over a thousand corpses trapped in the limited confines of the station concourse. Occasionally the pressure of the shifting crowds forced one of the lethargic figures up and over.

David joined her up on the top step. 'Oh, fuck.'

'That's an understatement.'

'How are we supposed to get through that lot?'

'You tell me. I'm all out of ideas.'

Omar had wormed his way up now to try and see what was going on. Half David's height, he stood up and looked out. 'Fuck me,' he said under his breath.

'Get back down, mate,' David told him. 'Too risky up here.'

'We could do with Sam right about now. He'd know what to do.'

'Yeah, well, Sam's gone.'

'He'd get them lot to go downstairs so we can go up.'

David and Vicky looked at each other. 'That might actually work,' David said.

'We could try and force the bodies down the escalators and relieve the pressure up top,' Vicky suggested. 'Can't think of a better idea right now.'

'But there's less room down there than there is up here.'

'It would reduce their numbers at least, give us a fighting chance.'

'Hell of a risk. I can't see us getting through.'

'What other option do we have? We can't get back out through the station entrance. The only way we can go now is forward.'

'Can't we just—' Omar started to say, but Vicky wasn't finished.

'There's got to be another way we can thin them out. What if a few of us try to get over to the other side, maybe? Take out a couple of ticket barriers, then lead the dead out onto the tracks.'

'What, and risk dumping a ton of corpses into the compound?

The same compound we're trying to get into? That's going to mightily piss Dominic Grove and his pals off, if they're even still there.'

'Dumb idea,' Omar said, annoyed that he'd been silenced. The others still weren't listening.

'You're right, though,' David said, 'we don't have any other option. Get as many of the dead down onto ground level as we can, then see where we go from there.'

'Agreed.'

David went back down several steps to talk to the others. 'We've got a problem.'

'Tell me something I don't already know,' Marianne said.

'There are loads of them trapped up there. Dominic did tell us they hadn't done anything with this place because it was pretty well sealed up.'

'And you decide to tell us this now?'

He ignored her and continued. 'The only way we can see to get rid of them is to force as many as we can downstairs to reduce the pressure, then make a run for it. We'll stick to the staircase, then try and funnel the dead down the escalators.'

'Seriously?' Damien said from the middle of the crowd.

'Yes, seriously. Keep as close together as you can, and if any of them come at you, kick the fuckers down to the ground floor. Got it?'

He took their silence as agreement.

David, Sanjay and Vicky climbed over onto the escalators. Working almost blind in the minimal light, they began to disassemble the blockage which prevented the dead up there from dropping down. Sanjay shoved his hand deep into the mess of remains. He screwed his face with disgust and rooted around in the jelly-like slime for something he could grab hold of and pull. He wrapped his hand around a bone and yanked it towards him, doing everything he could not to think about what he was holding on to. The other two began doing the same, dragging parts of corpses out and hurling them down the escalators.

Endless grabbing hands reached out for them from above, the dead reacting, snatching at the air just above their heads. Vicky caught one of them by the arm and threw it down the escalator like a martial arts master.

Sanjay had his hand wrapped around another bone that was stubborn and wouldn't budge. There were masses of them, and their jumbled pile reminded him of jackstraws, an ancient kids' game he remembered. He adjusted his position then gave it a hard yank towards him. The dam burst. Vicky grabbed him and pulled him to safety as an avalanche of rot rolled down the escalator. Some of the dead that rushed forward were so decayed as to almost appear liquid, flowing unevenly down the metal steps, spurting down under immense pressure. Other, more recognisable body shapes began to fall as the creatures filling the station concourse surged through the gap.

David scrambled over the divide between the escalators and the staircase, then helped the others to get back. 'Well, that seemed to work,' he said.

The relief was short-lived. One of the people nearest to the bottom of the steps shone a torch into the crowds of fallen dead. They were up and moving with surprising speed and tenacity. Vicky immediately understood why.

'They've been shut away in here, protected from the wind and the rain and everything else that's eating away at them outside,' she said, still breathless.

'But they're still dead. They're still rotting,' Sanjay protested.

'Yes, but some of them look like they've deteriorated far more slowly.'

There was hardly any room to move on the staircase, and those people stuck at the bottom of the steps were now doing everything they could to climb higher. The fallen dead were dragging themselves upright to attack the living. 'We need to keep moving,' Marianne said to David, stating the obvious.

'Don't you get it? We can't.'

'We have to,' she hissed back at him.

Gary was down at the bottom, too tired to climb. He did what he could to restore some order, but the desperate souls around him were broken people, ruined people, and they had nothing left. They'd been forced out into the open today and offered a lifeline to get to the Monument group, but every turn they took just led them to another dead end.

One of the corpses grabbed hold of a woman's ankle. She screamed and tried to get away, dragging the cadaver along with her. Other people recoiled, primarily interested in self-preservation. Gary grabbed hold of the dead thing and prised its fingers open, then kicked it back down. The woman was hysterical. He tried to cover her mouth and she bit down on his hand. He yelled out with surprise and pain, his cries loud enough to fill the whole damn station.

At the top of the stairs, David shone a torch out over the constantly rippling crowd. He made no effort to stay hidden any longer. There was no point. The damage had already been done.

Marianne was next to him. 'Christ, David, what do we do?'

He didn't answer; there was nothing he could say. The ruckus at the bottom of the staircase continued, and the reaction of the mass of cadavers on the crowded concourse above them increased. Out front, more corpses hammered against the station entrance, desperate to get at the living trapped inside.

David's torch only illuminated the closest of the undead, but he knew that what he was seeing here would likely be replicated throughout the entire station tomb. Not only were the dead fighting with each other to get closer to the light and noise on the staircase, but the release of pressure at the top of the escalators had also caused them to surge. That surge had, in turn, resulted in another bottleneck forming as hundreds of corpses tried to force their way through a gap only wide enough for a few at a time.

Marianne dragged David back down. Most of the group were bunched together in a huddled mass in the middle of the staircase, packed in tight. At the bottom, he saw Gary repeatedly lashing out at corpses, but for every one of them he destroyed, there were many more ready to take its place.

'We're fucked,' David said, keeping his voice low.

'There must be something we can do,' Orla whispered, close behind him.

'You think? We're trapped. No way up, no way down. Stranded.'

'We can try again later, can't we?' she suggested. 'Wait for them to calm down and forget we're here?'

'We're long past that being an option,' David said. 'Have you not heard them? They're hammering on the front of the station down there, and they're fighting with each other up here. It's self-perpetuating. It'll take days for them to quieten down, and as soon as we make a move, we'll set them off again. Back to square one.'

'Is everyone safe?' Vicky asked. 'As safe as we can be, anyway.'

'I'm not even sure if everyone's here,' David said.

'There's nothing we can do for them if they're not,' Sanjay said, dejected.

There was another ripple of movement on the staircase as someone buried in the middle of the group climbed up. It was Selena. 'Anyone seen Omar?'

36

He was on his hands and knees, crawling through a dark and terrifying forest of decaying legs which seemed endless. Omar had climbed into the crowd when no one else was looking, figuring he'd do what Sam would have done. No way would Sam have just been sitting in the dark waiting for help to come. No way would Sam have let them get into a mess like this without a get-out plan. Omar had tried to tell them, but no one wanted to listen.

The floor was slippery, and it stank. When Omar's hand slid from under him, he ended up flat on his belly with the dead walking over him, not even knowing he was there. He had his face pushed right into the toxic slop now. He wanted to throw up or scream, but he knew he couldn't do either. He felt one of them put its foot right in the middle of his back, and he bit down on his lip to stop himself from yelling out in pain. As soon as it stepped off him he started to move again, sliding across the station floor on his belly.

He could hear the others panicking and fighting. Didn't they get it? Hadn't they listened to anything Sam had told them? Idiots. They just needed to shut up and wait.

Daylight.

Finally.

It felt like he'd been doing this for hours. The light was intermittent, visible now and then between the crisscrossing legs. He wanted to get up and run and had to stop himself. *Not yet; not close enough.* He put his hand in something awful and slid again but he didn't shout and he didn't scream and he didn't panic.

He just kept moving, head down.

He smacked the top of his head against a ticket barrier and

yelped with pain, then curled up into a ball and covered his mouth with his slime-covered hands. Had any of them heard him? He screwed his eyes shut, not wanting to look, but eventually he had to.

Safe.

No reaction.

No problem.

He braced himself, knowing that the second they saw him, everything would change.

He tried counting down from ten but got halfway then bottled it. He didn't want to move. He was scared - terrified – and now he wished he hadn't been so stupid. He should have stayed with the others. He should have stayed safe.

He remembered last time he'd been planning to stay safe. He'd spent weeks on his own in the flat, just waiting, and if he hadn't spotted Sam that day, he might still have been there.

If he hadn't spotted Sam, they'd have never got to the hotel. And if they hadn't got to the hotel, the others probably would never have ended up coming here. And if they hadn't come here, then when the dead bodies had broken into the hotel, this lot would likely have been killed.

It struck Omar that sitting back and playing it safe just wasn't going to cut it anymore. Sam had proved that again today.

Omar knew he had to man up.

Before he could talk himself out of it again, he got to his feet, pushed away the corpses that lashed out at him, then clambered up onto the top of the ticket barrier, ready to jump.

Just as he leaned forward, the dead pulled him back into the rotting crowd.

They were all over him in a heartbeat, yanking at his clothes and hair, scratching at his skin. Omar started thrashing and kicking and punching... fighting back and doing anything he could do to break free. He pulled one arm out of the sleeve of his jacket, then slid the other one out, then fell forward and hit the deck.

No way are you going to beat me, you dead fuckers.

He scrambled back up and hurled himself over the barrier before any of the corpses could react. One of them caught his ankle. He kicked out and felt his foot make contact with a dead thing's chin. It let go and he slid over the other side of the metal barrier and dropped down. He hit the ground hard, but the pain didn't register. He was in open space at last. Omar picked himself up and staggered away from the endless sea of monstrous faces that glared back at him with utter hatred in their dark, sunken eyes. But was it hatred...? It could have been pain, agony. Part of him almost felt sorry for them. What had happened wasn't their fault, was it? They reached out for him, furious that he'd escaped while they remained trapped, pinned behind the line of ticket barriers. More of them thudded against the metal and glass, crushing those in front and preventing any of them getting through.

Omar turned and raced to the end of an empty platform, then jumped down and ran along the tracks, his feet churning the gravel between the rails. There was a derailed train ahead of him, its upturned carriages blocking the line, dozens of dead commuters inside, still fighting for release. He dropped down and crawled again, flattening himself to squeeze through a gap under a carriage on its side that looked impossibly narrow. Emaciated hands hammered against the windows above him, vacant eyes continuing to watch his every move. Omar picked himself up and ran on again, the way ahead now completely clear.

He stopped when he heard voices.

There were people close, very close, but he didn't know where or how to get to them. He leant over one side of the tracks, but all he could see was more death, another endless crowd, tens of thousands strong, corpses filling the streets, stretching away forever. His heart sank. If this was the place they'd fought to get to, then there'd been no point. It was as dead here as everywhere else. Dejected, he crossed the tracks and looked over the other side.

Now Omar saw space.

And he saw people.

Living people.

He ran back the other way until he found a way of getting down to street level, a makeshift metal staircase. He didn't think, he just kept running, looking for someone to help him. But they all looked as scared and confused as the people he'd left behind in the station. The air was filled with the familiar sounds of panic. Was this the safe haven they'd been so desperate to reach?

Directly ahead, he saw the Tower of London. He recognised it from a school trip a couple of years ago. The building looked the same as he remembered, but nothing else looked like it had back then. He ran towards the Tower then pulled up when a car raced across in front of him. The driver blasted their horn and Omar stopped, realising he was in the middle of a road. It had been so long since he'd seen traffic...

'What the hell are you doing?' a woman on the other side of the road shouted at him, on her way to the Tower. She gestured for him to follow her and he did, only catching up as she disappeared through the ancient building's entrance. He stopped running, stunned. There was a crowd of people in here that seemed ten times bigger than the size of the group he'd turned with today.

'Omar?'

The mention of his name cut through all the noise and confusion of everything else. He looked around and saw a man he thought he recognised. It was that irritating old guy he'd met in the church with Sam.

'What's going on, Stan?' the woman Omar had just been following asked.

'This lad... he was with my lot. Christ, Lynette, they must have made it after all.'

'We need to tell Dominic. Someone go find him.'

'Where are the others?' Stan asked Omar.

'Trapped. They're stuck in the train station.'

37

The people on the staircase were increasingly hemmed in, the dead closing in on them both from above and from below. At the bottom of the stairs, more corpses continued to climb, while up on the concourse, countless more of them surged towards the top of the escalators. For the living, there was no escape in any direction. To their right, the escalators had become clogged with death. To their left, a sheer drop back down to ground level. The group was confined to a progressively limited space, almost fifty of them trapped on just a few steps.

Gary stood up. Marianne grabbed his arm and tried to pull him back down. 'What are you doing?'

'Leaving.'

'But you can't...'

'What's the alternative, Marianne? Shall I sit here and wait for them to kill us? If this is the end, I might as well go out fighting and take a few of them to hell with me.' He picked up a shovel and climbed towards the sickly pack at the top of the staircase. They began to react to his movement and noise. It didn't scare him, it spurred him on. He turned back to face the others. 'Come on. We haven't come this far just to roll over and die, have we?'

'Fuck it,' David said. 'He's right.'

'I'm with you,' Vicky said, and she climbed up to the top step and peered into the gloom. She wished she could see more, but she was equally glad of the shadows that hid the worst of the horror.

'We might even be able to do this,' David said, though he sounded less than convinced. 'It'll take time to get rid of all of them, but I guess time's the only thing we've got left now.'

And he swung his baseball bat through the air and brought it crashing down on a dead man's skull. Vicky shoved the end of her crowbar into another's eye, then Gary thumped the blade of the shovel into another creature's chest. 'Three down,' he said, yanking the shovel free again. 'Several million to go.'

They hacked and slashed at the closest of the dead. Bodies began reacting to the carnage and came towards them, almost as if they were queuing up for slaughter. Sanjay, Damien, Marianne... more climbed the steps to fight alongside the others, desperate to do something – *anything* – to stay alive. Vicky sensed that Selena was next to her now, and the ferocity with which the teenager began to fight was inspiring.

Vicky shoved the closest corpse in the middle of its chest and sent it flying back, giving her a little space to move, then went deeper into the dead. Sweat-soaked and already panting with effort, she began to swing and lunge with the crowbar again. She was determined, but hopelessly outnumbered. Right now, she had nothing left to live for but this very moment.

It was do or die.

Two of them came at her at once, one from either side in a completely random but shockingly effective pincer movement. She took the first one out with ease, but the second managed to wrap its arms around her and it wouldn't let go. Its grip was surprisingly tenacious. She caught it by the throat and drove the end of her crowbar down into the crown of its skull, but by that time she'd another four of the fuckers hanging off her. She dealt with two more of them, but five more took their place. The ground was greasy and she lost her footing and went down, twisting her knee as she sank into the liquefied remains of those she'd already hacked down. She tried to get up again, but her lone battle had become the focus of so many corpses that it was impossible. She'd become isolated from the rest of the group and the undead turned on her in huge numbers, swarming all over her.

And then the outer wall of the train station exploded.

There was a deafening blast that made the whole building shake, and a shockwave that blew hundreds of cadavers off their feet and into pieces. Vicky was sent flying, cushioned by corpses below her, then buried under many more. She was trapped. Paralyzed. Unable to move, barely able to breathe.

Sanjay had been blown halfway down the gore-soaked escalator. He picked himself up, ears ringing, and started to climb. More corpses dropped down onto him from the concourse above, and he clung onto the rubber handrail, terrified that if he let go, he'd fall and drown in the lake of decay below him around the station entrance.

And then they stopped falling.

He started to climb again, and when he made it back up to the first floor, it was immediately obvious what had happened. There was a bigger distraction than the small group of survivors now. Up here, the whole world had changed. The pressure had lifted, the air was colder, the light was clearer... Dazed, he stood upright and saw that an ugly hole had been torn through the side of the station. The dead on this level – those that were still physically able to keep moving – were now being drawn towards the light and were ignoring the living. When they reached the hole, they either fell through or stopped and were pushed over the edge by others behind. The station concourse was rapidly emptying, a deluge of rotten flesh being vomited onto the pavement outside.

Sanjay's head began to clear.

He looked around and saw others... Marianne, Damien, Orla... He saw Selena and David still fighting just a couple of metres from where he was standing, and he waded over to help. They were grabbing corpses off the floor and re-killing them, one by one.

As the dead gravitated towards the light pouring in through the hole, so the living sought safety in the shadows. The rest of the group had emerged from the staircase now and were moving towards the ticket barriers. Other cadavers tried to attack, but their numbers were far fewer, and they were dealt with easily, put out of their misery.

Yet David and Selena continued to fight.

'We need to go,' Sanjay told them. 'It's done. Come on.'

Selena glared at him. 'Not yet. Vicky.'

When Sanjay realised what they were doing, he threw down his weapon and started to hunt through the corpses – and the parts of corpses – that carpeted the station concourse. Though the explosion had allowed much more light into the ruined building, on the ground the shadows remained impenetrable. Sanjay didn't know what he was treading on. The crack of bone beneath his boots felt the same, regardless of who or what it belonged to. He felt a handful of fingers crunch when he stepped back and he panicked in case it was her, but when he moved his boot to relieve the pressure, he put it through a ribcage instead. And when he shook himself free from the ribcage, he saw his other foot was on someone's leg...

Selena dropped down onto her hands and knees, feeling her way through the vile soup in desperation. Her hand rested on something solid, but it was just a shoe, and then she grabbed a handful of hair but when she tugged it, it came away from the scalp it had been attached to. There were other people helping now. She saw some dragging their feet along in the hope of coming across Vicky, some herding the few remaining mobile corpses towards the hole in the wall, others picking up individual bodies to check, one by one...

And then her hand rested on something. It was the back of someone's leg, but she could tell immediately from the muscle tone and size that it wasn't one of the dead.

'Got her!' Selena shouted, and both Sanjay and David raced over and began digging Vicky out. As they began to shift the mass of bodies she'd been buried under, she started to move.

'I'm okay,' she said as Selena helped her to her feet.

'You don't look okay. You look frigging awful,' Selena told her, and she took her arm and led her away.

The group helped each other over the ticket barriers and staggered out into the daylight. Dazed, they walked in silence towards the derailed train that had blocked the tracks. As they approached the wreck, other people appeared from the opposite direction, climbing over and around it to help the new arrivals. Vicky's eyes struggled to adjust to the brightness outside, but she gradually began to make out detail and was able to recognise some of the faces. There was that brutish guy, Piotr, and others she'd seen around the table with Dominic Grove. She saw Ruth and Liz, the doctor.

Once they were on the other side of the train, they were helped down into the heart of the base. It was so good to see the Tower of London up close again, and to realise that it still held strong and hadn't been overrun as she'd feared. Selena finally let go of Vicky's arm, but Vicky grabbed hold of her and held her close. The kid hugged her back just as hard. Vicky hadn't expected that.

'You okay?' Vicky asked her.

'Yeah, I'm good,' Selena said, dismissive, and that was the end of the conversation. Typical bloody teenager.

David was talking to Dominic Grove. She passed them as she crossed the empty space. 'We made it,' David said.

'Most of us.'

'Almost all of us.'

She just nodded. 'Omar?' she said quietly.

'It's thanks to him you're here,' Dom said, smiling. 'Good to see you again, Vicky.'

Vicky nodded once; she no longer had words past that. She continued to walk down towards the river, keen to wash away the clinging stench of death.

Then she stopped. Turned back.

'Thank you,' she said, and she gestured up at what was left of the station. 'For that.'

He started to say something – he was always saying something, she thought – but she was too tired to listen. She continued down to the pier and looked into the murky waters of the Thames. The current was carrying debris away from the centre of London: flotsam and jetsam, human remains, whole bodies floating together like a burst logjam. Standing there alone, she felt no relief, just a new kind of nervousness. She knelt on the pier and washed herself clean.

Looking up, she could see London Bridge, choked with bodies. In places they were backed up, their numbers such that they were forced up and over the sides of the bridge. Close to the north bank, she could just make out an indistinct mass. That had to be the bus, she presumed, but there were no details visible, no flashes of signature London red to confirm her suspicions. It had been completely buried under rot.

38

In the final hours of a day that had seemed never ending, the combined groups gathered together as one for the first time in the spacious atrium of Tower Place. The new arrivals had been temporarily billeted in office space and they'd had chance to wash and change, scrubbing away the stench of death that was so prevalent outside the walls of this precious safe haven. Food had been shared. A fragile calm had been restored.

Dominic was delivering a war report. That was what it felt like, anyway. 'Does that fucker never stop to take a breath?' Vicky asked David. He laughed.

'Does it matter? If he gives this lot some hope, let him keep going until he's all out of words.'

'I don't have that long to wait.'

'You got anywhere better to be?'

'I wish.'

'Today was hard, and it's cost us dearly, but in the end, this was a positive day,' Dominic said. 'I know we've had losses and I know we've paid a high price, but all in all, the benefits outweigh the disappointments.'

'People died out there,' Gary said, cutting the politician off mid-flow. 'Are you saying they're "disappointments?"'

'No, no... not at all. I just—'

'And how exactly do you measure success?'

'We're safe and we're secure.'

'You think?'

'And we're trapped,' Vicky added.

'From what I've heard, you're in a far better position than you were this time yesterday. Yes, we've suffered some massive setbacks, and yes, there are more of the dead surrounding us now than ever, but there are more of us than ever, too.'

'Do we have enough food and water for everyone?' she asked.

Dominic looked for a particular face in the crowd. 'Mihai?'

'We've got enough to last a couple of months, I expect, maybe longer if we're careful,' Mihai answered. 'Hard to say offhand, with so many extra mouths to feed.'

'It's not a problem,' Piotr announced. 'We have the whole of London. We'll go and fetch more. Yes, there are more of those rotting fuckers here, but winter is coming. They'll deteriorate. They'll freeze. We'll cut our way through them if we have to.'

'Prick thinks he's in *Game of Thrones*,' David said under his breath.

'Piotr is right,' Dominic continued. 'We've made it through the hardest days of this nightmare. Sure, there will be more challenges ahead, a few more tough months, but after that the world will be ours for the taking. The future is ours now.'

He looked like he was expecting some kind of jubilant rallying cry from the crowd in response to his words, but he got nothing.

David got to his feet, keen to make his people's voice heard. 'We want to thank you for helping us today. We're glad to be here. But if there's one thing we've learnt, it's that none of us can afford to take any risks until we have some certainty. We had our backs against the wall, but we couldn't risk leaving the hotel until we knew for sure that we had somewhere else to go. Even then, we nearly didn't make it. I think we're all in that position now. It's hell out there, and that's not going to change overnight. I think we all need to work together to make sure this place stays safe and provides protection and security for every single one of us.'

'Totally agree,' Dominic said.

'And with what David says in mind,' Orla said, 'what the hell happened here today? Were we attacked? Could the same thing happen again?'

Dominic was keen to calm nerves. He gestured for quiet, the crowd unsettled. 'Since you left us, Orla, we've had an issue with another group,' he explained.

'I heard they killed Ash.'

'They did. And they killed others too, but the fighting ended today. They took exception to what we were doing here. They saw us as a threat, but there's nothing to worry about now. We dealt with the issue.'

'Seconds before we arrived, by the look of things,' Gary said. 'We were almost here when they blew your barricades to shit.'

Piotr was not impressed. 'The area is secure. We lost a little ground, but no harm done. Like Dominic says, the problem has been sorted out. The explosions were a parting shot.'

'Why should we believe you?'

'Why would we lie?' Dominic asked. 'I've told you what happened. We inadvertently caused problems for another group of people. We tried to make peace with them, but they weren't interested. We had to deal with the situation, so that was what we did. We didn't want to, but we did it.'

'How many people?' David asked.

'Just two of them, but they were trying to give the impression there were many more.'

'Both dead,' Piotr added quickly. 'We killed one of them before dawn. The other one planted their bombs before we could get to him, but he got caught in one of the blasts. We found what was left of him.'

'What about the explosion in the station?' Vicky asked.

'That was us,' Dominic said. 'When your lad Omar showed up and told us where you were and how many of the dead you were dealing with, it was the quickest way we could think to release the pressure and get you out of there.'

'And we appreciate what you did,' David said. 'Thank you again.'

Dominic again tried to wrestle back control of the meeting. 'Look, we're all on the same side here, and we need to remember that. We're not two groups in one place, we're one group. We live together, we work together, we survive together. Right now, this place is our entire world. We have to accept that we're staying put and make the most of it. Things are tough right now, but don't lose sight of the fact that we're in a far better position than most. We've survived while millions of others have died. We just have to bide our time. The bodies that are still out there will eventually rot, and we'll be able to take back London.'

'I'm not staying in London,' Selena said. 'I'm going to Ledsey Cross. We should all go.'

David shook his head. 'Will you just quit with all this Ledsey Cross nonsense? The entire world is dead, Selena, and you need to accept that. There's no mystical, self-sufficient village up North, and even if there was, there's definitely not a community of people still living up there.'

'There is,' she said, indignant.

'Get your head out of the clouds. Like Dominic says, we have to focus on what we've got here.'

'Thank you,' Dominic said. 'Okay, tonight we rest and get our breath back, then tomorrow we start to rebuild. We've lost ground today, but it's land we can reclaim if we need to. We have plenty of space here still. We have the apartments and the Tower, and we're going to focus on clearing out a hotel over by the docks, which will give us almost double the amount of living space. Lynette and Marianne have agreed to work together to coordinate that, so when we—'

Selena was standing right in front of him, holding up a phone. The bright, artificial light from its screen was harsh against the fading natural light of everything else.

'How have you still got a working phone?' he asked.

'Power bricks. Got a couple of solar ones, and another one you wind up. I need to keep this phone alive. It was Kath's. It's all on here.'

'What is?'

'All the details about Ledsey Cross.'

Dominic took the phone from her and began to scroll through the things she wanted him to see. 'This is impossible,' he said. He shook his head and double-checked himself. It was a full exchange between Kath and her friend Annalise, preserved in time. 'This doesn't make sense,' he said.

'What is it?' Lynette asked, and she took the phone from him.

'Those pictures and messages... look at the date stamps, Lynette.'

She squinted to make out the details. It had been weeks since she'd held a phone and she struggled to hold it the right distance from her face. It felt like it was the first time she'd used one. 'Bloody hell,' she said. 'This all happened after everyone died.'

'I told you,' Selena said. 'None of you believe me, but Kath never lied. There's a load of people up at Ledsey Cross, and they're waiting for us.'

Lynette said nothing. She just stared in disbelief at the photograph on the tiny screen in her hands: an image of a group of survivors who'd gathered together at Ledsey Cross in the days that had followed the end of the world.

39

Piotr and Dominic in the boardroom. No one else. Late.
  'Well?'
  Piotr sighed. 'No sign. He could be anywhere.'
  'But you think he's still here?'
  'Most likely. Where else would he go?'
  'Think they bought our story earlier?'
  'No way. Don't worry about it. I'll find him.'
  'And how will you do that, Piotr? You don't know what he looks like. We've had a shedload of new people turn up today, for crying out loud. He could be hidden among them.'
  'They'd have known.'
  'Yes, but we wouldn't. We don't know all the new faces, and they don't know the old ones. Taylor could be walking around in plain sight here, and we'd be none the wiser. I might assume he's a new arrival, and someone like David Shires might think he's one of us. You've put us in a hell of a position, Piotr.'
  'I didn't have any choice.'
  'Do you actually believe that? I'll check with Georgie and find out who she's got records for. The only saving grace was that last blast. For whatever reason, it was clearly designed to help.'
  'You think he's something to do with the other group?'
  'I don't know. For now, I'm taking the fact that the barriers are still intact as a positive sign. I think that was his way of showing us who's boss.'
  'That fucker could take out the railway at any second.'
  'He could, but don't you think he'd have done that already if he was going to?'
  'Perhaps.'
  'You destroyed his building, Piotr, and you killed his friend. He

doesn't sound like the kind of person to put up with something like that, but right now, I think he needs this place as badly as we do.'

'I'll find him.'

'You'd better, because until we get rid of him, Taylor's in control here and he knows it.'

THE STORY CONTINUES
THE LONDON TRILOGY: BOOK II

autumn
INFERNO

ABOUT THE AUTHOR

A pioneer of independent publishing, David Moody first released Hater in 2006, and without an agent, succeeded in selling the film rights for the novel to Mark Johnson (producer, Breaking Bad) and Guillermo Del Toro (director, The Shape of Water, Pan's Labyrinth). Moody's seminal zombie novel Autumn was made into an (admittedly terrible) movie starring Dexter Fletcher and David Carradine. He has an unhealthy fascination with the end of the world and likes to write books about ordinary folks going through absolute hell. The publication of a second trilogy of Hater stories cemented his reputation as a writer of suspense-laced SF/ horror, and "farther out" genre books of all description.

Find out more about his work at:

www.davidmoody.net
facebook.com/davidmoodyauthor
instagram.com/davidmoodyauthor
twitter.com/davidjmoody

"Moody is as imaginative as Barker, as compulsory as King, and as addictive as Palahniuk." —*Scream the Horror Magazine*

"Moody has the power to make the most mundane and ordinary characters interesting and believable, and is reminiscent of Stephen King at his finest." —*Shadowlocked*

"British horror at its absolute best." —*Starburst*

"As demonstrated throughout his previous novels, readers should crown Moody king of the zombie horror novel" —*Booklist*

CPSIA information can be obtained
at www.ICGtesting.com
Printed in the USA
LVHW030501180621
690565LV00016B/751